HATEFUL HEROES

GIFTED ACADEMY BOOK THREE

MICHELLE HERCULES

INFINITE SKY PUBLISHING

1

———

BRYCE

The power to unmake Idols. The words bounce around in my skull like metallic balls in a pinball machine. No one says anything for several beats. I can't speak for my brother or my friends, but I can guess they're just as shocked as I am. I turn to Daisy. She's frozen on the spot, and despite the gloom, I can see her face has gone ashen. The need to comfort her is immense, but I hesitate. When she touched me, I felt my power ebb away. It didn't hurt, but it left me with a sense of wrongness. I know she didn't do it on purpose, but it doesn't change the fact that I can't give what she needs right now.

"What does that mean?" she finally asks.

"It means you can strip the power of an Idol away," Mr. X replies.

"Permanently?" Morpheus moves closer to her.

"Yes," the asshole Knight responds. "I know this is a lot to take in, and you must have a thousand questions. Let's go in so we can discuss our next steps."

"*Our* next steps?" Rufio takes an aggressive stance. "Do you think we're working for you now?"

"I didn't say that, but surely you must know how important Daisy is," the man replies.

Cold dread licks my spine. Daisy is a newly minted Idol with the ability to render anyone powerless. I can see how an organization like the Knights would like to take advantage of her.

Over my dead body.

She shakes her head. "I'm not going anywhere with you. You kidnapped Bryce, spied on me, and who knows, maybe you even paid Mr. Rogers to toss me out of the window."

Shit. She could be right about that little detail. I throw my ire at the man, ready to strike him again. If he had anything to do with her attempted murder, he's as good as dead.

"Mr. Rogers has no affiliation with us. He's part of the Neo Gods, a radical group that preaches Idol supremacy. We're fighting against them."

"So you say," I retort. "But you knew exactly how long you should keep me trapped. So even if what you say is true about Mr. Rogers, don't deny you had intel that he was going to try to kill Daisy that day."

"Of course Gunther didn't know what Mr. Rogers's plans were." Mr. X looks at Daisy pleadingly. "You know I'd never let anything happen to you, sweetheart."

"Don't call her that," Phoenix snaps.

"This is too much. I wanna go home." Daisy hugs her middle, shrinking into herself.

Phoenix moves closer to her, but she steps away, almost as if she's fearful of what she could do by accident. My heart constricts in my chest. I hate seeing her like that and not being allowed to offer her any comfort. Damn everything to hell.

"Daisy, we really should ta—" Gunther begins.

"No! You've manipulated me long enough. We're leaving," Daisy grits out, projecting an energy field so strong it raises the small hairs on my arms.

Shit. She's not only an Idol, she's a high-level one, possibly more powerful than me.

~

DAISY

The silence inside Rufio's car is absolute. Once again I'm sandwiched between Bryce and Phoenix, but this time there's no holding hands. Since Mr. Silverstone dropped the bomb that I have the power to unmake Idols, the change in the guys has been impossible to ignore, just like the gap between our bodies is now. I can't blame them. No one knows how my gift works. What if I accidentally take their powers away with a mere touch?

I dip my chin and wriggle my hands together. Killer hands. I slashed and struck two men without mercy or thought. Now their deaths sit heavily on my conscience, despite what Bryce said. I can't reconcile the idea that they were evil because they worked for Phoenix's father. Vargas, the butler, also worked for the vile Idol, knowing what he did to Phoenix. But in the end, he called for help.

But if he knew what his employer was doing to his own son, and he was actually working for Xavier, why didn't he try to help Phoenix sooner? Ugh! There are so many questions that need to be answered, so many pieces missing in this giant puzzle, that thinking about it is splitting my skull in two. I press the heel of my hand against my forehead and close my eyes.

"Daisy, sweetheart, are you okay?" Phoenix asks. The term of endearment is like a balm over my bruised heart.

I open my eyes and turn to him. "I'm getting a headache. Nothing major."

His face is still a mess of welts and dried blood. Gazing at him makes my chest hurt like a mother. I raise my hand to touch his cheek, but I catch myself just in time. I drop my arm and look away.

"You can touch me," he says before he tries to grab my hand.

In a kneejerk reaction, I twist away from him, which sends me flush against Bryce. There's an energy convergence where we touch; it crackles and makes the small hairs on my arm stand on end. I pull away from him almost immediately.

"Sorry," I mumble.

"Daisy—" Bryce starts.

"What was that?" Rufio asks with a hint of alarm in his voice.

"Nothing. Keep your eyes on the road," Bryce grits out, almost as if he's angry about something.

My stomach coils tightly, and the sense I've done something awful increases. I shrink into myself, biting my lower lip to keep the tears at bay. I've never felt more wretched in my entire life. I should have called shotgun. No risk of me bumping into anyone by accident.

Morpheus turns in his seat and stares at me. "You look distraught. Are you in pain?"

At once, everyone is looking at me, including Rufio in the rearview mirror.

"Are you?" Bryce asks, his voice tight.

"No. How far are we from campus?" I ask to change the subject.

"Ten minutes or so."

I drop my eyes to my lap and ignore their scrutinizing stares. When we got on the road, I was tempted to ask Rufio to take me to Rosie. But considering how we parted ways, and the fact that I'm now an Idol, I decided against it. How am I going to tell my sister I turned into something she hates? Maybe that's what's troubling me the most. I've lost so much already; I can't bear to lose Rosie's love too.

The ten minutes feel like an eternity. No one speaks the rest of the way, and when we arrive at Gifted Academy, I don't make eye contact with any of them while I walk to my room. They leave me alone during the trek, but as soon as I stop in front of my door, Phoenix touches my forearm.

"Daisy—..."

I jerk away from him. "Don't touch me!"

He winces as if I'd slapped him, and the glint of hurt in his eyes is almost too much to withstand.

"I'm sorry," I say quickly. "I don't want to risk... you know."

"You're not going to take my powers away."

"You don't know that." With shaking hands, I try to open my door. Impossible.

"I don't think you should be alone right now. Why don't you spend the night with us?" Rufio suggests.

My heart lurches inside of my chest. I'd give anything right now to be able to find comfort in their arms, but I can't.

I shake my head. "No. I need to be alone."

Finally, I manage to unlock the door and escape into the confines of my room. When the lock clicks shut again, I lean against the wall, feeling guilty as hell. We've all been through a lot, especially Phoenix, but I can't offer them solace, not when I'm hollow inside. I choke on a sob, biting the inside of my cheek to keep the tears at bay for a while longer. I can't let them hear me bawling my eyes out with their super hearing.

Crap on toast. That's an ability I now possess as well.

It's easy to discern each of their steps as they walk away from my door toward their apartment. I hear the soft click of their lock as clearly as if I were standing in front of their door.

Suddenly, I can't breathe right. My lungs constrict, and there's a huge lump in my throat. I brace my hands on my knees, fighting the bolt of anxiety attack with everything I have, which isn't much. I'm spent. Dark spots appear before my eyes, and my head feels light. I think I'm going to pass out.

Forcing my legs to move, I stumble toward the bed. I'd rather collapse on my mattress than the floor. By a miracle, I reach my destination. Toppling forward, I hit my face on the soft pillow with my eyes already closed. It's the last thing I remember doing before I'm dragged into oblivion.

~

MORPHEUS

"I don't like this. Daisy shouldn't be alone right now," I say, tempted to go back out and knock on her door.

"She has a lot to process. We all do." Bryce walks toward the window, shoulders visibly tense.

Without a word, Phoenix heads for his room. Damn. Here I am only worrying about Daisy while one of my best friends has survived an ordeal I can't even begin to imagine. But I don't say a word or try to stop him. Phoenix, more than anyone else, needs time alone.

When I turn to the living room, I find Bryce and Rufio staring in the same direction I was. Both have matching furrowed brows and hard-set jaws.

"I can't believe that son of a bitch was abusing Phoenix all these years and we didn't know about it. It makes me so fucking mad." Rufio grabs an empty beer can from the coffee table and turns it into dust in the blink of an eye.

"It was probably the tattoo he had on his wrist that prevented him from speaking," I say. "The mark of the binding god Ogmios. It had power over him."

"Daisy was able to figure it out." Bryce looks away again, folding his arms in front of his chest.

I push my long hair back, but what I really want to do is yank it hard. I'm so frustrated with everything.

"What are we going to do about the Knights?" I ask to stop

berating myself for failing Phoenix. "Can Gunther Silverstone be trusted?"

"No," Rufio and Bryce reply at the same time.

"All right, then we're on the same page. But what do we do? They've been keeping tabs on all of us for years, it seems. Shit, they knew Bryce had the ability to heal. How did they know that?"

"I suspect my mother is responsible for sharing that intel." Bryce turns to me, his eyes narrowed to slits.

"But how could she have known?" Rufio asks in turn.

I snap my fingers as the realization hits me. "Your lineage. There must have been someone in your family who had the ability to heal."

"So what? That wouldn't guarantee I'd be the one to inherit the ability. It could have been Rufio."

"There must have been signs when you were growing up," I reply. "If they believed Daisy was meant to regain Magia's power, they wouldn't gamble with her life without knowing for sure you would be able to heal her."

"I could have failed or not arrived in time," Bryce replies through clenched teeth while his power increases tenfold, coiling around his frame like a living thing. The lights flicker for a moment before returning to normal.

"What if we play along with the Knights for now to see what they truly want?" Rufio has a dangerous glint in his blue eyes.

"What about Daisy?" I ask. "They want to use her."

Rufio runs a hand through his hair. "Fuck."

"She's an Idol now with an extremely dangerous gift. Do you know how many people would want her dead if they knew?" I continue.

"If they want Daisy, they'll have to come through me," Bryce states.

"And me," Rufio adds.

I stare in silence at the two brothers who are usually like night and day, but today they're the same in their determination to protect Daisy. Any fool would be able to read the devotion in their eyes. They've fallen in love with her. Her status change would send lesser Idols running, but not them. And not me either.

I can't explain what I feel for her. But if anyone tries to harm her in any way, they'll wish they were never born.

2

___

DAISY

The sand is soft and warm under my feet. The water lapping at my heels is cool, though not to the point of giving me shivers, and the light breeze blowing my hair feels like a caress against my skin. In front of me, the white shore stretches for a few yards until thick tropical vegetation rises into a wall of green and luscious foliage. Without fear, I move toward it, despite the fact that I can't see what's inside the rich forest. Any danger could be lurking behind the almost impenetrable barrier.

My feet sink into the sand as I walk forward. With each step, my heartbeat increases until it's drumming so fast, it's all I can hear pounding in my ears. As I approach, the forest trembles, and like magic, the trees and shrubs part down the middle, revealing an idyllic landscape that takes my breath away.

A beautiful azure lake reflects the light from the sun. Its crystalline water is peaceful and beckoning. Colorful huts surround the lake, and right behind the cluster of happy homes, tall trees rise to the sky, forming a protective wall around the settlement. They're connected by bridges and vine cables. At the top of those trees, more colorful structures stand on thick branches. But the most alluring detail of all is the people. Norms, Fringes, and Idols, all living in complete harmony. I can feel their peaceful energy rolling out in waves toward me. I'm staring at a paradise where races don't matter.

This must be Starlight Island. I can't believe that after all these years, I've finally found it.

I run toward it, eager to join the sanctuary, when the trees close in again, cutting me off from the village. The sky that until a minute ago was clear and bright blue changes into dark and ominous clouds. Everything turns obscure, and the only source of illumination comes when lightning strikes the gray canvas, followed by the terrifying roars of thunder.

Seized by sheer terror, I turn around to flee, but there's nowhere to go. I'm on an island, and there's no boat out of here. Cold rain falls from the sky, fast and furious. The droplets hit my skin like pellet bullets. This is no ordinary rain. I should run for cover, but the only option is the oppressive forest behind me.

I know I shouldn't enter it, but if I don't, I'll be flayed alive. With a curse through my teeth, I bolt toward the unknown. The moment I breach the forest, I hear a burst of evil laughter that turns my blood cold. A shiver runs down my spine, and I'm all too aware of the malicious presence nearby.

A low growl echoes not too far from me, making my heart skip a beat. I should pivot and face what's stalking me, but I can't move. Twigs break and dry leaves crunch before hot and foul breath fans over the back of my neck. I close my eyes while my body is taken over by uncontrollable shakes.

"There's no running away. You're mine now," the beast says before it strikes.

～

I JOLT AWAKE, sitting up in the process. My accelerated heart feels like it's going to explode out of my chest. Blinking fast, I do a quick sweep of my room to make sure I'm safe. Sunlight is pouring from my window, but the sense of foreboding still hangs in the air.

"It was only a nightmare, Daisy," I murmur.

It takes me a good minute before my breathing returns to normal, and then I finally realize I fell asleep wearing my evening gown. The fabric is deep red, but even so, I'm able to see dark splatters on my bodice and skirt.

Blood.

Sudden nausea hits me. I bolt out of bed and run for the bathroom, barely making to the toilet in time. I can't remember the last time I ate, so there's not much in my stomach to empty, and I'm soon dry heaving. When it's safe for me to pull away from the bowl, I stand on shaky legs and push my matted hair off my face.

I scrutinize my reflection in the mirror, and finally the magnitude of what happened last night, of what I did, hits me like a cannonball. My stomach twists painfully, but there's nothing else to expel. I move closer to the mirror, touching my face, stretching the skin under my eyes. I look exactly like I did before Bryce healed me and inadvertently reawakened the Idol spark in me.

I'm a killer.

The thought pops in my head unbidden, and immediately my legs become weak. Placing my hands on the sink, I lean forward, dipping my chin. It's not the first time I've killed. But I didn't feel any remorse when I skewered the gangbanger who hurt Felicity. And maybe that was the reason; he hurt my friend and deserved what he got. But those Fringes were only doing their jobs. There's no way to know if they were aware Mr. Westbrook was a monster. The uncertainty is what's bothering me.

In a fit of rage, I yank the ball gown off my body, careless that I'm tearing the delicate fabric off. I'll never wear this dress again. I hop into the shower and attempt to wash away all the guilt and turmoil swirling in my chest. A loud sob erupts from my throat, and this time I don't fight the tears. I let them out until I feel hollow.

When I finally emerge from the bathroom, my skin is red thanks to all the rubbing I did. My stomach groans, reminding me that I haven't eaten in a long time. I put on a pair of sweatpants, an old T-shirt, and sneakers. It's the best I can do. I grab my debit card, praying the scholarship funds have hit my account already; the last time I checked my balance, I only had enough money to buy a bag of peanuts from the vending machine.

Lost in my thoughts, I open the door without looking, unprepared for the body that topples down against my legs. I let out a yell as I jump away. Morpheus falls on his back with a soft thud.

"Ouch," he says.

Pressing my hand against my chest, I exclaim, "What the hell! What were you doing sitting against my door?"

He sits up first and then jumps to his feet. His hair is pulled back into a messy bun, and there's scruff on his chiseled face. The roguish look suits him, and slowly my shock morphs into craving. I'm consumed by the urge to run my fingers over his chin, but it's a desire I must fight. The last time I touched him, I made his shadows disappear. Now I know why.

"I was waiting for you to wake up," he replies sheepishly.

My heart does a backflip, but I try to ignore it.

"And you couldn't have waited inside your apartment?"

"I wouldn't have been able to sense you were awake."

"I've been up for at least half an hour." I cross my arms in front of my chest before my traitorous body decides to reach over. Why am I so tempted to connect to him? Could it be because now I can't?

The corners of his lips twitch upward. "I dozed off."

"Did you sleep at all last night?"

His grin wilts and his eyes take on a haunted glint. "Not really. Lots to process. How about you?"

I drop my gaze to the floor, ashamed that I slept like the dead despite everything. "Yup. I passed out, actually."

"It's understandable and quite normal."

I look up again. "Why is that?"

He shoves his hands in his jeans pockets and shrugs. "It was the first time you used your powers. That takes a toll on your body. You'll get used to it."

A bout of anxiety pierces my chest, and I'm afraid I'll start hyperventilating again. The moment I step foot inside the school building tomorrow, everyone will know I'm an Idol.

"What's the matter, Daisy? Your face turned white all of a sudden."

My stomach decides to protest just then, reminding me of the reason I was heading out.

"You need food," Morpheus states. "Come on. Things always look better on a full belly."

"And after coffee," I add.

He smiles, showing me his adorable dimples. The haunted look in his eyes fades away. He points toward the hallway. "After you."

I hesitate for a second, biting my lower lip.

"What is it?" he asks.

"I might have to borrow money from you. I'm not sure if I received my financial aid yet."

Morpheus pinches his lips and frowns. "Seriously, Daisy? You're not paying for breakfast."

"Nonsense. I can pay."

"I invited you. Therefore, it's my treat."

I finally move, locking my door for good measure. It's pointless to argue with Morpheus or any of the guys. To them, paying for stuff isn't a big deal, but if I start accepting it, it'll make me feel like a moocher.

"All right, but please don't take me anywhere super fancy where they charge an arm and a leg for a plate of bacon."

"Good grief. You really have the wrong idea about me," he replies with a chuckle.

"You go here." I shrug to save face, but the truth is I know nothing about Morpheus besides he has a scary gift.

When we reach the garage, I discover I did indeed peg him wrong. I thought he was just like everyone else around here, swimming in riches. But Morpheus's car isn't brand new like the ones his roommates drive. It's an old Jeep with a few scratches and a bent bumper. I stare at the front of his car for a moment.

"I have to ask, is it safe to enter your vehicle?"

He follows my line of sight and makes a disgruntled sound. "Yes it is. I didn't crash my car, if that's what you're thinking. Phoenix did that."

"How?"

"He got bored and decided to make shit fly. My poor car was a casualty." He taps the metal hood affectionately before he circles around the front of the vehicle and opens the driver door.

The door unlocks on my side, so I follow suit, sliding in as well. Inside, there's no new car smell. The scent is smoky, metallic, and warm, a combination of lavender, lemon, cedar, vanilla, and rum that's all Morpheus.

Damn. I was never able to distinguish between different scents like this before. Talk about enhanced senses, and also intoxicating smells. I'm getting light-headed, and it has nothing to do with hunger. Or maybe it is—only I'm hungry for something other than food.

3

———

DAISY

Morpheus doesn't say where he's taking me, but I also don't ask, too busy trying to control the hormones that are wreaking havoc on my body. Is it possible that my newfound powers are also responsible for giving me an increased libido? Just freaking great. Like I wasn't already flirting with the line of sex addiction. I rub my legs together and look out the window. I hope he can't sense my arousal.

To take my mind off what's happening to me, I decide to ask Morpheus a practical question. "Do you know how to mask your Idol power?"

"I never tried, but I suppose I could if I wanted to. Why?"

"I don't want anyone in school to know about me."

Morpheus doesn't speak for several beats, making me curious. I look at his face, but I can't guess anything from his profile. "Do you think I'm wrong for wanting to keep it a secret?"

"No, absolutely not. I'm in complete agreement with you."

He signals to turn at the nearest exit, and after a few yards, he veers into the parking lot of a small diner. It's not even nine yet and the place is already packed.

"Popular spot," I say.

"Yeah, they serve amazing Swedish pancakes."

My stomach grumbles again, as if sensing nourishment isn't too far away. I reach for the door handle, but Morpheus touches my arm, stopping me. I tense in an instant and pull away.

"I'm sorry. I shouldn't have done that." He looks straight ahead, clenching his jaw hard.

Shit, I think I hurt his feelings. Morpheus and I have an undefined relationship. The attraction is there, at least on my part, but unlike his roommates, he's always kept his distance from me. He's standing firmly in the friend zone, and I'm unsure whether he wants to cross that line.

As crazy as it sounds, I want him to do it.

"No, Morpheus, it's not like that. I don't know how my newfound powers work. I'm afraid to accidentally unmake you."

He peers into my eyes with his brows furrowed. "You're not going to accidentally unmake me."

"You don't know that." I nibble on my lower lip.

Morpheus's eyes drop to my mouth, and I belatedly realize what it must look like. My face is on fire now. "Let's go in. I'm starving."

"Wait. The reason I stopped you is because I wanted to tell you something."

"What is it?"

"I can't possibly begin to imagine what you must be feeling right now. I was born an Idol, and most of the time my power feels more like a burden than a gift. So, if you need to vent, curse at the gods, I'm here for you."

His offer turns me into a pool of goo. At the same time, my heart overflows with joy. I'd kiss him if I dared.

"Thanks, Morpheus. I really appreciate it."

He answers with a panty-melting smile, and I swear, the temperature in the car goes up by a hundred degrees. Before I combust on the spot, I get out, taking deep breaths to calm down. Morpheus circles around to the front of his car and waits for me to join him.

"Ready for this?" he asks.

"As ready as I'll ever be. It's not like I know anyone inside."

I totally jinxed myself.

The moment I enter the establishment; I recognize a few faces from school. Shit. And I haven't learned how to mask my power yet.

The group from Gifted Academy is sitting at a booth in the back. Two couples from senior year who, judging by their attire, haven't been to bed yet. The guys are still wearing their tuxes, albeit their ties are missing. The girls are in their skintight, sparkly evening gowns, but their makeup is more Halloweenish than glamourous. Hello, raccoon eyes.

My throat becomes dry. If they see me, they'll know.

Quick as a whip, Morpheus grabs my hand and drags me out of the diner before we're spotted. Stunned for a moment, I don't pull free from his grasp. His touch is warm and sure. But when something cold licks the back of my wrist, it sends an unpleasant jolt up my arm. With a gasp, I glance down. The shadows that sometimes cover Morpheus's wrists are writhing and spreading up both our arms.

I yank my hand away. Morpheus twists his face into a grimace and covers his wrist with his other hand.

"I'm so sorry," he chokes out.

"Are you in pain?" I take a step toward him.

With a grunt, he ambles toward his car. "No."

"Don't lie to me. What can I do?"

He rests his hand on the car's hood and dips his chin. "Shit. I think the god is coming back again."

"The god? What are you talking about?"

Morpheus looks at me, his face now completely white. "I can't explain right now. Can you drive?"

Hell. I can't say no. I really need to get my driver's license soon. "Yeah, sure."

I take the key from Morpheus, careful not to touch his fingers. I don't think I sucked the power out of him when we held hands, but I have no idea what triggers my powers, so who knows.

With my heart stuck in my throat, I slide behind the wheel and wait for Morpheus to take his seat. He grunts again, letting his head fall back against the headrest. His eyes are closed and his brows are furrowed, making a sharp V. A sheen of sweat covers his forehead, and with a quick glance, I see the shadows are restless and now all the way up to his elbows.

"Where should we go?"

"My parents' house. I need to see my mother."

"Okay. Where is that?"

"Ever... dale."

Crap. Everdale is an hour from here, and he can barely get words out. I put the car in Drive and peel out of the parking lot, burning rubber as I go.

"Should I call the guys?" I ask.

"They can't... help me."

Curling my fingers tighter against the steering wheel, I take deep breaths. They're meant to calm me, but I don't think anything can make my heart stop galloping at breakneck speed.

"Ugh!" Morpheus leans forward, clutching his head with both hands.

"Morpheus!"

"Don't... mind me. Just... drive."

I put the pedal to the metal, praying there aren't any cops on the way. I thank my luck that it's Sunday and traffic is barely nonexistent. I manage to make it to Everdale in half the time, during which Morpheus's condition only worsens. The exit sign for Everdale looms ahead, but I have no idea where to go.

"Morpheus, I need an address."

His head is still low and his eyes are shut.

"Morpheus, can you hear me?"

He pulls his cell phone from his jeans pocket and hands it to me, unlocking the screen with his finger before letting go. Guessing what he wants me to do, I search his contacts. I find his mother's information, but there's no address.

"Call—" His reply is cut short by another grunt.

I press the Call button, slowing the car down as I come onto the exit ramp. The phone rings several times, and I begin to lose hope. If she doesn't answer, then what?

"Hello?" a female voice says on the other side of the line.

"Oh thank goodness," I breathe.

"Who is this? Why are you calling from my son's phone?" Her voice becomes agitated.

"Forgive me. This is Daisy. I'm Morpheus's friend from school. He's not feeling well, and I'm driving to your house."

"What's wrong with him?"

"It's...." I turn to him, noting the shadows have covered his arms and are now expanding toward his upper body. "The shadows. They're everywhere."

She makes a disgruntled sound first before saying, "Get him here as quickly as you can."

"I'm in Everdale already. I need your address. Morpheus can't talk."

Instead of giving me the address, she guides me over the phone. Their upper-middle-class neighborhood isn't far from the highway, and within five minutes I'm parking in front of their house. A petite woman with dark curly hair runs outside. She opens the passenger side door and helps Morpheus out. I join them in front of the car but keep my distance from him.

"I can't believe this is happening again," she says almost to herself.

"How often do the shadows take control like that?" I ask, following them in.

She doesn't answer, making me think I've stepped over some boundary.

She takes Morpheus to his childhood bedroom; it still has toys on display on the shelves and a bedspread featuring a cartoon design. Morpheus is lying flat on his back with his eyes closed now. His mother sits on the edge of the bed and taps his cheek.

"Morpheus, darling, can you hear me?"

He groans something incoherent but doesn't open his eyes.

His mother turns to me. "What happened?"

"I don't know. We went out to get breakfast, and then suddenly, the shadows went out of control."

I don't tell her that I touched him, that my strange gift might've been the cause. This is so new, and I have no idea what I'm capable of.

"His bracelets have been reinforced recently. They should be holding. Something must have weakened their magic."

I swallow the huge lump in my throat. Not something, *someone*. I must have accidentally touched the bracelet and sucked the magic that controlled Morpheus's shadows.

"This is all my fault," I finally confess.

"How is it your fault?" She stands, watching me through slits now.

Fuck. I should have kept my mouth shut.

The doorbell rings, saving me from Mrs. Malek's wrath. She walks out of the room in a hurry. As for me, I don't move from my spot at the end of Morpheus's bed, guilt and fear keeping me rooted to the spot.

Mrs. Malek returns a moment later accompanied by two

older men wearing elaborate priest robes. Their gazes are vacant, and by how they don't focus on anything in particular, I realize they're blind.

They head straight to Morpheus's bed, though, implying they've been here more than once. Poor Morpheus. What a cursed gift.

The priests stand on each side of Morpheus's bed, stooping over to place their weathered hands over his bracelets. With eyes closed, they begin to recite a prayer of sorts. Their bushy eyebrows furrow in concentration, and minutes go by without any change on the blasted shadows. Mrs. Malek is standing by the door, clutching her pearl necklace and watching the scene with round eyes.

Perhaps sensing my stare, she turns to me, accusation flashing in her dark eyes.

Damn. Way to win points with Morpheus's mother.

The priests stop chanting, and the woman takes a step forward. "Were you able to reinforce the bracelets?"

"No, ma'am. The threads that held the magic together have been completely destroyed. Nothing will do besides forging new bracelets."

"But that'll take days!" she shrieks.

I look at Morpheus, almost completely covered by the shadows. If it weren't for the rise and fall of his chest, I'd think he's dead. Anguish twists my insides. I can't let him be devoured by darkness, especially since I'm the one responsible for releasing it. I approach his bed, and before I can talk myself out of it, I touch his chest.

"What are you doing? Step away from my son!" Mrs. Malek screams.

"I can help him," I grit out without taking my eyes off Morpheus's face.

"Let the girl try, Mrs. Malek," one of the priests says. "I sense great power coming from her."

I think only the priest's words are preventing Mrs. Malek from tackling me off Morpheus. If I can't help him, she's going to flay me alive. She's a Fringe, a fact that's obvious to me now that I have the special Idol senses. But she's as fierce as a lioness.

The shadows cover my hand at first, cold and harsh against my skin. I focus on sending them back to where they come from instead of wishing them gone entirely. My palm is sweating now, which I suspect has more to do with my nerves than any side effects of my ability. I feel resistance at first, but slowly the shadows recede, returning to the silver bracelets.

Odd. The priest said the accessories are useless now.

Morpheus opens his eyes with a gasp, which is my cue to pull away.

"Morpheus!" His mother drops to her knees next to his bed, touching his face. "How do you feel?"

"Awful." He looks at me. "Did you...?"

"Yeah. I had to. I'm sorry."

He sits up slowly, sporting a frown. "Why are you apologizing? You saved me."

I glance down, feeling undeserving of his praise.

"Oh my. You're still so cold. I'll bring you some hot chocolate and soup." His mother stands again.

"Mom, aren't you going to offer Daisy something to eat too?" Morpheus asks, and I want to disappear.

"It's okay—" The room begins to spin, and I have to press my hand against my forehead and close my eyes for a moment.

"Daisy," Morpheus says.

"Impossible," one of the priests mumbles.

Someone curls a hand around my forearm, steadying me. I open my eyes and am surprised to see it's Mrs. Malek who came to the rescue. She's watching me differently now, curious. It's better than the animosity from before, at least.

"Are you okay?" she asks.

"Yeah, it's nothing. I didn't have breakfast yet."

"Have a seat. I'll escort the Zions out and prepare some food."

"Okay."

The Zions, blind as they are, have their eyes trained on me. I wonder if they're truly blind. They don't budge until Mrs. Malek urges them out the door.

"Daisy, sit down. You look as white as a sheet."

I begin to move toward the desk chair, but Morpheus taps the mattress. "Sit here, next to me."

"I don't think that's wise."

"You just used your powers on me, and I'm still an Idol."

"How do you know?"

He gives me a droll stare. "Trust me, Daisy. If you had stripped my powers, I'd know."

I open my mouth to reply, but the angry and loud voice of a man coming from somewhere in the house makes me stop.

"What are they doing here?" the man asks.

"What do you think? Morpheus needed them," Mrs. Malek replies.

There's more grumbling and then the bang of a door shutting hard.

Morpheus stares at his bedroom door with a glower. "Great. My father is home."

4

RUFIO

I didn't think I could sleep despite being bone-tired. The fight at Mr. Westbrook's mansion took a toll on me. At first, we thought we were only dealing with Fringes, but the asshole also had Idols working for him. It's the reason it took so long for Morpheus and me to storm the place.

To my surprise, I did fall asleep, even with all the thoughts whirling in my head. And apparently I slept like the dead, because it took relentless banging on our front door to jar me awake. I jerk to a sitting position with my heart stuck in my throat. My first thought is about Daisy, naturally. But it's another girl who's calling out from the hallway.

I don't recognize her voice right away; my head seems to be stuffed with cotton candy. When I get to the living room, Bryce has already beat me to the door.

"Who is it?" I rub my eyes and yawn.

"Renata Pomme," Bryce grits out.

I'm alert in an instant. What the fuck is Drusilla's minion doing here?

Bryce yanks the door open. "What do you want?"

"I need your help."

I push Bryce out of the way so I can glower at the girl. She's still wearing an evening gown, but her appearance is disheveled. Her eyes are red and puffy, and her mascara has run down, making her look like a zombie.

"You have some nerve showing up here," I sneer.

"I wouldn't have come if I had any other choice. Drusilla has gone crazy."

Bryce scoffs. "That's rich. Fuck off before I decide to make you pay for everything you've done to Daisy."

Renata's eyes turn as round as saucers. "I'm sorry about Daisy. I don't have anything against her. I was—"

"Following Drusilla's orders. Like that's an excuse." My power swirls in my chest, and energy crackles between my fingers. The only thing keeping me from pulverizing the girl is the school rules.

With a sob, she replies, "I'm sorry. You have no idea how hard this school is if you're not part of a clique."

"You're not seriously trying to gain our sympathy with that pathetic story, are you?" I ask. "You followed Drusilla's orders because you're just like her: a jealous, mean-spirited cunt."

Renata winces, taking a step back. "Call me all the names you want, but Drusilla is out of control. She made me do this to myself." She pulls her strapless gown down, revealing cuts all over her breasts. The sight is gruesome and renders me speechless.

"Why?" Bryce asks.

"I don't know!" Renata covers her chest again, losing her shit. Fat tears run down her cheeks, and I don't believe they're fake. Not after what she showed us.

"We went back to our apartment after the ball, and she started acting strange," she continues.

"Strange how?" I ask.

"Almost as if she was high. She was spewing nonsense about gods and destiny, how chaos would descend upon us.

Then she started to bleed from her eyes and nose. When she looked at me, there was no recognition in her gaze. That's when she started to torture me."

"How did you escape?" Bryce poses the question now.

"She collapsed. I didn't wait to see if she was okay. I ran away."

"And what do you want us to do about it?" I keep glaring, clueless to why she thinks we should care about her or her odious friend.

Renata hugs herself and dips her chin. "I don't know. Maybe because you're the strongest Idols in school and... I don't want Drusilla to get in trouble in case she took some stupid drug."

"Wait here. I'll get dressed." Bryce whirls around, and I follow him.

"I can't believe this. Are you going to help her?" I ask, already angry at my brother.

Bryce looks at me like I'm dimwitted. "Drusilla has the same mark we do. What if her condition is related to the god who owns our asses? Aren't you curious?"

Damn. My hatred for the girl blinded me to that. "Okay, let me check on Phoenix first."

I head for his room, not bothering to knock before I go in. His bed is unmade, but he's not there.

"Phoenix?" I head for his bathroom, but he's not there either. Fuck.

I meet Bryce in the living room. "We have a problem. Phoenix is gone."

He pinches the bridge of his nose and lets out a string of curses. "We'll call him on the way to Drusilla's." He looks to Morpheus's bedroom. "Is he still asleep?"

Frowning, I go check. Unless he took something last night, he'd be up thanks to all the ruckus. No sign of him, and his bed is made.

"Morpheus bailed too. Maybe he and Phoenix are together."

Bryce strides out without sparing me a glance, but when he walks in front of Daisy's door, he glances at it, pausing for a split second. As much as I want to find out what the deal is with Drusilla, checking on Daisy is more important.

"Shouldn't we—" I start.

"She's not there," Bryce answers through clenched teeth and resumes his brisk pace.

Right. Now that Daisy is an Idol, she has a signature that we can sense even through closed doors. I check just in case, but her apartment is empty. Where the fuck is she? She doesn't own a car, and her buddy Toby didn't spend the night on campus.

Stop worrying about her like you're a whipped boy, Rufio. Most likely she's with Morpheus and Phoenix. I pull my cell out and call Morpheus first. It rings until it goes to voice mail. It's the same deal with Phoenix. I can't call Daisy because she doesn't have a phone. A problem I have to fix as soon as possible. I have to be able to reach her at any time I want or I'll go crazy.

Fuck. When did I become so needy?

Drusilla and Renata's apartment is in a different building than ours since they aren't seniors. It's a five-minute walk, which we make in two. Bryce is as eager to deal with the situation as I am.

Only it's much worse than I thought.

Drusilla is in the common area, terrorizing a group of Fringes in front of an audience. The sound of her cackle and her manic appearance puts me on high alert. Her hair is a mess, and there's dried food and other crap all over her face.

The Fringe girls are all on their hands and knees, licking the floor. The sight wouldn't have given me a second thought a few weeks ago, but now it makes me see red.

I'm ready to put a stop to it, but Bryce beats me to the

punch. Without a word, he sends Drusilla flying across the area until she crashes against one of the vending machines. The crowd immediately parts so Bryce and I are on full display. If they knew what was good for them, they'd leave. But the prospect of a showdown between two powerful Idols isn't something these idiots would miss. They have a taste for blood, just like I used to have. We're no better than savages.

Bryce stalks toward Drusilla, who's already getting back on her feet. She pushes her mangled hair off her face, standing on unsteady legs. Now that I can see her properly, I realize the gunk on her face is blood that poured from her eyes and nose. Her gaze is bloodshot and downright crazy.

"Oh, Bryce. I should have known you'd make an appearance. You've now become the knight in shining armor to all the worthless bitches in this school."

"You're out of your mind. What did you take?" he asks.

"What did I take? The best fucking thing in the world. The nectar of the gods. I'm invincible." She throws her head back and laughs.

The Fringes, momentarily free from Drusilla's compulsion, begin to rise from the floor. But she catches the action and yells, "Who told you to stop licking? Back on your knees!"

Immediately the girls drop down.

This needs to stop.

I take a step in her direction when she lets out a wail and her legs fold from under her. Murmurs reign supreme all around us, but so far, not a single member of school faculty or security has shown up. Useless leeches.

"What's wrong with her? Maybe we should call the nurse," some random girl says, but I don't stop to see if anyone will follow through.

"Get up, bitch," Bryce commands. His voice trembles with barely contained rage, and I don't even need to look to know his body is crackling with raw energy. He's about to fucking unleash his full blast on Drusilla. I don't care about her well-being, but if he hurts her in front of all these witness, he's fucked.

I reach Drusilla and drag her to her feet. She digs her long nails into my forearms hard enough to pierce my skin. "Don't make me hurt you," I grit out.

"Oh, I'm banking on it," she replies, but her voice sounds different, deep and—

Son of a bitch. She sounds like the god!

Damn it. I need to render her unconscious, but I don't think whacking her over the head will do the trick.

"I want to die, Rufio. Use your powers on me."

In an instant, my powers manifest of their own accord. It takes me a split second to understand Drusilla used compulsion on me. But I was never affected by it before. *Damn everything to hell.*

"Rufio, let her go!" Bryce yells.

"I can't!"

My fingers tingle as my gift ebbs freely from them. Drusilla is still clutching my arm, and there's nothing I can do to stop her from crumbling to dust before me. Distraught gasps echo all around me, followed by Drusilla's demented cackles as she disintegrates. I break free when her arms collapse, but there's no stopping her complete destruction now. I gave her what she wanted, what she compelled me to do. In a few more seconds, she's gone.

5

—————

PHOENIX

Once the adrenaline wore off, I couldn't face my friends. Shame took over me. They know what that bastard did to me. Even after death, he can still make me feel worthless, dirty. Like a coward, I hid in my room. But being alone just meant I had no distraction. Memories of the abuse returned to haunt me, smother me.

I was fucking glad I had a stash of Silver-voltage in my drawer. The dosage I took was enough for a week, but damn it, I took it all. Even so, oblivion was hard to come by. So I focused on the only bright spot in the nightmare that was tonight.

Daisy.

Fearless and furious, she charged in that room of torture like a warrior goddess. She defied my father, not knowing she was an Idol. It's no surprise I feel what I do for her. I don't even know what it is, only that it's overwhelming and absolute.

I don't care that she has a dangerous gift, that she could strip away my godly powers with a mere touch. If I had to make a choice between not being with her or living my life as a Norm, I'd choose the latter.

Slowly, the numbness starts to spread through my body.

Finally, the drug is doing its job. I pull my cell phone out and turn it on. The asshole switched it off when it wouldn't stop ringing last night. It's a miracle he didn't smash it.

As I suspected, there are several missed calls from my friends, but there's also a call from an unfamiliar number. They left a message. I don't know what prompts me to listen to it now, but I do. It's the fucking cops. They want to take my statement about my parents' home invasion and my father's disappearance.

We don't know what happened after we left. I didn't care then, and I don't care now. The police can kiss my ass.

I head for the shower and spend an absurd amount of time under the scalding hot jets. But no matter how hard I scrub, I can't get rid of the filth. I don't think I'll ever be free of the stain on my soul.

When I return to my room, the space feels confining. The walls are caging me in. Daybreak is a few hours away, but I need to get out.

Mercifully, the living room is empty when I head out. I don't know how long until I'll be able to look my friends in the eye. It's only when I hit the garage that I realize I don't have my car. Rufio drove us back, which means my wheels are still parked at my parents' house. No wonder the cops are hounding me. Fuck.

I stop next to Rufio's car and try the door. It's unlocked. He left the fob inside. Predictable. Not that anyone here is concerned about grand theft auto.

I start the car and drive out of the garage without a destination in my mind. I wish I could just keep going and never come back, but the thought of never seeing Daisy again makes my chest tight.

As soon as I cross the gates of Gifted Academy, I press down on the gas pedal, testing the engine's limit. The car goes from zero to sixty in less than five seconds. The lurch flattens my back against the supple leather seat, but it doesn't bring me exhilaration. In my current state, I'd have to be strapped to a rocket to feel anything.

Ten minutes into my aimless drive, I become aware that I'm a fucking glutton for punishment. My deranged conscience leads me to the last place on the Earth I should be: my very own hell. But I don't turn around when the first checkpoints come into view. I stop in front of the community's gate, since Rufio's car doesn't have credentials, and have an internal argument about what to do. I don't have ID on me, but it's needless when the security guard shines his flashlight on my face. Without a word, he lets me through.

Once inside the gated community, the need for speed vanishes; I'm driving so slowly that I'd be faster on foot. My stomach coils in anticipation. I have no idea what coming back to my place of torture will do to me. I'm obviously already unhinged. Am I going to lose my mind completely?

Sunrise has already begun. I kill the headlights as I approach the mansion's gates. They're closed, but I can see police tape all over the courtyard, and there are several vehicles parked in front of the house. The cops must be inside, combing my father's property inch by inch. The bodies of the slain security guards have been cleared away. In hindsight, maybe Rufio should have gotten rid of those too.

My phone begins to ring, the sound too shrill and irritating. With a frown, I glance at the screen. My mother is calling. Bitch. She knew exactly what my father was doing to me all these years, and she didn't once try to help me. Now that the bastard is gone, she's as good as dead to me too.

I hear the sound of voices coming from ahead. I can't be caught here by the police. My father was a very powerful man in the community, and the authorities need to find the guilty party as quickly as possible.

I put the car in Reverse, spinning it around too fast. The tires screech. *Way to go, Phoenix.*

I glance at the rearview mirror for signs of pursuit. No cars are behind me. I exhale loudly, relieved.

Too soon.

The community exit gate is shut, and in front of it are two black SUVs blocking my way. I could push them aside and blow up the gate with my mind, an option I consider for a split second. But in the end, common sense prevails. Rufio took care of my father's body, and I trust the fucking Knights cleaned up the rest. They want something from us, after all.

No, they want something from Daisy.

Shit. It would be much easier to manipulate Daisy if we weren't around. My brain has deserted me; that's the only explanation for my actions in the last hour. I shouldn't have taken so much Silver-voltage. It's too late now. A quick scan tells me those cops are Idols. They aren't messing around.

One of them stops next to my door and knocks on the window. I school my face into a neutral expression—a skill I mastered a long time ago—before I lower the glass.

"Good evening, Officer. How can I help you?"

"Mr. Westbrook, please step out of the vehicle," the unfriendly suit says.

"What for?" I narrow my eyes, fully projecting my level fifteen Idol essence. I want this idiot to know who he's messing with.

"Sir, don't make me ask again." He puts a hand on his hip, showing me his Taser. Idols are immune to bullets, but those suckers deliver an energy blast strong enough to fry an elephant.

I fight the urge to roll my eyes. I can get ahold of his stupid weapon before he can blink.

"Seriously? Is that supposed to intimidate me?" I ask, because why not? I haven't made a good decision in the last hour. Might as well keep the streak going.

The guy curls his lips into a sneer. "No. But maybe this

will." He places his hand on the door, and in only a few seconds, the car's frame turns bright orange and the temperature inside rises to almost the melting point.

"Fuck!" I send the door flying into the distance and jump out of the car before I turn into ashes. Too bad I didn't hit the jackass in the process.

Before I can do anything else, I'm hit on different spots of my body by several electrical shocks. I could have withstood one discharge but not several at once. I fall on my knees with my jaw clamped shut. A metallic taste fills my mouth while I try to ride the electric currents without passing out.

The motherfucker who melted Rufio's car stands in front of me. "You should have done what I told you."

"I don't follow orders from those beneath me," I grit out.

The guy chuckles, but he can't hide the rage in his eyes. So I'm dealing with an asshole in a position of power but with an inferiority complex. Just fucking great.

"It seems to me you're not as powerful as you think." He signals to someone behind me, and then cold cuffs trap my wrists. My powers become numb. *Fuck*. They must be using the same material the Knights had access to.

The cop who cuffed me helps me to my feet. But if they think I'm going let them take me away without a fight, they're fucking wrong. I may not be able to use my telekinesis ability, but my core power, the gift to give people illusions, is barely affected by their feeble restrains.

I could conjure up the nastiest scenarios—I have several from my own memories—but I opt for something simple and fast. I stick everyone around me into an endless void. The gasps that immediately follow give me a great sense of satisfaction. I prepare to bolt, but the infernal man who melted my mode of transport is staring at me through slits. He's unaffected.

How is that possible?

"Nice try, punk, but your illusions don't work on me."

"How the hell are you doing that? You're not powerful enough to block me. You're barely an Idol." I get back onto my feet.

"True, but let me give you a free piece of intel." He approaches me, still displaying a smug grin. "It pays to work for the right people." From inside his shirt, he pulls out a glass vial attached to a leather string, which he has around his neck. "Your father made sure I was immune to your gift in case you went rogue."

Knowing the motherfucker standing in front of me worked for that monster makes me see red.

"What the fuck is that?"

"What, you don't recognize your own blood? Your old man had plenty to spare. I heard he enjoyed pounding you on a regular basis."

With a roar, I charge the man. Hands cuffed behind my back be damned.

He was expecting that and swiftly moves out of my way. Distracted by his goading, I lose control of the illusion keeping his accomplices occupied. They recover fast and blast me again with their Tasers. Excruciating pain comes first before everything goes dark.

6

MORPHEUS

I want to go back to campus, but my mother is adamant that I rest for a few more hours. There's no woman more stubborn than Shereen Malek. Staring pleadingly at Daisy doesn't help.

"Don't look at me like that. Your mother is right. You need to rest," she says.

I sit back down on my bed with arms crossed and a frown. I can't blame Daisy for siding with my mother. I still feel like shit, so it's logical to assume I look like crap too. I'm not sure what the hell happened to me. The shadows broke free from the bracelets without warning, and it wasn't the god punishing me as I had thought initially.

"Why do you want to leave so suddenly anyway?" she asks.

"My father is home, and I try to avoid the man as much as I can."

"Why?" She sits on the end of the bed, eyeing me with curiosity.

Damn it. She's so pretty it hurts. I can see signs of the ordeal she went through last night in the dark circle under her eyes, but it doesn't change the fact that she's stunning. My heart begins to beat a staccato rhythm, and my mouth goes dry.

I realize I'm staring like a fool and didn't answer the question yet. "Because he hates me."

Her delicate eyebrows furrow together. "How can he hate his own son?"

My chest feels tight. My father has always treated me with contempt, and I didn't understand why until I overhead one of my parents' many arguments. I never told anyone the truth because it makes me so ashamed, even if it's not my fault.

I shrug and drop my gaze to my lap. "Beats me."

Daisy scooches closer but stops short of touching me in any way. "It's his loss. You're an amazing person, Morpheus."

I give her a droll stare. "Please. How can you say that after the way I treated you?"

"True. You were an asshole in the beginning, but I believe wholeheartedly that people can change."

"I haven't changed. I'm still an asshole."

Why am I trying to tell Daisy that I'm not a good person when I yearn for her so much? Maybe after all these years being told I'm an aberration, a mistake, I've started to believe it. It doesn't help that the god who marked me loves to put me down every time he's in my head as well.

Mom comes into the room again. "I've put a spread of hearty food for you and Daisy in the kitchen."

"What about Dad?" I ask.

My mother's expression falls. "He's in his study."

Daisy stands first, and I follow suit. Who knows, maybe I won't suffer my father's presence after all.

In the hallway, the smell of waffles reaches my nose, and my stomach reacts accordingly. Two distinct rumbles echo. One came from me. I look at Daisy with a grin.

"Sorry," she says sheepishly.

I chuckle. "Don't be. I promised you breakfast over an hour ago."

When my mother said spread, she really meant it. She prepared not only waffles but pancakes, eggs, soup, and even sausages.

"Wow, Mrs. Malek. How did you get this ready so fast?" Daisy asks.

"I suppose Morpheus never told you about me." She watches me with a playful accusation in her eyes.

"No, our friendship is new," Daisy replies and then smiles at me.

My face goes hot in an instant. I'm glad I don't blush. Hell and damn. Why am I acting like a shy schoolgirl around her?

"I'm a Fringe, as you can tell. My gift is speed. Mind you, I'm not as fast as any of you kids, but I can make things faster than the average person."

Daisy twists her face into a grimace, which my mother misses. I wonder what part of Mom's statement troubled her. Was it because she implied Daisy is an Idol?

"Now, sit down before the food goes cold." Mom motions for both of us to take our seats.

Daisy doesn't say a word as she fills her plate with a little bit of everything. She won't look into my eyes now, and I want to know what's troubling her. But I can't ask freely while my mother is around, hovering. When I manage to capture Mom's gaze, I plead with my eyes for her to leave. She shakes her head and grins, but before she can actually make herself scarce, my father stumbles into the kitchen. He's clutching a half-empty bottle of whiskey, and his eyes are bloodshot.

"What are you still doing here?" he slurs.

My spine becomes tense immediately. Fleetingly, I spare a glance in Daisy's direction. She's staring at my old man with round eyes.

"Tarek, please." Mom moves toward him, but he sidesteps her.

"Shut up, woman. Every time those damn Zions come into this house it's because something is wrong with that freak." He points at me with hatred in his eyes. I wince, even though that's not the first time he's insulted me like that. I suppose it's worse now because Daisy is witnessing it.

"Morpheus is not a freak," she defends me. "You should be glad to have a son like him."

"Who the hell are you to tell me how I should feel about that aberration?" Dad stumbles forward, and when Mom tries to pull him back, he shoves her. She hits the counter hard and winces.

I push my chair back and jump to my feet. "Don't you dare take your frustrations out on her."

"She's my wife, and I'll do whatever I please."

"Not in front of me, you won't." I purposely bring the shadows back from their confinement. They spring forth unbidden, despite the bracelets at my wrists. Daisy was the one who got them under control before, and it's clear the magical accessory is now useless.

"Morpheus, don't do it. He's not worth your life," my mother pleads, but I'm barely listening. The whooshing in my ears is almost drowning every other sound.

I lash out at the man who I had wanted to make proud since I was a little boy. But it's clear that's never going to happen. He can't see past my mother's mistake. His eyes bulge, followed by a gasp. He drops the bottle of whiskey to the ground, shattering it to pieces, before clutching at his chest.

"Morpheus, please. Let him go." Now it's Daisy who begs.

Her voice pulls at my heartstrings and I falter. My father drops to his knees, breathing hard. His heart is probably about to explode with all the fear I put there. Pure darkness seems to have invaded my body and consumed my soul.

Daisy was wrong. I'm not a good person.

Only when I sense her touch on my arm do I pull my gift back.

My father tumbles forward, propping his hands on shattered glass and spilled liquor. He lifts his eyes to mine, and his face is contorted in rage. "You filthy bastard. I curse the day you were born. Get out of this house and never come back."

"With pleasure," I say through clenched teeth.

"Morpheus, wait. You can't leave like that," Mom pleads.

"Yes I can. I don't belong here, Mother. I never have."

I march out of the kitchen, seeing nothing in my way. The ominous sound of thunder rattles the walls of the house, and when I burst out the front door, the sky decides to fall down in thick droplets of rain. How fitting.

"Morpheus! Wait!" Daisy comes running after me.

I stop next to my car, but I don't turn to her. I can't face her, not after what she saw.

She circles around, stopping in front of me. There's barely any space between our bodies. The rain is coming down fast, drenching us within seconds. Daisy doesn't seem to care about that as she stares into my eyes.

"I told you I was an asshole, Daisy."

"For defending your mother from a mean drunk? I don't think so."

"He's right about me, though. I *am* an aberration."

"Shut up. I don't want you to say that. You're not an aberration."

I lift my hands, which have completely disappeared under the shadows. "Look at me. I'm made of darkness, Daisy."

She grabs them, and immediately the shadows recede. We both watch the phenomenon for a few seconds before Daisy speaks. "Darkness isn't bad. Without it, there can be no light."

I curl my fingers around hers and then finally have the courage to do what I've been craving for so long. I pull her toward me and crush my mouth to hers. The kiss is demanding and harsh, full of need, but Daisy doesn't resist. She opens her lips and allows me to invade her mouth. The darkness I felt deep in my soul diminishes, but it doesn't disappear completely. In the back of my head, I think that maybe Daisy is using her power without knowing. But I don't care. As long as she lets me hold her, she can unmake me.

I grab her face between my hands and deepen the kiss, pushing her body against the car so I can meld my body to hers. An electric spark runs through my veins, turning me into fire. She clutches my shoulders and pulls me even closer to her, pressing my erection against her belly. Fuck, I want to do more than just taste her mouth.

She eases off a little and whispers, "Let's get out of the rain."

"Is it raining? I didn't notice." I capture her lips again, biting the bottom a little before switching my attention to her neck.

Daisy arches her back, and I take that as an invitation to pepper kisses toward the swell of her breasts. But then I remember where we are and stop. I'm burning up for her, but I can't let things go any further while we're standing in front of my parents' house.

I pull away and reluctantly say, "Let's get out of here."

"Do you want me to drive?"

"No, it's okay. I feel better now." And I need the distraction.

"Good. I don't have a driver's license."

"Really? We need to remedy that."

She smiles tightly before walking around the vehicle.

Shit. Did I say something wrong?

I slip behind the steering wheel, hating the feel of wet clothes against the leather seat. Daisy joins me inside, shivering.

I turn on the engine and crank up the heater. Then I remember I left an old sweatshirt in the back seat of the car. I twist around and look for the discarded piece of clothing, finding it on the floor. Great.

"Here. It's a little dirty, but at least it's dry."

"Thanks." Daisy takes the offering and sets it next to her. She then bites her lower lip before peeling her wet T-shirt off.

With a hard swallow, I force my gaze toward the road and put the car in Drive. My dick, which was at half-mast, is at full attention again.

We don't speak for several minutes until Daisy breaks the silence.

"Your bracelets are broken."

Of all the things she could say, that wasn't what I expected.

"I figured as much. The Zions couldn't fix it this time?"

"No. They said the magic in them was utterly destroyed. I'm afraid I did that." She looks out the window.

"How?"

"I think I accidentally touched one of them."

I suppose if Daisy can take away an Idol's power, she can break an ancient spell too.

"I had to eventually learn how to control my gift without help, so don't beat yourself up for it."

"It's not only that. I think that when we kissed, I started taking your powers away. What if I can't control it? What if I can't touch anyone without unmaking them?" Her voice rises to a shrill.

I turn on the blinkers and pull onto the side of the road.

"Why did you stop?" she asks.

I unbuckle my seat belt and face her. "You only had your full powers for less than twenty-four hours. It will take time to learn to master it."

"But what if I accidentally touch someone before I do?"

I grab her left hand tight, knowing she'll try to pull away. "Practice on me."

Her eyes go round. "Are you crazy? What if I unmake you?"

"You won't."

"How can you be so sure?"

Dropping my gaze to our joined hands, I take a deep breath. I never thought I'd be sharing this secret with anyone. "The reason my father hates me so much is that I'm not his biological son."

"Oh, Morpheus...."

I hear pity in her tone, so I'm quick to continue. "Please, don't feel sorry for me."

Daisy pinches her lips together and keeps watching me intensely. Her beautiful hazel eyes shine with emotion. "I feel sorry for him, not you."

Shaking my head, I laugh derisively. "I'm sure he wouldn't appreciate your sentiment."

"Do you know who your biological father is?"

"Not his name, but I know what he is."

"What?" She squeezes my hand tighter.

"He was a demigod, Daisy."

Her eyes get rounder and her bee-stung lips make a perfect O. "Oh my goodness. That means you have the strongest link to a deity possible. You should be stronger than Bryce."

"Yeah, I know."

7

BRYCE

"Rufio, what have you done?" I ask.

My brother turns to me with eyes wide and a pale face. He opens and shuts his mouth, but no sound comes forth. Around us, the crowd stares in stunned silence.

"You killed her," Renata murmurs, covering her mouth next.

Rufio's face contorts into an anguished expression, and it's what propels me to finally take action. I look around the room. There are twelve students, all of them with cameras in their hands. I don't think twice before I fry their devices with my mind and also disable the security cameras, sending a destructive electric current through the relays to make sure nothing is left of the footage. Unfortunately, there's nothing to be done about the witnesses. I don't have the power to alter memories, but at least there isn't hard evidence of what happened here.

I hope no one was broadcasting live. Fuck.

I grab Rufio's arm and steer him toward the exit.

"What are you doing?" he asks.

"We need to get out of here," I reply through clenched teeth.

"We can't just leave."

Once outside, I whirl on him. "Rufio, you just killed Drusilla. Do you know what's going to happen to you?"

"Bryce and Rufio, come with me at once," a familiar voice says from behind me.

"Mother, we don't have time for your bullshit," I grit out.

She takes a step toward us, her eyes flashing with anger. "Do not argue with me. To my office. Now!"

A violent gush of wind comes from her, creating a mini tornado around Rufio and me. She's never used her gift against us before, which means she knows exactly what happened, and she's furious.

"Fine. We'll come with you!" Rufio shouts to be heard over the howling wind.

The gale recedes, but our mother isn't paying attention to us now. She's glaring at the small crowd of students who followed us out.

"Get back to your quarters this instant. Any student found in the common areas today will be facing expulsion."

Shit. What the hell is she doing? Imposing a crazy curfew like that on a weekend. She's rattled, another first for her. That can only mean she doesn't have a solution to get Rufio out of the giant clusterfuck he's in now.

We follow her but at a safe distance. Her power is amplified, and it's rolling out in waves; one wrong word from us and there will be hell to pay.

She stops in front of the main building, and by the rise and fall of her shoulders, I can tell she's taking deep breaths. She whirls around, checking the perimeter. I do the same, noticing no one has followed us.

"I have to get you out here," she tells Rufio.

"Where am I going to go?"

"For now, we're going home. I have to think." She rubs her forehead and then resumes her brisk walk.

We circle around the building and head toward the staff's parking lot. There are only a few vehicles there, being the weekend and all.

"How did you know about what happened?" I ask as soon as we're all in her car.

"I saw the beginning of the altercation on the security feed. I raced here. If I had been on campus when it started, I wouldn't have let things go that far."

"The entire thing was caught on camera before I cut the feed. How come no security guards came to stop Drusilla?" I ask.

Mom clenches her jaw so tightly that a muscle on her jaw twitches. "It seems this was a setup. What I want to know is what possessed Rufio to kill that stupid girl in front of all those witnesses? Do you have a death wish? Is that what this is about?"

"She compelled me to kill her."

"That's impossible. Drusilla was a level twelve Idol. She wouldn't be able to compel you."

"She hasn't been a level twelve for a while," I say.

Mom takes her eyes off the road for a second to look at me. "What do you mean?"

"She leveled up," Rufio replies.

"Leveled up? What do you think this is, a video game? There's no leveling up in real life."

"We don't know how she did it, okay?" I lie.

I can't tell our mother about the island of horrors or the god who roams there. She's too cunning. That knowledge could potentially be disastrous in her hands. I don't know what her plans are, but I have no illusions that it's something good.

"I'm not lying about Drusilla. She compelled me to turn her into dust. I'm not stupid enough to off the girl like that."

"It doesn't matter if you're telling the truth or not. No one will believe you," Mom retorts.

"I destroyed the recording from the security feed and also all the phones in the room. That ought to count for something," I argue.

Mom snorts. "In this day and age, at least one video must have been uploaded online before you had the foresight to destroy the evidence."

"Are you implying Rufio will be prosecuted for murder?" My voice rises.

"Only if they catch him."

"I'm not going to run away and spend the rest of my life in hiding," he snaps.

"What do you suggest, Rufio? You killed the daughter of one of the most influential Idols in this country. He'll want your head."

She pulls up the driveway of our home. I was so engrossed in the conversation that I didn't even notice the ride. Mom must have driven like a maniac to make it here so quickly.

"If you want me to flee, this is the last place I should be," Rufio counters.

Mom gets out of the car without saying a word.

I turn in my seat to look at Rufio. "Just say the word and we're out of here."

"And go where, Bryce? Let's face it. I fucked up royally. I should have known better than to get near that bitch."

"Don't you dare blame yourself for what Drusilla did to you."

Rufio laughs derisively. "This wasn't even her doing. It was the god's punishment. He must know that Daisy is an Idol now. He was too keen on destroying her. He didn't want Magia's powers restored."

"One more reason to make sure the authorities don't get a hold of you."

Rufio's door gets yanked open suddenly and our father is standing there.

"Get out. Now!"

"Are you fucking kidding me?" I jump out of the car in a flash, ready to defend Rufio from our father's wrath.

Dad's breathing is coming out in bursts as he stares Rufio down. But my brother simply raises his chin and stares defiantly at him.

"You must be the stupidest kid alive," our father finally says. "No matter how much you hate someone, you don't kill them in broad daylight in front of witnesses."

"Unless that someone is a Fringe or a Norm, right?" I reply angrily. "Then it doesn't matter."

Dad whips his gaze to mine. "Don't even start with me. I know you and your brother have been cozying up with that Norm whore."

"Daisy is not a whore," Rufio grits out.

The slap on the face is swift. Rufio doesn't stand a chance to move out of range. Our father is also a level fifteen, and just like our mother, his gift is tied to the elements. In his case, he can control mineral materials. In a head-to-head confrontation, they would be equally matched in terms of power, but Dad has experience on his side. Plus, Rufio isn't thinking straight right now.

Covering his face with his hand, he glowers at our father. Dark sparks of energy coil around his body, the telltale sign he's about to blow. Fuck.

"Go ahead. Try to strike me," our father goads. "You'll not only miss, but you'll also seal your fate."

With a flick of my hand, I shove Rufio away from him. He slides across the courtyard, stopping a few yards from us.

"Bryce, what the hell!"

Ignoring him, I turn to Dad. "Drusilla compelled Rufio to kill her. You may choose not to believe me, but that's the fucking truth. The question is, are you going to help him or not?"

The man stares at me through slits for several beats, and it takes a herculean effort on my part to not squirm under his gaze. I'm stronger than he is, but years of oppression and brainwashing make me feel like I'm still a child.

"I'm aware of the circumstances. Your mother filled me in," he finally replies.

"I'm not running away," Rufio insists as he approaches. "If that's your idea, forget about it."

A glint of pride shines in our father's eyes. "I'm glad to hear that, boy."

"So what's your plan?" I ask. "Mom was fresh out of ideas."

"Forget about your mother. This is all her fucking fault anyway. If she had paid more attention to her duties as principal instead of mingling with the riff-raff, this wouldn't have happened."

"That doesn't change the fact that Drusilla is dead, and her father will more than likely want retribution," I say.

Dad sneers. "I'm not going to lose my son thanks to some deranged bitch. It's high time you two step up to the role you've been destined for."

Rufio furrows his eyebrows. "What's that supposed to mean?"

"You're coming with me."

8

PHOENIX

A splash of cold water on my face jars me awake. My hands are cuffed behind my back, and I'm strapped to an uncomfortable metal chair. I shake my head to get rid of the droplets of water stuck to my eyelashes, but it takes a few seconds for the blurriness to dissipate.

The smug cop who had a vial of my blood hanging around his neck is standing in front of me.

"Sorry to wake you so roughly, but time is of the essence."

"You can't keep me trapped like this. I've done nothing wrong."

He presses his index against his lips and tsks. "Really? You've done nothing? So refusing to cooperate with the authorities and assault is nothing to you?"

He turns to a figure hidden in a corner by the shadows. "Don't you hate how privileged kids are so fucking entitled?"

"It sounds to me like you have a problem with those better off than you," I say. "Jealous much?"

The cop's face twists into a scowl, but he attempts to mask his reaction with a forced grin. "I'm definitely not jealous of you, considering the charges you're facing."

Maintaining a mask of calm and innocence, I ask, "Charges? You have to do better than that, buddy."

"Let's start with home invasion and kidnapping."

"I have no idea what you're talking about."

He laughs without humor and begins to pace in front of me. "So that's how you want to play, huh? All right, I'll indulge you. At approximately one in the morning today, your father's property was invaded by a group of Idols who killed all the security guards. Their mangled bodies were left for us to clean up, but your father is missing."

I smile. "Boy, that's what you have going for you? Damn, you're not only scraping the bottom of the Idol scale, you're also fucking dumb."

The punch comes so fast, I have no warning. It sends my head back, and it would have toppled the chair too if it wasn't bolted to the floor. My head is ringing and my nose is throbbing. *The motherfucker better not have broken my nose.*

"I'd be more careful about the words you use with me, boy. You're my bitch now."

I watch him through slits, and at the same time, I test the strength of the cuffs around my wrists. They're still dampening my powers but not completely. I bet I can break free if I focus hard enough. And when I do, this asshole is fucked.

"Keep telling yourself lies if it makes you feel better. But you and I both know you can't keep me here. You have nothing on me, and I bet the security tapes you've confiscated from my parents' house showed zilch."

I'm totally bluffing. My mind was reeling when I left my father's property, and I have no fucking clue what was done to the tapes. But my gamble pays off. The asshole's brows scrunch together, and his lips become nothing but a thin flat line.

"Cut the bullshit, you little fuck. Where's your father?"

"I don't know."

"You're lying, and I have no qualms about using creative

ways to extract the information from you." He lifts his hand, which is now ablaze. "How about I start off by melting your pretty face away? I bet your lady fans would love that."

He's not bluffing. I seriously doubt this chump is an actual cop.

He approaches me menacingly, his eyes filled with mirth. I try to ignore the nearing flames, focusing instead on fighting the material that's dampening my powers. I don't need to overcome it completely, only enough to break free from the cuffs.

His hand is mere inches from my face now. "I'm going to ask you one more time. Where's your father?"

I don't answer because I need every ounce of focus. I picture those damn cuffs flying off my wrists, but I also sense the resistance. It's giving way, though.

"What is it, boy? Cat got your tongue?"

My nostrils flare when I give the final push. The barrier of dampening powers on the cuffs cracks, followed by the soft click of them opening. Faster than lightning, I jump off the chair, sending the cop flying back. He crashes against the interrogation room mirror, cracking the surface, and doesn't get up. His silent pal in the corner comes into view, a short bald man with a round belly. He's chewing on a toothpick, and he looks as dangerous as a stool. A quick scan tells me he's a Fringe, a low-level one.

"Do you want a piece of me too?" I ask.

"Nah. I was just here because Agent Torrance needs an audience when he's feeling particularly nasty." He turns to his unconscious coworker. "Nice job there."

The door to the interrogation room opens, and in comes someone I didn't expect to see at all—my mother. She's accompanied by another guy in a sharp gray suit. He's so tall and thin, he looks like death himself.

"Phoenix, are you okay?" she asks.

I don't know how to answer her question. It's the first time in my entire life that she's asked about my well-being. Not even when I was a small child did she show concern. Her eyes travel the length of my body before she looks over my shoulder. Her companion steps forward.

"Have you been interrogating my client without his lawyer present?" he asks the Fringe cop.

"Not me, sir. He was." He points at the asshole cop, still crumpled on the floor.

"On what grounds? My son has done nothing wrong," Mom states vehemently.

"To be honest, I don't know, ma'am. Agent Torrance believes your son is involved in your husband's disappearance, but he has no proof of that. Between you and me, he's got nothing."

"What's going on here?" Another cop comes in, eyeing the scene with suspicion. "Who authorized you to barge into an interrogation room unaccompanied?"

"The name is Mr. Frisk. I'm Mr. Westbrook's attorney. I was just informed that one of your agents has illegally detained and interrogated my client without any motive."

"What happened to Agent Torrance?" the man asks.

"He slipped and fell," the short guy replies with a shrug.

"And you expect me to believe that?" He puts his hands on his hips.

"It doesn't concern me what you believe or not. We're leaving, and make no mistake, we *will* be contacting the head of the bureau and demanding a thorough investigation of what has clearly been an abuse of power." My mother's lawyer turns to me. "Come on, son. We're going home now."

My spine turns rigid in an instant, an involuntary reaction to the word "home." But then I remember the reason that my stomach coils is no longer there to torment me.

I walk ahead of everyone, ensuring I don't make eye contact with the new agent who came onto the scene. I have a suspicion he knew exactly what Agent Torrance was up to, and I don't want to give him any reason to keep me trapped here.

As we make our way through the precinct, I feel everyone's gaze on me. This time I don't keep my gaze down. On the contrary, I sweep the room and take a mental note of every single agent who's glaring in my direction. Those are probably the ones who were in my father's pockets. Do they all know how to neutralize my core gift, or was that information only Agent Torrance had?

Fuck. One person who can block me is already one person too many.

The sun is already up, but dark clouds are approaching from the east. The smell of ozone in the air tells me a big lightning storm is coming. But is it a regular occurrence, or is that damn god coming for retribution?

I don't say a word to my mother, nor do I make eye contact. She's as bad as my father in my book. The last thing I want to do is get into a car with her, but the other option is to walk back to campus.

Mother's lawyer is driving, and we both sit in the back. I look out the window and pretend she's not there.

After several minutes of silence, she finally speaks.

"Phoenix, I can't begin to tell you how sorry I am about everything."

I scoff. "Please, Mother. Spare me the remorseful speech."

"I don't blame you for resenting me."

I whip my face to her. "Resenting you? I don't resent you. I *hate* you."

She winces and then drops her gaze to her lap. "I deserve that."

"I just want to know why. Why did you let him do all those awful things to me?" I choke out.

"I had no choice. I was marked too. I had the same tattoo you did."

I narrow my eyes to slits, not buying her excuse. "Since when?"

"Since I married him. He told me that in his family, it was a tradition for the wives to receive their husband's mark. I was so in love with him that I didn't hesitate. I thought the idea was terribly romantic. Little did I know what it really meant." She drops her gaze to her lap and wriggles her fingers together.

I don't speak for several beats while I process her story. All these years, I thought my mother didn't care about me at all. But she had been my father's prisoner, just as I had been. Bile pools in my mouth. Still, I can't accept the fact that she never tried to save me.

My vision is blurry, and the lump in my throat is making it hard to breathe. Covering my mouth with a closed fist, I look out the window. Fat tears run down my cheeks while tremors rack my body.

"I tried to take you away from him before he marked you. He found out, of course. But instead of punishing me, he took his anger out on you."

I close my eyes, remembering the first time my father laid his hands on me. He didn't rape me then, but he did almost kill me. I choke on a sob, hating that he can still make me feel this terrible even after his demise.

"I was terrified that if I tried again, he'd kill you." Her voice cracks at the end.

"He was close on many occasions," I reply bitterly.

"I'll never forgive myself for all the years you had to endure his torture. I'm so, so sorry, Phoenix."

She sounds so shattered, so remorseful, that it cracks my heart even more. We were both victims of a monster.

I turn to her. "Mom...."

She lifts her tear-streaked face to mine, and finally the dam breaks loose. I throw myself in her arms, and for the first time, she comforts me. The tears come faster and more violently.

They're like a waterfall of all my suppressed emotions, finally being allowed to break free. I don't know if I'll ever be able to build any kind of relationship with her, or truly forgive her, but right now, I'll pretend she's the mother I'd always wished she were.

9

———

DAISY

"**D**o the guys know?"

He shakes his head. "No. You're the first person I've told."

His confession makes my heart beat faster. Not even his closest friends know, yet he confided in me.

"Why is that?"

Morpheus's shoulders sag forward. "I didn't want them to know my mother was unfaithful. I know it sounds stupid, but it makes me so ashamed that she valued having an Idol child more than being true to her husband. No wonder he hates me."

"Oh, Morpheus. Don't make excuses for his awful behavior."

"It doesn't matter anyway. Now he finally has the guts to do what he's been dreaming about since I was born. He was terrified my real father would punish him if he kicked my mother and me to the curb. It seems alcohol has erased that fear."

"Was he also afraid of you?"

Morpheus laughs without humor. "Oh yeah. Very much so. But I'm not as powerful as he thinks I am. My mother didn't think things through when she decided to produce an Idol child at all costs. Because she's a Fringe, I can't handle all the power I inherited from the demigod who sired me. That's why when my powers began to manifest, she had these bracelets made."

"So that's why you think you can be my guinea pig? Because of your direct link to a demigod?"

"Yup." Morpheus releases my hand and removes the bracelets.

I hold my breath, expecting the shadows to leap forth and devour him whole, but they remain hidden.

"Morpheus, I still don't think that's a good idea," I say.

He reaches over, cupping my face. I should push him away, but my careless heart has other ideas. I lean into his caress, covering his hand with mine. My heart flutters, and radioactive butterflies break free in my belly.

"I want to kiss you again," he breathes.

"I want to kiss you again too."

The rain is still pouring outside, and we can't see anything beyond the gray curtain. We're trapped in our own cocoon, and there's nothing keeping Morpheus from crossing the distance between us. And he does just that.

Overwhelmed by desire, I do the same, meeting him in the middle. The moment our lips touch, an electric current runs through my body, igniting a furnace inside of my chest. It spreads rapidly like wildfire. My bones burn and my skin yearns for everything he can give me. I need him so desperately, it's almost like I want to take his entire essence into myself.

That's when I feel the wrongness of it. I'm sucking Morpheus's powers out of him.

I pull away suddenly, breathing hard.

His eyes are half closed but lust-filled. He leans forward, trying to capture my lips again, but I have no choice besides pushing him away.

"Morpheus, we can't. I'm sorry."

His gaze goes from smoldering hot to ice cold in a split second. "Why?"

"Didn't you feel it? I was taking your powers."

His eyebrows arch. "I didn't notice."

I face forward, hugging myself. "I'm like a succubus. This is awful."

"You're nothing like that. We'll figure this out together."

I look at him. "I didn't take it all, did I?"

"I don't think you took anything, to be honest. Let's test it out."

"How are you going to do that?" I cower away from him. "Please don't put fear into my heart."

An emotion I can only describe as remorse strikes Morpheus's features. "Daisy, I'll never do that to you again." He turns away, rubbing his face. "You have no idea how much I regret treating you so terribly before."

I nibble on my lower lip, hating the way the memory of my early days at the academy makes me feel. So much has happened since that it was easy to simply push those sentiments under the rug. Apparently, I'm not over it. But I don't want to be the type of person who holds grudges, who can't truly forgive. That kind of negative emotion will only turn me bitter.

"I believe you," I say, "but the memory is still too vivid in my mind."

"If I have to spend the rest of my life atoning for that, I will."

I glance at him, finding his eyes shining with so much sincerity, so much emotion, that I wholeheartedly trust him.

"How are you going to test if you have all your powers?" I ask to get back on track.

"Right." Morpheus stares at his bracelet-free wrists. "This is the first time that I'm not wearing the protection of the bracelets, and the shadows aren't tormenting me."

"But they did when I accidentally disabled them."

"True." He looks me in the eye. "I'm going to bring them forth."

"On purpose?"

"Yes. I did it before when I thought Drusilla had done something to you."

The memory comes to the forefront of my mind. Morpheus turned his shadows into a whip. It was absolutely terrifying.

"They almost consumed you then."

His lips twist into a sardonic grin. "Good thing you're here. If it happens again, just touch me."

I can't help but hear the double meaning of his words, which makes my cheeks warmer.

He switches his attention to his hands again, and a couple of seconds later, the shadows reappear, writhing like snakes. They coil around Morpheus's wrists slowly this time, not out of control like before.

Without warning, Morpheus flicks his left wrist, slingshooting the shadows forward. They hit the windshield, spreading through the glass until they block the view entirely. The inside of the car turns almost pitch black thanks to the now tinted windows.

"I'm still an Idol, which means...." He grabs my hand.

My heart skips a beat. I'm nervous for more reasons than one. The leather seat creaks as Morpheus moves. He leans forward, stopping an inch from me. "I think we should continue where we left off," he finishes.

The speakers blast the most god-awful ringtone, destroying the moment like a vengeful machete.

"What the hell!" He digs his cell phone from the car's console. It automatically got connected wirelessly to the sound system. The incoming call's number is also flashing on the car's display.

I frown, recognizing it. "Why is Toby calling you?"

"Is that who it is?" Morpheus asks.

"Yeah, I memorized his number."

At once, Morpheus answers the phone. "Hello?"

He turns to me with eyebrows furrowed together. "I'm not home, but actually, she's next to me. Hold on." He offers me the phone. "He wants to talk to you."

I take the device from him, already worried. "Toby? What's going on?"

"Finally! I've been trying to reach you for hours."

"Why? Is everything okay? Is Rosie with you?"

My plan was to grab breakfast and then ask Morpheus to drive me to see Rosie. But the situation with him derailed me completely. Now the urgency to see my sister returns with a vengeance. I have to talk to her.

"She's in her room. I'm calling you from your landlord's living room. She made me sleep on the couch, by the way."

Like I was truly worried about Toby and Rosie sleeping in the same bed, considering everything that's happened in less than twenty-four hours.

"You sound agitated."

"I need to speak with you in person, but I don't want to leave Rosie alone. Can you get a ride here?"

"I'm on my way. Toby, you're scaring me. Why can't you tell me over the phone?"

"I—shit, I can't, okay? When do you think you can get here?"

Morpheus must have heard every single word Toby said, because he lifts his arm and the shadows covering the windshield return to him. The rain is no longer coming down like it's the end of the word, and visibility is much better.

"In an hour or so," I reply.

"Good. I'll see you then." He ends the call before I can ask any more questions.

"Is everything okay?"

"You heard him, right?"

Morpheus nods. "Sorry. He was loud."

"Did he sound nervous to you?"

"Yeah, a bit."

"He wants to talk to me in person. Do you mind driving me to my old place?"

"Not at all." Morpheus adjusts his pants, reminding me of what we were about to do. The throbbing between my legs is also a tell.

I'm disappointed and glad for the interruption. I was ready to succumb to my feelings for him, disregarding his safety. He may be confident I can't take away his powers, but I'm not so sure.

"When did you give your phone number to Toby?"

"I don't remember ever giving him my digits, but Toby was involved with several school organizations last year. It's possible he got it from the school administration. He said he called Bryce, Rufio, and Phoenix first, but I was the only one who actually picked up the phone."

"That's strange. Do you think they're all right?"

"They were all in their bedrooms before I left, and it's still quite early." His gaze lands on the digital clock on his dashboard.

"It's almost noon. How can you think that's early?"

"It's Sunday, Daisy. And no one had any sleep last night," he replies, but his words sound hollow to me, almost as if he doesn't believe them.

"I'm mostly concerned about Phoenix." I look out the window.

"We all are. He wouldn't talk to us last night. He locked himself in his room as soon as we got into the apartment."

"You never suspected?"

"I only started to notice something was off recently. As a matter of fact, it was when you came into the picture."

I don't know what to make of that statement. "Uh, okay."

"I'm not saying this as a bad thing. I think you were meant to save us, Daisy."

"Don't be crazy. I'm not a savior."

"You're a warrior, dauntless, fierce. That's probably why we wanted so much to destroy you in the beginning. You upset the status quo. You challenged us."

"I was only trying to survive."

"I know." He reaches over and takes my hand. This time, the electric shock is mild, barely noticeable. "You're not alone anymore."

My heart squeezes tightly. Losing my parents at such a young age put me in survival mode and forced me to build a shield around it. My parents' death left a hole in my chest. If I pretended it wasn't there, I could face another day. But everything changed when Morpheus, Rufio, Bryce, and Phoenix came into my life. I couldn't have known how much they would mean to me in such a short period of time.

"Can I make a confession?" I ask.

"If you want to."

"I think I'm more afraid now that I'm an Idol than before when I was a hopeless Norm."

"Is it because of your ability to unmake Idols?"

"In part. I feel I've been manipulated my entire life and this is only the beginning. The Knights want something from me. What if I don't want to cooperate with them? What's going to happen to me then?"

"Daisy, I want to make something very clear to you. No one is making you do anything you don't want to. I don't care if they're Knights or the gods themselves. I won't let them."

"Would you challenge a god to protect me?" I ask in disbelief.

He takes his eyes off the road for a second to look at me. "I've already done it. We all have."

10

RUFIO

After our father dropped the statement that it was high time for us to fulfill our destinies, I knew it didn't mean anything good. It might have taken me a while to see the man for who he is, but I know now that all the years he preached about the supremacy of Idols was a load of bullshit. Daisy made me see that Norms and Fringes are people just like us. They aren't vermin undeserving of living.

Hate isn't something you're born with. It's taught. And Bryce and I couldn't have possibly had a better teacher than Daddy dearest.

We don't go into the house; instead, our father urges us toward his vehicle. Bryce aims for the passenger seat, but Dad stops him. "No. I want both of you in the back seat."

"Why?" my brother asks.

"Because I said so."

He waits next to the car until we obey him and then orders us to wear the blindfolds we find inside.

"Are you kidding me?" I glare at the piece of black fabric in my hand.

"You haven't earned the right to see where I'm taking you yet. Don't argue with me, and put that thing on, damn it." He slams the back door shut and walks around the car.

"Where do you think he's taking us?" I ask Bryce.

"I have no idea, but I say we do exactly as he commands."

I open my mouth to offer a retort, but Bryce cuts me off. "Do not argue with me, and follow my lead."

He ties the blindfold behind his head and sags against the leather seat. Reluctantly, I do the same. Going to a mysterious location with our father beats getting arrested for killing Drusilla. I still can't believe I fell right into her trap. I'm the stupidest person alive.

When I hear my father slide behind the wheel, I ask, "How long until we get where we're going?"

"You'll know when we get there."

The silent engine turns to life; the only telltale are the soft vibrations beneath our seat. A lurch forward tells me we're on the move.

A minute later, my father speaks again, though not to us.

"Delta, I have a job for you."

Who the hell is Delta?

"I just sent you several images. I need you to get a team of Sweepers and follow the standard procedure on every single person in those pictures. Call me when the job is done."

"What the hell was that all about?" Bryce asks.

"I just did what your incompetent mother should have done from the get-go."

"What the hell are Sweepers?" I ask in turn.

"Idols who can scrub minds. Bryce thought fast and destroyed the security tape footage and the cell phones of everyone present, but there's still the issue of their memories."

"Isn't scrubbing minds forbidden by law?" Bryce pipes up again.

"So is killing an Idol," Dad replies sternly. "I'm cleaning up the mess Rufio made by whatever means necessary. Do you have a problem with that?"

"No."

"What if someone broadcasted that live?" I ask.

"Who do you take me for, Rufio? It was the first thing I took care of. The only loose ends now are those witnesses. Next time you decide to kill someone, do me a favor and don't have an audience."

"Don't plan to," I grumble.

It seems that not being able to see where we're going makes the trip much longer. Also, without visual stimuli, all I can think about are the events of the night before. Does my father know about what happened to Mr. Westbrook? They weren't friends, but Saturn's Bay is a small town, and everyone knows everyone. Damn it. We shouldn't have trusted Mr. X's associates with the cleanup. What if they missed something?

I don't think my father will be so willing to help if he finds out we invaded Mr. Westbrook's home and killed a bunch of Fringes and Idols in the process. Don't get me started if he discovers that I helped get rid of that monster's body. I don't regret any of it, and I'd do it again if given the chance, but it's best to face one bad situation at a time.

No one speaks for the remainder of the trip, but I know Dad is headed for the mountains by the vehicle's inclination and the way it keeps swerving left and right. The motion is making me carsick thanks to the blindfold. I clamp my jaw shut. Puking all over my father's pristine car won't help me one bit.

Finally, the car begins to slow down, and a minute later, it stops. There's a whirring outside, which I immediately associate with the sound of a gate sliding open. The tires crunch against loose gravel as we move forward. A second later, the car dips at a forty-five-degree angle, if I were to guess.

"We're here. You can remove the blindfolds," Dad says after a minute.

I blink my eyes several times to adjust them to the brighter lights. Bryce opens his door and gets out, prompting me to do the same. If I didn't know we'd traveled through several hills, I'd say we're underground. But since we did, we're most definitely inside a mountain. A vast space with a high domed ceiling greets us. The walls are smooth concrete, but after ten feet or so, they stop abruptly to reveal the rough-cut rock.

Ahead of us, the stainless steel doors to an elevator stand almost lonely in the background, if it weren't for the Idols wearing combat uniforms and sunglasses standing on each of its sides. A quick scan doesn't tell me their level on the power scale; they're masking it. There's only one reason that comes to mind for their trouble: they want people to underestimate them, which means they're packing power.

Without a word, our father strides toward the elevator. The guards remain frozen as if they were marble statues. The doors slide open and my father steps inside. Bryce and I follow him, but I make a point to stare at one of the guards to see if I can get a reaction from the guy. Nothing. Not even a jaw muscle twitch.

"What is this place?" I ask as soon as the doors shut again.

"This is where the birth of a new era for Idols will take place."

My stomach twists savagely as if I had eaten something rotten. His words remind me of what our mother said to me not too long ago, that a shift was coming and we had to prepare for that. I wonder if she told Bryce the same thing. It's a pity I can't read minds.

The elevator goes down and down. It almost feels like we're going to the center of the Earth, or worse, Hell. It stops suddenly, and when the doors slide open again, they reveal nothing but a long and narrow corridor. A golf cart is parked next to the elevator, but Dad doesn't veer toward it. Instead, he leads us to a single door to our left with a scan pad next to it. He leans forward and a blue light runs overs his right eye. Damn, a door secured by a retina scan. I wonder what we'll find inside.

"Go in," my father says while he waits by the door.

We enter a small meeting room with a long rectangular table that has six chairs on each side and one chair at the end. Not what I imagined, and I'm disappointed. All that modern technology to secure a meeting room? Seriously?

Two Idols are in the room, sitting at the end of the table. The door slams shut behind us, sealing Bryce and me in the room with individuals who aren't masking their powers. The man on the left is a hulking albino with short cropped hair and pink irises. He's wearing a dark suit that's straining against his beefy arms. His traps are so developed that they almost make his neck disappear.

The Idol at the head of the table is, for lack of a better word, ancient. The man has so many wrinkles on his face that he resembles a shar-pei. He sits stooped in his chair, sinking against the supple leather as if his frail body frame can't support his head. But despite his feeble appearance, he's the most powerful being in the room. He's a level seventeen, just like my brother, but the added years of experience make up for the difference, I'm sure.

My father strides in their direction and takes the seat to the old man's right.

"Those are your boys, heh?" he says.

"Yes, Master."

Wait. "Master"? Hell and damn. Is this a fucking cult?

"I thought you didn't know if you could trust them," the albino guy says, making my spine rigid in an instant.

Our father glances in our direction. "I have my concerns, especially after what happened today."

"What the hell!" I say, ready to burst out of here. This is looking more and more like a trap.

Bryce steps in front of me. "If you don't trust your own sons, why did you bring us here?"

I move out from behind my brother who, I have no doubt, is using his body as a shield to protect me. But I don't need his protection. I don't care if those Idols are powerful. I am too.

"To prove I didn't waste my time by marrying your mother."

"War is upon us, and alliances must be declared," the old geezer says. "Your father tells me you've been mingling with a Norm girl. Is she hot?"

The man gets a leery glint in his eyes, making me want to blow him to dust.

"Yes, for a Norm," Bryce replies coldly. "She was a toy thing we shared."

"Ah, toys are good. I've been known to enjoy Norm pussy in my good old days." The man flashes his yellow teeth. "As long as that's all they are, toys to be discarded after you get bored."

"Naturally. She means nothing to us," Bryce continues.

"So you say," my father replies. "But your mother also told me a similar lie, and in the end, she was fucking a Norm behind my back, so forgive me if I don't take your word for it."

"And you killed one of your own," the albino man adds.

"Drusilla wasn't one of us. Her best friend was a Fringe. She didn't share the same values we do," Bryce adds.

What the hell is he talking about? Drusilla was just like the other Idols in school, a Norm-hater, and I wouldn't go as far as say Cherise was her best friend. Bryce is lying through his teeth.

"Was that the reason you killed her, boy?" The old geezer looks at me.

Fuck. I can't tell those suckers that she compelled me. I can't look weak in front of them.

"She got under my nerves and I lashed out," I answer instead.

"Are you saying you lost control of your powers?" The albino man raises his white eyebrows.

"No, I said I lost my temper. Not the same thing," I grit out.

"Mr. Dharma is a powerful player in the Idol community. We don't want to lose that potential source of investment. A war costs money." He turns to the old man.

"I've already taken care of the incident. There won't be anything linking Rufio to her death by the end of the day," my father replies.

"Very well." The *master* links his hands together. "The young one has proven he can kill without remorse. That's a quality I greatly admire in an Idol. The question is, are you willing to prove your loyalty to the cause?"

"And what *is* the cause?" I ask.

"For years, Idols had to make concessions so weaker creatures like Fringes and Norms could coexist with us. The time has finally come for us to claim our gods-given destiny. They have blessed us with their gifts for one reason, to make this planet a better, prosperous place. To do so, we must eliminate the scourge."

Bile fills my mouth and my blood runs cold. I know exactly what's coming next.

"You're fighting for Idol supremacy," Bryce says.

"Exactly."

"And what do you want from us?" Bryce takes a step forward without showing an ounce of emotion.

"Jonathan is sure you would be loyal to the cause, but we can't take any risks, legacy or not. You must earn your place within our organization."

"How?" I ask.

"We've heard rumors the Knights have gotten a secret weapon, an Idol capable of unmaking our kind."

Shit. They know Daisy exists, but do they know who she is?

"You will find that Idol and kill him."

Him. They don't know it's her. A sense of partial relief washes over me, but not completely. I open my mouth to ask what happens if we don't, but Bryce beats me to the punch.

"Consider it done."

11
─────

DAISY

I didn't know what to make out of Morpheus's statement. What did he mean that they've all defied a god to protect me? But I don't ask in the car because I sense that's a conversation that needs to happen among all of us.

We don't speak much on the drive to my old neighborhood. To be honest, my head is filled with thoughts and worries. The most pressing one is obviously about Rosie, and the closer we get to Mrs. Wilmot's house, the more nervous I become. I don't know how to mask my powers yet, and even as a Norm, she'll be able to tell I'm different.

When Morpheus parks in front of the house, I don't get out of the car right away, just keep staring straight ahead. The rain has stopped, but the sky is still dark gray, matching my somber mood perfectly.

"What's the matter, Daisy?"

"Rosie and Toby will know about me as soon as I stand in front of them."

"We never got to practice masking your gift. I'm sorry."

"It's not your fault."

"In a way, it is. Let's try now."

"Do you think I can learn it that quickly?"

He gives me a little smile, showing just the hint of his adorable dimples. "It's not difficult."

I let out a shaky breath. "All right. Teach me."

"Close your eyes and imagine you're naked."

I squint. "What kind of exercise is that?"

His smile widens, and his eyes dance with amusement. "I swear I'm not trying to be a perv. Do you trust me?"

"Crazy as it sounds, I do." I close my eyes. "Okay, I'm naked."

Morpheus doesn't speak for several beats, which prompts me to open one eye to peek at him. His gaze is a little dazed, and I suspect he's also picturing me naked. Desire once again makes itself known, but I stomp on it for now.

"Hello? What's next?" I ask.

He clears his throat. "Right. Your naked image is your power, bright and obvious to anyone who looks at you. Get dressed slowly, and with each piece of clothing you add, you're covering your power from prying eyes."

I do as he says, even though the exercise is a little silly to me. I put on underwear, then a pair of jeans and a T-shirt. But even so, I'm not completely covered yet. I can still see the brightness peeking out from underneath my clothes. I add a thick sweater, a scarf, gloves, and top it all off with a ski mask. The only thing showing now is my eyes.

When I look at Morpheus again, the smile is still plastered on his beautiful face, but the shining in his eyes is pride.

"Did I do it?"

He nods. "You did. You masked your powers."

"Really? But am I going to be able to keep it masked for long periods of time?"

"Now that you've associated the mask with wearing clothes, you should be able to keep it on subconsciously."

I nibble on my lower lip while my thoughts stray. It sounds too easy.

"Please don't do that," he almost groans.

"Do what?" I focus on him again. He looks pained.

"Bite your lips like that. It makes me wish I was the one doing it."

Heat rushes to my face, and my body is once again on fire. He's not even touching me.

A loud knock on my window jolts me from the lust-infused fog that had wrapped around me. Toby is standing outside. He must have spotted Morpheus's car from the house.

"Here goes nothing," I say before I open the door.

"Hey, Daisy. How is everything? How's Bryce?" he asks, bouncing from foot to foot. He seems nervous.

"Toby, is everything okay? Did something happen to Rosie?"

"She's fine. Still shaken about what happened last night, but I think she'll get over it soon."

The sound of a door banging shut tells me Morpheus is also out of the car. He walks around the vehicle and stands next to me.

"You said you wanted to talk to me about something. What is it?" I ask.

He looks nervously in Morpheus's direction and then back to me. "I think Bryce did something to me when he healed me."

My eyebrows furrow together. "What are you talking about?"

Morpheus places a hand on the small of my back, sending chills up my spine. "Daisy, look at him closely."

I do as he says, but I see nothing different about Toby. He's projecting the faint energy Fringes usually do, but that's thanks to the device he has around his neck.

"I don't see anything out of the ordinary," I reply.

"His aura is different," Morpheus points out, and Toby's face blanches.

"It's because of his necklace," I say.

Toby shakes his head. "I'm not wearing my necklace, Daisy. That's what I'm talking about. I think Bryce turned me into a Fringe."

My jaw drops of its own accord while my brain spins at breakneck speed.

"Son of a bitch." Morpheus runs a hand through his hair.

"How did you figure that out?" I ask Toby.

"I thought I was losing my mind at first. I was trying to sleep on your landlord's uncomfortable couch when I heard her mumbling about her not getting paid enough to deal with so much bullshit. I opened my eyes a fraction and saw her looking through the mail. Her lips were nothing but a slash across her face, but I kept hearing what she was saying."

"Are you implying you heard her thoughts?" I ask.

"I don't know, to be honest. When Mrs. Wilmot went quiet, I thought I'd hallucinated the whole thing. Then I went to see Rosie. She was sound asleep, so I just watched her for a few minutes before I heard her voice in my head."

I take a step back, an involuntarily reaction that, unfortunately, Toby catches.

"You're afraid of me now."

"No, it's not that."

"Can you hear what I'm thinking right now?" Morpheus takes a step forward.

"No. I can't."

Morpheus turns to me, his eyes hard. "I think we have one more issue to add to our plates."

"What does that mean? Am I a Fringe for real now?" Toby's voice rises to a pitch.

Morpheus whirls on him. "A little louder so Daisy's nosey landlord can hear it."

I look over Toby's shoulder, and sure as shit, she's watching us from the window. "I believe someone paid her to spy on us."

"Who?" Toby asks.

I don't answer him. Instead, I trade a meaningful glance with Morpheus. My prime suspect is Mr. Silverstone. Xavier was the one who referred us to Mrs. Wilmot, and he works for the Knights' leader.

"Toby, you need to come back to campus with us right now," Morpheus says.

"What about Rosie? I can't simply leave her without saying goodbye."

"Wait here. I need to speak to her alone anyway," I say.

Mrs. Wilmot hides behind the curtain, and when I walk in, she pretends to be busy wiping the dust from the furniture.

"Daisy. What a surprise." She smiles tightly in my direction.

"Hey, Mrs. Wilmot."

She sets the duster on the table and approaches me. "I have to say, I was quite shocked that you allowed Rosie to bring her boyfriend home with her. She's only fifteen."

"I trust Rosie and Toby. I knew they wouldn't do anything inappropriate. He slept on the couch, didn't he?"

"Who can tell?" She shrugs. "He was sleeping on the couch when I went to bed, and I did find him on the couch this morning, but whether he stayed there the entire night is another matter."

I have to fight the urge to roll my eyes. "I'm going to talk to Rosie."

My tone was clearly dismissive, but Mrs. Wilmot follows me down the hallway. "How was the ball? Did you have a good time? Rosie wouldn't tell me anything."

"The party was nice."

I finally reach the end of the hall and turn to our landlord. "I'll talk to you later, Mrs. Wilmot."

She twists her expression into a scowl, perhaps catching the fake, overly sweet tone in my voice. I lock the door behind me, finding Rosie sitting at her desk and staring out the window.

She turns to me. "What are you doing here?"

"I came to see how you're doing." I walk closer.

"A little too late for that." She looks away again.

"Rosie, come on. Don't be like that."

With a huff, she swivels on her chair. "Don't be like what? Upset that my sister chose an Idol boy over me?"

"Shh. Keep your voice down. Mrs. Wilmot is most likely eavesdropping."

"I don't care if she hears it."

I sit at the edge of the bed and wait a couple of beats before I say another word, hoping Rosie's rage won't last too long. I can't talk to her when she's like that.

The silence stretches for a few more seconds before she breaks.

"That's it? You're just going to sit there and stare at me?"

"No, I'm waiting until you're ready to hear my explanation. I didn't mean to pick you over anyone, Rosie. As a matter of fact, it broke my heart that you thought that."

"Whatever, don't try to twist this around and put the blame on me. Confess you just wanted to spend the night with your boyfriend. I hope he was worth it." She crosses her arms over her chest and looks away with a pout.

Phoenix. Thinking about him makes my heart ache. How is he coping with everything that happened? How do we move forward? I care deeply about him, Morpheus, Bryce, and Rufio. What does that mean for the future, considering what I can do?

"My night was horrible, Rosie. I couldn't come home with you because a friend needed me."

Her eyebrows twitch together. "Friend? Toby is your only friend at the academy, and he was with me."

I'm torn about what to tell Rosie. I'd never kept anything from her before, but since joining Gifted Academy, the secrets keep piling up.

"I was talking about Phoenix. He was in tro—"

"Phoenix again. You're so full of shit, Daisy. It's almost like you've turned into another person since you joined that school. Your priorities are all screwed up!"

I jump to my feet, angry at Rosie now. "All I've ever done is try to protect you. My priorities are not screwed up. The only thing that's changed is that you're not the only person I love anymore."

Rosie's green eyes round, right before she turns them into slits and her complexion becomes beet red. "Screw you, Daisy!"

She grabs the snow globe on her desk and throws it in my direction. It would have hit me straight on my forehead if I hadn't made it fly at slow motion. I step out of its trajectory before time resumes to normal. The object hits the bed, bouncing on the mattress.

"How the hell did you do that?"

Shit. I used my powers in front of Rosie, and now she's staring at me like I'm a monster.

"Oh my God. You're one of them now."

12

DAISY

"Rosie, wait. Let me explain." I raise a hand in her direction, but she steps out of my reach.

"Stay away from me."

Before I can stop her, she bolts to the door and bursts out of the room. Mrs. Wilmot was standing right outside and gets pushed aside when Rosie storms through. Shit. She must have heard what Rosie said. Of course, just because I suspect she works for Mr. Silverstone doesn't mean that's true. She could be working for someone else with a darker agenda.

I don't stop to help the woman. Getting knocked down is what she deserves for spying on us.

Rosie heads straight to the front door, but suddenly Morpheus is standing there, blocking her way. His wild hair is framing his face, and he's not trying to tame his power. He's the personification of what used to give us nightmares, only now he elicits something else from me instead of fear.

But it's not the same for Rosie. She halts just short of colliding with him.

"What are you doing in my home? Get out!" she shrieks.

Morpheus raises both hands, trying his best to project a nonthreatening posture. He's even masking his power; the first time I've ever seen him do it.

"Rosie, you don't need to be afraid of me. I'm Daisy's friend, and I'm not going to harm you."

"Bullshit. You're an Idol, and you're all bad," Rosie accuses.

Toby walks around Morpheus and moves closer to her. "What happened?"

Rosie gasps, and I know she's sensing the difference in her boyfriend. "Where's your necklace? Tell me you're wearing it."

Toby's guilty expression says it all. "Rosie, don't be afraid. I'm still me."

He tries to grab her hand, but she walks backward. "Don't touch me." She whirls on the spot, facing me. "You stay away from me too."

"Rosie, you need to calm down," I tell her gently.

She shakes her head while fat tears stream down her cheeks. "No. I'm not going to calm down. I knew going to Gifted Academy was a terrible idea. And look at you now. You're a monster. They made you one of them!"

I wince, crying now too. I knew it would be difficult to make Rosie accept what happened, but I couldn't have foreseen how much her rejection would hurt me.

"Son of a bitch." Toby looks at me. "You've also changed."

Movement in my peripheral catches my attention. Mrs. Wilmot is behind Rosie, and before I can stop her, she stabs my sister's neck with a needle. Rosie's eyes roll back in their sockets, and then she collapses in our landlord's arms.

"What the fuck!" Morpheus advances but stops short of attacking the woman since she's now using Rosie as a shield.

"What did you do?" I grit out, trying to control my rage. My body is shaking so hard it's rattling my teeth.

"Don't worry, Daisy. Andrea didn't harm your sister," a

familiar voice replies from my right. Principal Fallon joins us in the living room, wearing her usual sharp suit and resting bitch face. "She only gave her a mild sedative."

"What fresh hell is this?" Morpheus glowers at the woman. "What are you doing here?"

"Hello to you too, Mr. Malek," Principal Fallon replies in a cold tone. "I see that you're doing much better now."

I trade glances with Morpheus. Is she referring to the incident at the diner this morning? Has she been following us?

"Why are you here?" I question.

"I came because I need your help."

The anger is still running rampant through my veins, but her words give me pause. Help with what?

"Great. One more person wanting a piece of Daisy," Morpheus replies angrily.

"It's not for me. Rufio and Bryce are in trouble."

My heart skips a beat before it begins to beat madly inside of my chest. "What happened to them?"

Principal Fallon turns to my landlord. "You can set the girl down and leave, Andrea."

Mrs. Wilmot lays Rosie on the sofa and, without making eye contact with me, disappears down the hallway. At least now I have one of my questions answered. My landlord was being paid by Principal Fallon to keep tabs on Rosie and me. But for what purpose? I thought she was in cahoots with Xavier.

"What's going on? What happened to Bryce and Rufio?" Morpheus asks.

"An incident occurred this morning in the juniors' dorm. Rufio accidentally killed Drusilla Dharma."

"No," I breathe. Rufio wouldn't kill a student like that, even if that person was Drusilla.

"What did she do to him? He would never be foolish enough to kill anyone," Morpheus chimes in.

Principal Fallon switches her attention to Toby, who's kneeling in front of Rosie's unconscious form.

"You can speak freely in front of him," I say.

"Rufio claims Drusilla compelled him to kill her. I want to believe my son, but everyone knows Drusilla wasn't strong enough to affect him. But that's not what I'm worried about. My husband took Rufio and Bryce somewhere, and I'm afraid nothing good will come of it."

I haven't had the displeasure of meeting the man, but I know he killed my uncle, which forces me to agree with Principal Fallon.

"What do you want me to do?" I ask.

"For starters, we need to return to campus as soon as possible."

That's not what I expected her to say.

"You came all the way here to tell us to return to campus? Are you kidding me?" Morpheus scoffs.

Principal Fallon squints in his direction. "Watch your tone, Mr. Malek. I'm still your principal."

"You drugged my sister and paid my landlord to spy on us. You'd better start giving me answers if you want my cooperation," I say.

"I drugged your sister because she was hysterical. You're no longer a Norm, Daisy. You're an Idol now, so you'd better start acting like one."

"Daisy is an Idol?" Toby unfurls from his crouch. "Holy shit. This has to do with Bryce healing both of us, right?"

Principal Fallon turns her keen eyes on my friend. "It's possible, but only two instances don't give us enough evidence to draw conclusions."

Bullshit. Of course it does. Bryce is the only common factor in both situations.

"It seems you've leveled up to Fringe status," Principal Fallon continues. "What can you do?"

I want to urge Toby to keep his mouth shut, but he's not looking at me. With squared shoulders, he answers, "I can read minds, maybe. At least I think I can."

"Really?" The woman raises an eyebrow.

Damn it, Toby. Why did you have to tell her the truth? After finding out his father's employer is involved with the Knights, how can he so carelessly give that information to another Idol in a position of power?

"Are you for real?" Morpheus snaps. "Your son killed another Idol, and my guess is it happened in front of witnesses. That's punishable by death, yet you're more concerned about a newly minted Fringe?"

Principal Fallon's nostrils flare, and there's a flash of pure hatred in her eyes. Damn. Morpheus hit a sore spot, but what I'm truly stuck on is the part about the death penalty. I know Idol-on-Idol killing is considered the worst of crimes, but the fact that Rufio might die because of it makes me icy cold with fear.

"How dare you imply that I don't care about my son," Principal Fallon retorts.

The front door bursts open and a gust of violent wind breaches through, disheveling my hair. This is her doing; I can sense her power controlling the molecules of air, bending them to her will. On instinct, I raise my hand. The wind parts, going around me. Principal Fallon reins in her powers, and they recede like a wave.

"So the prophecy was true. You did inherit Magia's gift," she says. "Do you have any idea what that means?"

"With all due respect, ma'am, I'm not interested in hearing about some glorious future you have planned for me. I want you to leave my house at once."

"But—"

"I said leave!"

She flinches, right before her face turns into a grimace. "Can I expect to see you tomorrow at school?"

"We'll see."

13

PHOENIX

I'm still numb when I return to campus. As much as my mother's revelation helped ease some of the pain, it doesn't change the fact that my own father tortured me for years and she didn't help me. I'd like to think that if I knew someone was hurting my kid, I'd move mountains to kill the person responsible.

I stop briefly in front of Daisy's door, but I don't sense her inside. She's not home. A splint of worry enters my chest, but I try to ignore it. I can't become one of those people who over-protects the ones they care about. Daisy is a survivor, a fighter; she doesn't need a damaged Idol like me as her protector.

The apartment is empty when I arrive, which I see as a blessing. Eventually I'll have to face my friends, but I'll avoid them for as long as I can.

I head for the kitchen because I haven't eaten anything in more than twenty-four hours. I'm not particularly hungry, but I know I can't starve myself. My stint in jail is just a prelude for what's to come. I have no illusions that me killing my father will go unpunished.

I prepare a sandwich, mindless to the ingredients I'm

adding to it. I'm about to sit down and eat when I hear the sound of an incoming call. Since my phone was fried together with Rufio's car, the call can only be coming from my laptop. Curious, I head to my room to check it. A quick swipe shows me Morpheus's mug on the screen. I debate not answering him for a split second, but then I realize that for Morpheus to be trying to reach me via video message, this must be an emergency.

I click on the Accept Call button.

"Damn it, Phoenix, it's about time. Where have you been? Your phone is going straight to voice mail," Morpheus barks.

"Fuck, you don't want to know. What's the emergency now?"

"I *do* want to know, but you can tell me later. Are Bryce and Rufio with you?"

"No. I just got here. The apartment is empty."

"Son of a bitch." Morpheus runs his hand over his long hair, yanking it back.

I hear Daisy's voice in the background and my heart lurches forward, despite the heaviness there.

"Where are you going?" I ask, noticing they're in Morpheus's car.

"To Unearthly Desires. You have to meet us there."

"Wait, what? Why are you going to the strip club? Are we meeting with... you know, the guys from last night?"

I can't risk saying "Knights" over the internet. Who knows who might be listening?

"I can't tell you right now. Can you make it there or not?"

Shit. Rufio's car is a pool of melted metal thanks to that asshole agent, and my car is probably impounded for investigation. I have to find another mode of transport. I suppose adding grand theft auto to my rap sheet won't make my situation worse. Nothing beats patricide.

"Yeah, I'll be there ASAP. How is Daisy?"

Morpheus glances to the back seat and then hands his phone to her.

"Phoenix, are you all right?" she asks.

I notice her hair is damp, and she's wearing one of Morpheus's sweatshirts. A spike of jealousy pierces my heart, but I try to ignore the sentiment. Daisy is already involved with three of us, so what if Morpheus joins in the mix?

"I'm fine," I lie. "How's everything with you?"

"Adjusting. But don't worry about me, okay? Just get to Unearthly Desires safely."

Hell, I've never wanted to kiss a girl as much as I want to kiss her right now. It seems my feelings for her have tripled in the last twenty-four hours.

"Okay, babe. I'll see you soon."

She smiles and sweet baby Martians, there are fucking butterflies in my stomach now. Even after her image vanishes from the screen when the call ends, I'm still picturing her in my mind.

I jump off the chair, ready to bolt, but a quick look at my reflection in the mirror makes me pause. My clothes are filthy, soiled with mud and soot from the altercation with the cops. I also stink of smoke and sweat, so I head for the shower instead. I may be depressed, but I ain't walking around like a fucking bum.

I'm ready to go in less than five minutes. At the door, I spare one quick glance at the sad sandwich I made and, with a grunt, grab it to eat on the go. I take a bite as I walk, but I could be eating drywall as far as I know. The damn thing is tasteless.

Turning a corner, I collide with someone who was striding in the opposite direction.

"Hey, watch it," I snap.

It takes me a second to notice he's not a student. He's an older man with white hair, a patch over his right eye, and a nasty scar running the length of his right cheek.

I'm tense in an instant. *Fuck, another agent sent to collect me.*

Only the guy barely glances in my direction as he continues on.

What the hell? If he's not here for me, then that can only mean....

I retrace my steps and watch the stranger as he strides down the hallway. He doesn't change his pace as he walks past Daisy's door, continuing all the way to the end and then making a right. Instinct is telling me the guy is up to no good, but he's not here for Daisy or me, so fuck it, he's not my problem.

By the time I get to the garage, the strange Idol is already forgotten. I do a quick scan of the assortment of vehicles at my disposal. Since it's Sunday, most of the cars are gone, but one in particular catches my attention—Bryce's SUV. If he didn't take his car, and Bryce and Rufio aren't with Morpheus, where the hell are they? Damn it. I wonder if that's the reason Morpheus was chasing after me and he wants to meet in person.

Without a second thought, I stride toward the white SUV. Unlike Rufio, Bryce didn't leave his fob inside. But it doesn't matter. A quick command with my mind has the door unlocked in a second. Getting the engine to start takes another minute. I'd be easier if I could control energy like Bryce does, but I've learned to move more than objects with my mind throughout the years.

Almost silently, the engine turns to life. I don't peel out of the parking garage like a maniac this time, too aware that stealth is more important than speed. That fucking agent won't give up on me just because I lawyered up. But the question is, how do I get rid of him? I suppose going to Unearthly Desires is the right call, despite Morpheus's motives. Last night, I was too stunned to ask a lot of questions. Today, I'll get straight answers from Mr. X.

Ten minutes after I leave the campus grounds, I notice I'm being followed. It's not an official car but a maroon station wagon. That doesn't mean it isn't that fucking cop again. It doesn't matter. I gotta lose the tail.

There isn't a lot of traffic on the highway today, so I have to get creative. First, I make sure the driver is indeed following me, swerving to an exit at the last minute to see if the station wagon will do the same. Sure as shit, it follows me.

Okay, then. Now I can carry on with my plan without remorse.

Shit. I was never one to be concerned about regret, yet here I am making sure I don't hurt an innocent person by mistake. Daisy's changed me in more ways than one. She made me care about her, for starters. Never in a million years did I think I'd fall in love with a Norm.

The sudden realization freezes me for a second. Son of a bitch. I'm in love with her, and that's the fucking truth. No wonder I felt such jealousy earlier.

And now I care about strangers too. Whatever. The motherfucker in that maroon car is definitely following me, so I won't hold back.

I let him tail me until we reach the Ardia bridge, which connects the north and south sides of Saturn's Bay, then slow down to way below the minimum speed limit. The car behind me will either keep up with my pace or he has to overtake me.

He chooses to slow down too, but not before he gets close enough for me to see who's behind the steering wheel. It's not the asshole cop who arrested me last night, but it's one of his coworkers from the precinct.

That's all I need to know.

Before he has the chance to change lanes and increase the distance between our cars, I put everything I have into sending the station wagon against the bridge's safety railing. He crashes hard against the metal, the friction creating sparks, before he loses control of the vehicle and spins. That's when I press the pedal to the metal and take off, leaving him eating dust. It's too bad I had to slow down to perform that little trick; if he'd been driving a little faster, he would have gone over the bridge.

My blood is pumping with adrenaline, and the euphoria lifts the fog that had been dragging me down for so long that I forgot what it was really like to feel alive. I turn on the radio, tuning it to a heavy metal station and blowing up the speakers. I scream from the top of my lungs in sync with the current song.

I don't ease off the gas pedal, almost wishing a cop would try to pull me over. But I already crossed the invisible line into Norm and Fringe territory. No cops will dare to stop me here. They know only Idols would be driving this car.

The number on the speedometer doesn't decrease until I hit downtown. Then I sober up and check if I have another tail. I was a little reckless for assuming I'd have only one, but after driving in circles for fifteen minutes, I'm satisfied no one else followed me. It's safe to head to my final destination.

Now my heart begins to beat faster for another reason. Daisy. It's been less than twenty-fours since we saw each other, but I'm craving her like a junkie craves their next fix. I don't think I'll be able to keep my distance from her, even though she's afraid to touch us now.

There are a few cars in front of the upscale strip joint, but I circle around the building to park in the back. Morpheus's car is there already, sitting next to a black sedan I assume belongs to Mr. X. Two men guard the back door, but they don't stop me or ask my name. Both are high-level Fringes.

"Mr. X is waiting for you," one of them says as he opens the door.

The second security guard walks ahead of me, and I follow him wordlessly. I've never been to this part of the club before.

The guard stops in front of a door and knocks. "The last guest has arrived, sir."

The door opens inward and Mr. X fills the frame. At once,

shame washes over me. He also knows what my father had been doing to me in that basement. The man barely spares me a glance, though, simply moves out of the way and lets me in.

My eyes immediately zero in on Daisy, who's sitting on the couch. Her sister, Rosie, is asleep on her lap.

Okay, that I didn't expect.

"You're here," she says.

"Yeah. You didn't think I would come?" I move closer. Too bad her sister is in the way or I'd crush Daisy in my arms.

"I knew you would. But...." She trails off, and I get what she doesn't say. Time is perilous now for everyone in this room.

"What's up with your sister?" I ask.

"Their landlord sedated her," Morpheus replies from the corner of the room. I didn't even notice him.

"What? Why?"

"Because she found out about me and freaked," Daisy replies.

"It was probably the shock of discovery. She'll come around. We started dating when she believed I was a Fringe, remember?" Toby says from the other side of the room.

I quickly glance in his direction, ready to return my attention to Daisy, when I sense a strange energy around him. *Wait a minute.* I look closely at him.

"What happened to you?" I ask.

"Eh, I—"

"He's a Fringe now. For real," Morpheus replies.

I whip around to face him. "Come again?"

"I need you all to stop talking at once." Mr. X walks to his desk, sporting a seriously pissed-off expression. He touches the ring on his left hand and the bookshelf on his right swings open, revealing a secret passage. "Everyone, get in there."

My spine goes rigid. "Hell to the fucking no. I'm not falling for that bullshit."

"This isn't a trap, kid. It's a safe room where we can talk without fear of being overheard."

"And we're just supposed to believe you?" Morpheus takes a step forward.

The man narrows his eyes to slits. "May I remind you that you called me? I also assume you have a thousand questions. Do you want answers? Get the fuck in there!"

My hands curl into fists. I'd punch his face if he wasn't Daisy's uncle, and if we didn't need answers.

"What about Rosie?" Daisy asks.

"I think it's best if she stays here," Mr. X replies in a much softer tone. Either he's an excellent actor or he does care about Daisy.

Even so, her shoulders tense. "I can't leave her."

"She'll be okay in my office, honey," he adds. "But it's best if she doesn't learn any more information she can't handle."

"I'll stay with her," Toby offers.

I can see that Daisy is still torn, but honestly, I'd prefer if the ginger is also not privy to the conversation we're about to have.

"All right, then." Daisy scooches sideways, careful not to jar her sister too much. The girl doesn't even stir.

She finally stands and Toby takes her place on the couch. I don't waste a second. In one long stride, I reach her and pull her into my arms. She gasps softly but doesn't try to break free. Instead, she buries her face in my chest while her arms go around my waist. Ignoring the audience, I kiss the top of her head and breathe her in. Tingles run all over my body, and the damn butterflies from before are having a fucking party in my belly.

Suddenly I'm hit by a dizzy spell, and my legs feel like they're made out jelly. *What the hell!*

"Daisy! Step away from him," Morpheus warns.

I sense her trying to move, but my arms are locked tight around her. I don't want to let her go.

Someone finally yanks her away from me, and the motion affects my balance. I stagger back as the world spins, forcing me to shut my eyes.

"Son of a bitch," Mr. X mutters behind me. Then his hands are on my elbows, steadying me.

When I blink my eyes open, there are dark spots in my vision. But I can still see Daisy staring at me wide-eyed and terrified.

Fuck. Did she do this to me?

14

BRYCE

Our father drops us off in front of our dorm building and strangely doesn't tell us anything else. The sense of wrongness doesn't leave me after he departs, though. It feels like an itch in my brain that I can't scratch.

Rufio waits until the car disappears down the driveway to whirl on me. "What the fuck, Bryce!"

I know exactly why my brother is giving me the death stare. The hothead can't grasp why I agreed to help the Neo Gods.

"Give me your phone," I command.

"What—"

"Give me your fucking phone, Rufio!"

Grumbling, he shoves his device into my waiting hands. "Here, asshole."

I look at the screen, and sure as shit, there are several missed calls from Morpheus. I don't bother unlocking the phone, though. I simply fry its system.

"Why did you do that?"

I toss his now dead phone back at him, and then I do the

same thing with mine. "For all we know, these devices are now compromised. We'll get new ones on the way."

"Where are we going now?"

I stride toward the garage without answering him. On the way here, I made a mental note of all the players we've encountered so far, and the only one I don't completely distrust is Mr. X, Daisy's uncle. I have to believe his affection for her is genuine. If I'm wrong about him, then we truly don't have anyone to turn to.

Rufio catches up with me but doesn't continue to pester me with questions until we're in the garage. "Bryce, I swear if you—"

I stop abruptly, and Rufio collides with my back.

"Fuck!" I say.

He walks around me, rubbing his face. "What now?"

"Take a look. Do you see anything amiss?"

"Not rea—son of a bitch. Where the hell is my car?"

With the garage practically empty, it's easy to notice his car and mine are both missing.

"Mine is also gone."

"Do you think that Delta guy our father called is behind this?"

"I don't know. But staring at an empty garage isn't going to help us." I spin around and retrace my steps.

"Now we can't even call a cab thanks to you, idiot."

I don't reply. If it makes Rufio better to call me names, so be it.

Once out in the open, I veer toward the school gate.

"You're not going to our apartment? We can call a car using one of our laptops."

"No. It's best if we don't."

"So how do you propose getting to where we need to go? On foot?"

"Don't be ridiculous. Of course not. We're taking the bus."

From the corner of my eye, I catch Rufio's jaw drop. "You do know what that is, right?" I ask just to be antagonistic.

"Bite me, asshat."

The guard stationed at the check-in point does a double take when Rufio and I cross the gate, then asks, "Where are you going, fellas?"

"Across the street." I point to the bus stop.

He furrows his eyebrows and then shakes his head. "Crazy rich kids."

Once on the other side, Rufio stares at the information board attached to the bus sign pole. "Do you even know how this works?"

"What do you mean?" I sit on the bench, resting my elbows on my knees.

"I've never taken a bus before. How do we even pay for it?"

"You're pathetic," I mutter.

Suddenly, the bench I'm sitting on disappears underneath me and I fall flat on my ass. "Son of a bitch. Are you fucking kidding me?"

Rufio stares at me with a grin on his face. "Who's pathetic now?"

I jump back to my feet, wiping the dust from my jeans. I'm tempted to retaliate, but the sound of the approaching bus stops me in my tracks. "You're lucky," I tell him.

Rufio flips me off before hoping aboard the bus. "How much for a ticket?" he asks the driver.

"It depends. How far are you going?"

"Uh, give me a sec." He turns to me. "Bryce?"

I walk around him and push a hundred-dollar bill toward the driver. "This oughta cover. Keep the change."

The bill disappears in the driver's greedy hands. Wordlessly, I head for the back of the bus. I dampen my Idol power, but it's too late. The few Norms on board have noticed what we are and are now watching us with fear in their eyes.

I pick a seat in the last row by the window. Rufio joins me, still sporting a scowl. Some passengers who were sitting near us move to the front of the bus.

"Wanna bet they'll hop off at the next stop?" Rufio asks.

I snort. "Like I'm going to bet on that. I know they will."

Sure as shit, all but one passenger exits the bus at the next stop. I feel bad for scaring them off, but masking my powers around Norms isn't something I'm used to. It doesn't happen automatically.

"I'll be damned. We have one courageous Norm among us," Rufio mutters.

I angle my body forward to see what the man is up to. "He's asleep."

"Of course he is." Rufio props his legs on the seat in front of him, crossing them at the ankles. "Now can you tell me where we're going?"

"I figured that after last night's shenanigans, you'd be in the mood for some distraction." And that's all I'm going to give Rufio. If he can't figure it out on his own, then he's a moron.

He squints. "Really? That's your big idea?"

"We're out of options, brother."

"But he works for... you know." Rufio turns to the sleeping man. Maybe we shouldn't be having this conversation here.

"Let's not talk about it now." I point at the Norm, to which Rufio responds with a groan.

"How long until we get there?"

I shrug. "Beats me. Two hours maybe?"

"Two hours? That's crazy." He shoves his hand into his jacket pockets and then curses. "Damn it. I forgot you fried my phone. How am I supposed to keep myself entertained?"

"Did you just seriously say that? What are you, a toddler?"

Rufio crosses his arms over his chest and pouts, illustrating my point.

This is going to be a long fucking trip.

RUFIO FELL asleep thirty minutes in. All the stress must have taken a toll on him. I should be glad that I don't have to deal with his pent-up aggression, but his ill humor served to distract me from my thoughts. What's swirling in my head is not something I want to dwell on too much. I honestly don't know how we're going to get out of the mess we're in. We have Knights, Neo Gods, and Mom all wanting to use us for their nasty plans. Yeah, I vowed to kill the new weapon the Knights acquired, and if my mother asks me to do something for her—which will most likely be the opposite of what my father did—I'll pledge my alliance to her as well. But how long will I be able to bull-shit them?

I didn't have much choice when it came to those assholes preaching Idol supremacy. Unfortunately, thanks to Rufio's mistake, I had to promise them something that makes me sick. Even if the weapon wasn't Daisy, I'd never complete the mission. As far as I'm concerned, they're the ones who need to be exterminated.

The bus is about to make another stop, and the driver yells, "Hey, Harry, your stop is coming up."

Not only does the sleepy man jar awake but so does Rufio. He looks at his surroundings, almost as if he's dazed, and then he glances at me. "Fuck. This isn't a nightmare."

"It's good that you're up. We should be at Unearthly Desires soon."

Harry stands up and heads for the exit door, which is near us. He looks at us through bloodshot eyes. No wonder he didn't move a muscle during the trip—he reeks of alcohol. "Did you say Unearthly Desires?"

I tense instantly but try not to show it. "Yeah. So?"

"Don't you care about your soul, young man? Here, you

should visit our church." He reaches inside his wrinkled jacket and pulls out a flyer.

"Thanks." I take the paper from the man so he won't gift us with a sermon.

But the bus stops then, and even if he wanted to convert us to his religion, his time is up. He misses a step and would have ended up with his face on the curb if I hadn't helped him with a little telekinesis.

"What a weirdo," Rufio says as soon as the bus door shuts. "I don't know why you bother with those losers."

"Trust me, my motives were self-serving." I glance at the flyer in my hand. It's the picture of an old store and a sign that says Church of the Bold and the Fearless. Whatever.

I flip it between my fingers, ready to toss it out the window, when I catch the scribbled note on the back.

"What's that?" Rufio takes the flyer from my hand.

"'Long live the Rinnegati.' Shit. Isn't that the name of the family linked to Magia?"

"Yup." I grab the flyer again and shove it in my pocket. "Come on. Our stop is next."

Rufio looks out the window. "How do you know?"

"I pay attention to my surroundings when I'm driving. I recognize that convenience store."

It's our luck that it starts to rain as soon as we exit the bus. We could take cover inside a store, but more than ever, I'm keen to reach our final destination.

Let's hope Mr. X is there.

15

DAISY

It turns out Xavier had an entire other room underground. The bookcase opened to a set of hidden stairs that led to a meeting room with a round table, another set of leather couches, and a liquor cabinet. We're sitting around the table with gloomy expressions and faraway looks. We just told him about what happened at Mrs. Wilmot's, and Phoenix told him about his arrest.

It's no surprise that not a word has been spoken for several minutes. I keep my eyes glued to the table while I wrestle with my guilt. A simple embrace almost cost Phoenix his powers. I could feel his essence coming into me, but I couldn't stop or move away from him. My experiment with Morpheus made me careless. He can withstand my power because he's stronger than me. I have to remember that.

Xavier rubs his face and then knocks once on the table. "There's no stopping this now. Jodie has finally made her play."

"Did you know she was paying Mrs. Wilmot to spy on Rosie and me?"

"No I didn't. I wouldn't have allowed it if I knew. But going behind my back is on-brand for Jodie."

"That woman is a piece of work, isn't she?" Phoenix grumbles.

"Why did you return to the scene of the crime?" Morpheus asks him.

I glance at Phoenix, and when our gazes connect, my heart crumbles. He's hurting so much still, and I can't even give him comfort.

He breaks the connection first and looks in Morpheus's direction. "I don't know. I guess I'm a glutton for punishment."

"I'm not surprised your father had connections in the bureau. But don't worry, we swept the place. Besides the bodies we thought it was best to leave behind, they won't find any evidence of what happened there."

"What about Vargas? Can he be trusted to keep his mouth shut?" Phoenix asks.

Xavier nods. "Yes. He's committed to the cause. He won't say a word."

"What *is* the cause? What do the Knights want?" I ask.

"Equality."

Phoenix snorts. "They must have taken too many hits of Silver-voltage. The Idols in power will never accept equality among races."

"That's where Daisy comes in." Xavier looks pointedly at me. "She's the Equalizer."

"What?" I squeak.

"I don't like the sound of that," Morpheus chimes in.

"What does that mean? Is she going to be at the forefront of this war you're planning to rage against an entire society of powerful beings?" Phoenix asks.

"Your existence was foretold, Daisy," Xavier states. "I'm not sure if you'll have any choice in the matter."

"Stop talking like I'm a child," I retort. "And I *do* have a choice. I have zero interest in turning into a weapon for the Knights."

"I don't want that for you either. But I'm afraid it's only a matter of time before other people find out that Magia's powers have returned."

"You can't expect her to be your war's champion. She's only one person!" Phoenix slaps the table hard.

"I'm not fighting in a war," I say stubbornly, but deep down, I know Xavier is right. I won't have a choice. The hounds are already sniffing around.

The intercom in front of Xavier begins to ring. With a frown, he presses the Accept button. "Yes?"

"I got two Idol kids here who wish to speak with you. They say there're Daisy's friends."

I sit straighter in my chair.

"What are their names?" Xavier asks, staring at me.

"Bryce and Rufio Kent."

"Thank fuck they're all right." Morpheus collapses against the back of his chair.

"Where are they now?" Xavier asks.

"At the back door. Should I let them in?"

"No."

"What do you mean, no?" I jump out of my chair, ready to get out of here and allow them entry myself.

"Instruct them to enter the premises through the front door and get comfortable in the club. I'll be with them shortly."

"Why did you do that?" I ask.

"Because if they were with their father, it's possible they were followed."

"Do you think Mr. Kent knows about Daisy?" Morpheus stands as well and places a hand on my lower back. Phoenix follows the movement and narrows his eyes. The energy surrounding him changes in nature, becoming aggressive. I gasp out loud, not used to feeling things like that with my new Idol abilities.

The furrow eases from Phoenix's face, replaced by an arch of his brow. "What's the matter?"

"Nothing."

Xavier heads for the door. "You stay here. I'll go talk to them."

"Hell to the no. I'm coming with you." I step in front of him.

"Daisy, it's best if you're not seen here."

"Why not? I worked here before. As a matter of fact, that's the perfect cover."

"One look at you and everyone in that club will know you're not a Norm anymore."

I use the technique Morpheus taught me, and when Xavier's eyes widen in surprise, I know it worked again.

"How did you learn to do that so fast?" Phoenix asks.

"Morpheus taught me."

My answer doesn't comfort Phoenix for whatever reason. I'm getting serious jealous vibes from him, which is odd. He was the one who forced me into a meeting with Bryce and Rufio, after all, and he didn't seem to mind then that I was seeing the three of them at the same time.

"Fine. You can come, but you have to wait in my office. There's no need to parade you in front of my clientele," Xavier replies.

"Most definitely not," Phoenix agrees.

I have several sassy responses on the tip of my tongue, but I keep them all bottled up. Phoenix is hurting so much right now that if being antagonizing is helping him cope, then he can be an ass.

We all follow Xavier back to his main office, but when we walk out of the hidden passage, Toby and Rosie are gone.

"Where is my sister?" I shriek.

"Fuck. This can't be happening." Xavier is on the phone in an instant. "Where the hell are the two kids I left in my office?"

I'm ready to bolt and search for them, but reason tells me I should wait to learn more.

"I see," Xavier continues. "I don't care. You should have alerted me immediately."

He ends the call and looks at me. "They're fine. It seems Toby called Gunther to collect him and your sister."

"That son-of-a-bitch Knight?" Phoenix barks.

I'm livid, but I attempt to control my anger for now. "Did Toby say where they were going?"

"I think he left a note." Morpheus hands me a piece of paper he found on the couch's arm.

I read the text quickly and then turn it into a tight ball. "Stupid ass."

"What did the note say?" Phoenix moves closer but stops short of touching me.

"He was afraid Rosie would wake up here and freak out even more. He took her back to his place."

"So he says. He has powers now. Who knows what's going on in his mind," Phoenix retorts.

"Toby wouldn't lie to me like that." I'm quick to defend him, but not even I believe my bullshit. Toby lied not only to me but to everyone at school.

"I'm sure Rosie is safe with Toby," Morpheus says.

"Since when are you the sensible one?" Phoenix asks angrily.

"Okay, enough with the testosterone contest," Xavier barks. "Stay here while I see what your other boyfriends have to say. I can't have another situation in my club."

Xavier is about to head out when the door opens and Bryce and Rufio fill the frame.

"Son of a bitch. How did you get here?" he asks angrily.

Rufio enters first, followed by Bryce, who shuts the door behind him. Both of them look at me, and the longing in their gazes hits me hard. But the memory of what I did to Phoenix in this very office reminds me I can't touch them.

"Hello? I'm waiting for an answer." Xavier waves his hand in front of the guys.

"Please. Like your security can stop us," Rufio answers.

Looking at the floor, Xavier presses the bridge of his nose. "Please tell me you didn't create a commotion. It's not like I don't have a bull's-eye on my back already."

"We were discreet," Bryce replies, then moves his attention to me once more. "Daisy, are you all right?"

"Yes, and you? I heard about what happened earlier." I glance quickly at Rufio.

"I'm not sorry that bitch is dead, only that she compelled me to do it." He shoves his hands in his pockets and shrugs.

"What does that mean for you, though? Weren't there witnesses? Aren't you a wanted man now?"

Rufio gives me a lopsided grin. "Relax, babe. I'm not an outlaw... yet."

"Your mother said you spent the afternoon with your father." Xavier watches them closely.

"Is it safe to talk here?" Bryce asks.

Almost as if we're in a mystery movie, Morpheus, Phoenix, and I trade a meaningful glance. All we're missing is the ominous soundtrack.

"Shall we go back to the secret meeting room?" Morpheus asks Xavier.

"No," he answers. "You're going back to the academy."

"We came here because we have something important to tell you. Now you're sending us home?" Rufio throws his hands up in the air.

"I know what you want to say, but you can't tell me. You can't tell anyone. Do you understand? Go back to the academy and act normally. Daisy, you must keep your powers concealed at all times no matter what."

"I know," I say.

"Why can't we tell anyone where we were today?" Bryce asks.

Real fear shines in Xavier's eyes. "You simply can't. Not even Daisy, Morpheus, or Phoenix."

"What kind of bullshit is that?" Phoenix turns on him, once again projecting his aggressive energy.

"Just trust me on this. You don't know how dangerous Jonathan Kent and the people he works for are."

"You know them?" Rufio asks Xavier.

"I know of them, and that's enough."

16

BRYCE

I wait until the apartment is quiet. I don't know if my roommates are sleeping or not, so I walk on my tiptoes. On the way back, Daisy called Toby and gave him a tongue lashing for leaving Unearthly Desires with Mr. Silverstone. I don't know what excuse Toby gave her, but by the end of the call, she was even more depressed.

As a matter of fact, the mood of our entire party was foul. By unanimous agreement, we decided a good night of rest was in order before we hatched a game plan. But I only agreed to let Daisy slip away once again because I had every intention of doing what I'm about to now.

But as I stand in front of her closed door, I don't know what to do. We've been through so much in the last few days. I've apologized for my despicable behavior, I poured my heart out as best as I could, but it wasn't enough. I still sense the rift between us. And now with the weight of what I have to do, I can't carry on without her knowing what I truly feel.

I held back yesterday when I realized what her powers could do. It was a terrible mistake. Instead, I should have held her close to me and reassured her that everything would be all right. I was too careful, too afraid of the consequences. But Rufio falling for Drusilla's trap and the hours we spent with my father's associates served to bring things into perspective.

Flattening my hand against her door, I let my head drop between my shoulders. *Please open the door, Daisy.* I lift my face when I hear the sound of her footsteps on the soft carpet. My heart leapfrogs to my throat when the bolt unlocks, and then Daisy is standing there, like a vision.

"How did you know I was here?" I murmur.

"I heard you."

I open and close my mouth but no sound comes forth. A few seconds go by with me staring in silence at her. Finally, when I find my voice, I reply, "I didn't say it out loud. I was gathering the courage to knock."

Her eyebrows arch, and her sweet bee-stung lips make a perfect O. Tremors run through my body as nervousness takes over. She can unravel me with a mere glance, and that's more powerful than any gifts she might have inherited from Magia.

Wordlessly, Daisy opens the door wider and lets me pass. Only the nightstand lamp is on, casting spooky shadows everywhere.

The door locks again, and Daisy finally speaks. "Why are you here, Bryce? It's the middle of the night."

I turn around, and the first detail I notice is how she's standing close to the door, hugging her middle. The room is too dark too see her face properly, so with a thought, I turn on the lights. I'm not sure if I'm happy with what I can see now. She's terrified.

"Are you afraid of me?" I ask.

"No. I'm afraid of what I can do to you."

I take a step closer, but when she backs up, I stop. "You don't need to be afraid of your powers, Daisy. You can learn to control them."

"I know. But until then I'm a menace to you."

I scan her energy field, something I hadn't had the opportunity to do thoroughly until now. Daisy is a powerful Idol, but I don't think she's stronger than me.

"I can handle it," I reply.

"You don't know that. Earlier today, I was close to taking Phoenix's powers away. He almost fainted."

"Only because he hadn't recovered from what he suffered at the hands of that bastard."

"Maybe. But I don't want to risk it."

"You have to risk it, Daisy." I take another step closer, and now her back is against the wall. "You have to."

"Why?"

I place my hands on each side of her head—a position that's quickly becoming our thing. "Because you can't ask me to keep my distance from you. It's like asking me not to breathe. It's agony."

Her breathing is shallow, and her gaze is trained on my chest. "It's agony for me too. But I have to fight the pull, because if I hurt you or the others, I'd never be able to forgive myself."

I place my index finger under her chin and lift her face to mine. "You're not going to hurt us. You can control your gift. I trust you."

"You do?"

Her question is loaded, and it hurts. I didn't trust her before. I accused her of the most horrendous things.

"Wholeheartedly. I'll prove it to you."

I take her hand and place it over my chest. Almost immediately, I feel her gift pulling, stripping my powers from me.

"It's happening again." She tries to pull her hand away.

"No. Focus on not taking, Daisy."

"I can't. The more I try not to take, the more I do."

"Change your thoughts. Don't think about what you're doing. Think about what you *want* to do."

"Bryce, please. Let me go." Her plea almost breaks me, but I don't crack. I won't give up on her that easily.

"No. I won't let you go. You can do this, Daisy. I have faith in you."

"Why?"

"Because I love you."

Daisy looks at me like a deer caught in headlights. She doesn't speak, but tears roll down her cheeks. She also stops taking from me.

"See? I knew you could do it." I smile to hide the fact that my heart is beating like a drum. I just laid myself bare to her. What if she doesn't reciprocate?

"You love me?" she asks, as if she doesn't believe it.

I cup her face with my free hand, wiping her wet cheek with my thumb. "More than anything in the entire universe, Daisy."

She jumps into my arms, crushing her lips against mine. Her attack is so sudden that I almost lose my balance. Laughing, I say, "Whoa, crazy girl. Take it easy. You're an Idol now."

A shadow of worry crosses her eyes, and I curse my big mouth.

"I'm sorry. I don't know what came over me," she says.

I pull her closer to me. "Don't ever apologize for your passion, Daisy. I love it. It injects fire into my veins. It makes me feel... *everything*."

"Do you think things will be different now?"

"What things?"

Blushing spreads over her cheeks. "You know... *things*."

I'm smiling from ear to ear, guessing exactly where her thoughts went.

"I really don't know what you mean. I guess you'll have to show me."

"Oh, shut up and kiss me." She holds my face between her hands and pulls me to her. There's nothing more erotic than a girl taking charge.

Before I know it, we're tumbling down on the mattress and making torn strips of fabric out of our clothes. Daisy has always been a fiery girl, but right now she's lust personified. It crosses my mind that getting into possession of her powers all at once may have heightened all her senses, including her libido.

With our lips and tongues locked together in an ardent dance, she straddles me. We're both still wearing our pants, but the friction below is maddening to the point that I'm afraid I'll combust. I reach for her breasts, cupping them with my greedy hands. Daisy moans against my mouth when I run circles around her nipples with my thumbs. But when she begins to rock back and forth, it takes a herculean effort to not come on the spot.

I wrap my arms around her tiny waist and flip us over.

"Bryce!" she squeaks.

I silence her with the sweep of my tongue while pressing my erection against her sweet pussy. *Damn it. Not good enough.* I abandon her mouth to leave a trail of wet kisses down her body. Daisy arches her back, offering me her luscious breasts. As tempting as they are, I keep going south until my hands and mouth are at her waistband. I'd peel her pajama pants off slowly if I weren't burning up.

Daisy lifts her hips to help. We're on the same page, both hungry, impatient.

As much as I want to plunge my cock inside of her, I can't resist a taste. Grabbing her hips, I sweep my tongue across her clit, loving how she trembles with the touch.

"For all the stars, Bryce. I can't handle this."

I chuckle. "Yes, you can." I lick her again, sucking her clit into my mouth.

Daisy cries out so loudly that I'm sure everyone on this floor heard her. Her trembles turn into violent shakes, and the new energy that surrounds her intensifies. My skin tingles everywhere it touches her while desire curls around the base my spine before shooting to my cock. Damn it, my release is just around the corner, but I can't go over the edge yet.

When the wave of her release recedes, I make the trek back up her body with my lips and tongue, stopping on the way to lavish her breasts with attention. I'm definitely a glutton for punishment, because I'm more than ready to explode inside of her.

Daisy grabs a fistful of my hair and pulls my face closer to hers. "Stop teasing, Bryce. I want all of you."

"You have all of me, sweetheart. But I also want something." I kiss her long and hard before I continue. "Ride me."

Her lips break into a wicked grin while her eyes dance with glee. "As you wish."

She's the one who flips us over this time, and hell, I can't get used to Daisy 2.0. She jumps out of bed, and I almost drag her right back to me but stop when I see what she's up to. She pulls a condom wrapper from the nightstand drawer and winks at me.

"I'm glad you're still thinking straight. I totally forgot about that."

She rips the foil package and pulls the rubber from within. "It's easy to forget when you're not the one to face the consequences."

I open my mouth to argue that I'd never skirt my responsibility, but Daisy's hand is on my cock now, and fuck, I have to use all my concentration to keep from coming too soon.

"What's the matter, babe? Are you in pain?" She guides my erection to her entrance and rubs the head back and forth against her warm pussy.

Squinting, I grab her by the hips and bring her down. She's so wet that I slide in all the way, sheathing myself completely inside of her.

"Oh my God," she cries out, holding my shoulder.

She tries to ride me, but I can't help but take control. The headboard starts to bang against the wall, and the bedsprings creak loudly. The noises mingle with our own grunts and moans. We're definitely not going for subtle here.

I close my eyes, a vain attempt to prolong this moment, but Daisy's pussy is too fucking good. When I feel her shake again, feel the raw energy that rolls off her body, I lose my fight. Blindly, I sit up, pulling her to me to taste her lips as I empty myself inside of her. She keeps gyrating her hips, which only intensifies my orgasm.

My muscles are liquefied a moment later when I fall back onto the mattress, dragging Daisy with me. We're still joined, but neither of us moves an inch as we breathe erratically and in sync.

I lose track of time, but eventually I help Daisy off me, then get up to dispose of the condom. When I return to the bed, Daisy is curled up in a fetal position and asleep.

I take a minute to appreciate the view. I'm not sure how many more moments like this we'll have in our future. Before the heaviness of what awaits us smothers me, I lie down, folding my body against the curve of hers.

"Bryce?" she asks softly.

"Yes, darling."

"I love you too."

I hug her tighter, hiding my face and my tears behind her neck.

17

DAISY

I wake up to the sound of birds chirping, but that can't be right. I'm in my bed, not in a forest. Then Bryce moves behind me, curling his arm tighter around my belly, and I melt against his warm body. Maybe happiness is making me imagine things.

I turn in his arms to make sure he's real.

"You're here." I touch his cheek.

"Of course I'm here," he replies without opening his eyes.

"I can't believe I'm touching you without taking anything from you."

Bryce opens one eye. "I'm an excellent teacher."

"And cocky too." I laugh.

My alarm clock blares loudly, ending our moment. The irritating noise forces me back to a reality I'm not sure I'm ready to face.

Bryce groans, rolling on his back and covering his eyes with his arm.

"It's too early," he complains.

"We agreed we would have a meeting before class." I sit up, pulling the sheets with me to cover my naked chest.

"And who had that asinine idea?"

"You." I smirk.

He drops his arm and levels me with a mocking glower. "I don't recall making the suggestion."

I also don't remember if he was the one who suggested it, but we were on board last night.

"Come on. We *do* need to talk. You haven't told us where your father took you and Rufio yesterday."

The amusement vanishes from Bryce's eyes. He sits up as well, throwing his legs to the side of the bed and giving his back to me. "You heard what your uncle said. I can't tell you."

I nibble on my lower lip. Xavier was adamant that Bryce and Rufio keep the information to themselves. He seemed to know exactly where they had been, but if that's true, why the secrecy?

"Since when do you trust my uncle?" I ask.

Bryce looks over his shoulder. "I don't trust him, but considering our options, he's the one I feel is least likely to betray us."

I break eye contact, letting my shoulders sag forward. "I'd like to say you can trust him, but I can't. But I think he does care about me, and that's saying something."

Bryce places a hand on my shoulder, squeezing it lightly. "At least he's family."

I snort. "Yeah, family. There's something you need to know about Xavier."

"What is it?"

I turn, looking Bryce straight in the eye. "He's a Morph."

His eyes widen a little. "Really? I've never met a Morph before."

"Wow. Like never?"

"No. Morphs are super rare nowadays."

"Why is that?"

"They were perceived as extremely dangerous individuals. Think about it, Daisy. They have the ability to change their appearance. So a little over a hundred years ago, they were hunted down like animals."

I feel the blood drain from my face. That information was missing from Dad's diary. He must have known Xavier was a Morph, right? Maybe that's why Dad didn't go into detail about them for fear the wrong people would find out about Xavier's ability.

"I didn't know that," I finally reply.

"Thanks for telling me. And don't worry, we'll keep this information between us."

A loud knock on the door is followed by Rufio's voice, "Daisy, are you up?"

I look down at the sheets covering my naked body and sigh. "Yeah, I'm up. Hold on."

"I can get the door while you change," Bryce says.

"Thanks. I'm going to hop in the shower." I bolt to the bathroom, locking the door behind me. It's not until I'm under the hot water that I remember I didn't bring any clothes with me. Great. I'll have to face Rufio, Phoenix, and Morpheus wearing only a towel.

What's the big deal, Daisy? Most of them have seen you naked already.

Shut up, slut.

When I return to my room, the guys are each standing in a different corner, and the atmosphere is a little heavy.

"What's going on?"

No one answers with words, only discontent grumbles. Bryce stares at the others and shakes his head. "They're a little upset that I spent the night with you."

"We're not upset about that," Rufio retorts.

"You could have fooled me." Bryce shrugs.

While Rufio is busy glaring at his brother, I try to find the answer in Phoenix's and Morpheus's gazes, but Phoenix purposefully looks at the floor, shutting me out. When I glance at Morpheus, I feel guilty, and I don't know why.

"Rufio and Phoenix are mad because we woke them up with the noise."

My face bursts into flames. "Oh my God. You heard us?"

"You weren't even trying to keep it quiet," Rufio replies, exasperated, and points at Bryce. "Next time you decide to have a midnight rendezvous, you'd better tell me so I can come too."

"What?" I squeak, clutching my towel tighter.

Phoenix finally raises his eyes to mine. "Oh look. Daisy is blushing."

There's no warmth in his comment, and his gaze is as hard as stone.

"I take it that you learned to control your powers," Morpheus says.

"Yeah, I did."

"Cool. Let's test it out." Rufio strides in my direction, and I become tense in an instant. Maybe it's because once again, the guys just caught me post-sex. Or it could be that I'm involved with all four and don't yet know how to handle it.

"What are you going to do?" I ask.

His eyes drop to my lips, and my stomach coils tightly. Is he going to kiss me in front of the others? He takes my hand instead and places it on the center of his chest. Automatically, my power flares up. Damn it. I thought I'd learned to control it.

Rufio twists his face into a grimace and grunts.

"No!" I yank my hand back.

He bends over, wheezing. "Fuck. That was intense."

"I don't understand. I was able to stop stripping Bryce's powers yesterday. Why did it not work with you?"

Bryce is staring hard at his brother, and I can almost see the gears whirring in his head.

"It's possible it has to do with your power scale," Phoenix

supplies. "You're packing juice, Daisy. You're probably a level seventeen."

"Which means what?"

Bryce rubs his face. "It means that maybe you didn't stop taking. Maybe I blocked you."

Disappointment washes over me. I really thought I was starting to get a grip on this strange gift I didn't ask for.

"We'll keep practicing," Bryce adds.

"She won't progress if she practices with you," Morpheus interjects. "You'll keep blocking her, and she'll never learn to master her powers herself."

"You don't know that. I can stop blocking her," Bryce rebuffs, frowning.

Morpheus shakes his head. "No, you can't. Survival instinct will override your wishes."

"Well, I guess you'll have to keep practicing with the rest of us," Phoenix says.

"No, I can't. The chance that I'll unmake you before I learn to control my gift is too great."

"There's gotta be a way, Daisy. I can't not touch you forever," Phoenix replies, surprising me. I thought he was angry with me.

"I'll help her," Morpheus announces.

"She'll suck you dry too," Rufio retorts, making me wince. Once again, the image of a succubus comes to mind.

"I know!" Phoenix snaps his fingers. "We'll round up all the nasty Idols in this school and use them as practice. If Daisy accidentally unmakes them, too bad."

Bryce and Rufio stare at him like he's lost his mind.

"I don't think your solution is practical, even if it has merit," Morpheus replies. "And no, Daisy won't suck me dry like you fear."

"Why is that?" Bryce raises an eyebrow.

Morpheus glances at me, and I see it then. He's going to tell them the truth.

With a deep breath, he says, "I'm not a level fifteen as I was led to believe. You see, the bracelets I've worn since I was a boy not only kept my shadows contained but also dimmed my powers." Morpheus closes his eyes, and a moment later, a surge of energy sprouts from his chest, spreading throughout his body. The shadows manifest, but Morpheus is in control of them.

"Holy shit!" Phoenix yells.

"You're a level eighteen? How is that possible?" Rufio asks, staring at his friend like he's never seen him before.

Bryce moves closer to Morpheus, stopping in front of him. "Mr. Malek isn't your real father, is he?"

"No. My biological father was a demigod."

"I'll be damned." Rufio walks to my window. "You were an eighteen all this time and didn't know."

"And we should keep it that way," Bryce says. "It's bad enough our mother and the Knights know about Daisy."

"I can keep my powers on the down-low." Morpheus shrugs.

"You're not even wearing your bracelets anymore. When did that happen?" Phoenix asks.

Morpheus and I trade glances, but I answer in the end. "I broke his bracelets by accident."

"How could you... oh, I see." Phoenix stares at Morpheus intently.

"Can we get back to the subject of my training, please? I think Morpheus is the best person to teach me how to stop unmaking anyone I touch. And by the way, that isn't the only thing I can do. I think I can also bend time."

"The stronger the Idol, the more gifts they have. You might discover you have other abilities," Bryce adds. "But what makes you think training with Morpheus will be any different than training with me? Won't he block you as well?"

I pinch my lips together. I hadn't thought about that.

"I didn't block her when we tried yesterday," Morpheus explains. "In fact, I let her take until I thought I had nothing left."

I glare at him. "You didn't tell me that."

"My head wasn't in the right place. But you didn't unmake me. You simply stopped on your own, and then my power was there, stronger than ever."

"She didn't take everything because you're stronger than her." Bryce rubs his chin. "I think I'm blocking her automatically because we're at the same level."

"That's settled, then." Phoenix claps his hands. "Morpheus will be Daisy's teacher on Power Control 101, and in turn, Daisy will teach Morpheus how to count."

"Bite me, asshole," Morpheus grits out.

"That was mean. Morpheus did really well on his last math quiz." I cross my arms and pout. "I'm an excellent teacher."

"Hmm, I think I want you to be my tutor too." Phoenix is acting like a complete ass, but at least he's laughing. I know it's his coping mechanism, but it's better than anger.

"That's settled. What are we going to do about Dad and his —" Rufio lets out a scream and clutches his head. He drops to the floor and begins convulsing. He's having a seizure.

"Someone call Nurse Ellen now!" Bryce drops next to him and tries to stop him from shaking.

"No. Don't hold him. Turn him on his side and make sure he's not biting his tongue," I say.

I place a hand on his back to keep him in position, and energy immediately whooshes from him into me. Fuck, I forgot I can't touch him.

A split second before I pull my hand away, I notice something different about the energy flowing from him. It's not his power. It's something else.

A few more seconds later, the shaking stops, but it takes another minute for Rufio to open his eyes.

"Motherfucker," he says.

"Did you get the nurse?" Bryce looks at Morpheus.

"It's ringing."

"End the call," Rufio croaks and tries to sit up. "I don't need medical attention."

"Bullshit. You just had a seizure. That doesn't happen to Idols," Bryce retorts.

"Exactly. I think I know why Mr. X told us not to say anything about our day with Dad. I was about to, and look what happened."

"Are you saying they did something to you, like they gave you a gag order or something?" Phoenix asks.

I can tell by Bryce's and Rufio's blank expressions that if that happened, they have no recollection.

Who the hell is their father working for?

18

DAISY

The pre-class meeting was helpful in some ways, but we still have so much to figure out. Who do we trust? What do we do? So Bryce and Rufio can't say anything about their father and whoever he's working for. That's scary shit. And it also proves that his father doesn't trust them. No wonder Xavier was so nervous about their presence in the club.

I don't know about Rufio, Phoenix, and Morpheus, but my head is most definitely not in class during the first period. When the teacher asks me to solve a problem on the screen, I totally blank. Surprisingly, no one teases me. And not because my guys are giving off protective vibes. It seems to me that most students aren't truly present in math class today. It's only when the bitchy Idol girl who sits next to me gossips with her friend that the coin drops.

Shit. Drusilla. Rufio killed her. I had forgotten all about that.

The gossip is that Drusilla is missing and Renata is in a psych ward. All Bryce could tell us is that his father took care of the problem. But how? I'm pretty sure that by third period, I'll have heard ten different versions of that story.

I look over my shoulder to see if the lies being spread are affecting Rufio in any way. His expression is blank, neutral, but his hands are curled into fists. He looks at me, and I see the truth in his gaze. He's pained, but I'm not sure about which part—killing the Idol or being indebted to his father. There's no love lost between him and that horrible girl. She tried to kill me, and while maybe it's petty of me not to feel an ounce of sadness that's she gone, I don't care. Good riddance.

I can't wait for class to be over so I can slip away and see Rosie. There was a reason a decision was made to make it to class this morning. With so many tragedies on campus in the last week alone, getting a pulse on the student body is vital. We don't know where the next threat is going to come from. But hell, even if the apocalypse is coming, it can wait. I have to see my sister.

Morpheus is the only one who has a car at the moment, and I couldn't make him miss math. We didn't really learn anything by staying, though. I don't doubt his head, just like mine, wasn't in the lecture. As soon as the bell rings, announcing the end of class, I turn to him.

"I can't stay. Would you take me to my sister?"

"Yes, of course."

"We should all go. Being here is giving me the creeps." Rufio stares down anyone who dares look in our direction.

"You don't need to tell me twice. Anything is better than being trapped here until afternoon," Phoenix adds.

As soon as we hit the hallway, I get another surprise. Toby is here. What the hell is he doing at school? What about Rosie? Fury takes over me, and when I march toward him, I have to remember to keep my powers concealed. *Clothed Daisy. Clothed Daisy.*

"What are you doing here?" I get into his space, not hiding my anger.

"Daisy, I—"

"Did you leave my sister alone?"

"No, I didn't. She asked me to take her to that former coworker of yours. Felicity."

I pinch the bridge of my nose, fighting the sudden urge to cry. Of course Rosie would seek out Felicity. She's the only adult who Rosie can trust.

A warm hand on my lower back pulls me from my misery. Morpheus is standing next to me, his eyes filled with compassion.

"Come on, Daisy. Let's go see your sister."

"Okay."

He laces his hands with mine, and together we follow Rufio and Phoenix, who have taken the lead and are now opening a path for us. As usual, people stare and gossip. Their attention is making me jittery. What if I forget to keep masking my power?

"Are you okay?" he asks.

"Why?"

"You're crushing my hand."

"Sorry. I'll feel better when we're out of here."

Bryce joins us in the hallway, sporting a frown. "Where are you going?"

"To see my sister," I reply.

He looks over my shoulder and squints. "You'd better hurry. My mother is coming our way, and by the determination on her face, she wants to have a talk with all of us."

"Speaking with Principal Fallon is the last thing I want to do right now. She was spying on us. Her lackey drugged Rosie," I say through clenched teeth.

"I know. Go. I'll cover you."

"Thanks, Bryce."

He leans closer and kisses me on the cheek. A girl to my

right gasps and another asks, "Is she sleeping with all of them now?"

It takes a great effort on my part to not respond to the malicious comment. But priorities. We have to escape Principal Fallon's clutches.

~

BRYCE

I shouldn't have kissed Daisy in front of everybody. It was an automatic gesture. I heard the comment, but I followed Daisy's lead and ignored it. Now I'm bracing to deal with my mother.

"Where do Daisy and your roommates think they're going?" she asks when I block her way.

"To get fresh air. You're not going to stop them."

She narrows her eyes and purses her lips. "Fine. I'll have a word with her later. I needed to talk to you alone anyway."

I follow her as she marches down the hallway, exuding her authority to the max, barking commands to students who aren't moving fast enough to their next classes. When we enter the office, her assistant looks up from her computer screen, startled.

"Principal Fallon. Did something happen?"

"No. Hold all my calls. I don't want to be interrupted."

I take a good look at my mother's assistant. I've never once given her much thought before. I know she's an Idol, but she's mastered the art of being invisible. Something odd in her gaze catches my attention, though, and it gives me the shivers.

Mom is already behind her desk when I enter the room and close the door. Once again, she reaches for the stone pyramid paperweight on her desk. She always likes to play with that particular object when the subject matter is serious.

"Where did your father take you yesterday?" She gets

straight to the point. It must have killed her to wait so long to interrogate me.

"I can't tell you."

Ire flashes in her gaze. "Oh, so he helped clean up Rufio's mess and suddenly you're on his side?"

"I'm not on anyone's side but my own. But I will give you this piece of free advice. Tighten your leash at Gifted Academy. Drusilla was high on some potent new drug that made her crazy. Cherise Blake was seen during Saturday's ball, and coincidently Toby was almost killed. Too many misfortunes in such a short period of time has to be concerning the board members."

"Are you afraid I'm going to get sacked?"

"I'm surprised you haven't already." I raise an eyebrow.

A chilling smile appears on her face. "Do you think your father is the one with all the powerful connections in this world? He was a nobody before I married him. A newly made millionaire. You ought to remember that."

"Don't worry, Mother. I haven't forgotten anything about our family history. But like you said before, times are changing, and the war you've so famously foreseen is closer than you think."

That's as much as I can say about the Neo Gods without triggering a seizure. Silence drops in the room, heavy and suffocating. Mom doesn't say anything for several minutes as she scrutinizes me.

"And where do you stand if a war between Idols, Fringes, and Norms break out?" she finally asks.

I don't even have to think before I answer. "By Daisy's side."

Her eyes narrow. "You foolish boy. You've fallen in love with that girl."

I lift my chin higher and square my shoulders. "Yes, I have. But unlike you, I'm not going to turn my back on her or let her be killed."

The window opens violently as a gush of strong wind invades the room. I bend my knees and lift my arms to protect myself from the angry gale Mom unleashed on me. It's so strong, I begin to slide backward. Damn it. I had to go and piss her off more. If I struck her with lightning, she'd stop, but then I'd be declaring open war against her, and I can't cut all ties with the woman yet.

Through the howling winds, I hear Miss Walkers's voice. She came in to check if everything was okay, no doubt. The wind stops suddenly.

Mom smacks her desk hard and leans forward. "I told you I didn't want to be interrupted."

"I'm sorry, ma'am. I just thou—"

"Get out," she grits out.

The assistant looks at me with round eyes before she closes the door softly. She seemed fearful, but I'm not buying her charade. She's not a meek employee. That's for sure.

"How dare you imply I killed William," Mom continues.

"He died because of you, didn't he?"

"He died because your father killed him. And he'll kill Daisy too if he learns she's the Equalizer."

A huge lump forms in my throat. She doesn't need to remind me, not when I'm tasked with killing her. But I'd level this city to the ground before I let anything happen to Daisy.

"He's not going to find out about her as long as she keeps masking her powers."

Mom snorts. "Do you think that's an option, Bryce? I know the Knights have been in touch with you. They want to recruit Daisy, don't they?"

"You should know. Aren't you one of them?"

"We've collaborated in the past, but no, I'm not a Knight."

"Why not? We seem to have the same goal."

"We do, but I don't agree with their methods. Did you know

they've been distributing lightning-glass weapons to the under-belly of Saturn's Bay?"

Shit. The motorcycle gang that Rufio went up against had such weapons. "Why would they do that? Criminals don't care who they kill as long as they're Idols. That makes no sense."

"Exactly. It doesn't. So be very careful with the information you disclose to Gunther Silverstone. They're going to use Daisy as the ultimate weapon. The fewer Idols they have to face, the better."

"They said they want to bring balance to the world."

"Bullshit propaganda to recruit gullible youngsters. And there's another thing you need to be very careful about."

"What is it?"

"Don't let them know what you're capable of, Bryce."

"They know I can heal, Mom."

"But they don't know you can make Idols."

"I can't make Idols. Daisy's case is different."

"You healed that ginger boy, Toby, and now he has abilities."

"He's only a Fringe."

"Yes, but for how long?"

"What do you mean, for how long?"

"I've scanned him twice. Once when his powers had just developed and again this morning. He's not a Fringe anymore, Bryce. He's an Idol."

19

DAISY

I'm still fuming, and we've been on the road for forty minutes already. I don't understand why seeing Toby at school pissed me off so much.

"Uh, Daisy. Are you okay?" Morpheus asks.

I turn to him with an angry retort on the tip of my tongue. But seeing the worried expression etched in his face, I don't bite his head off.

"No, I'm not okay. I'm so mad at Toby, I could scream. First, he takes off with Mr. Silverstone without saying a word, and then he simply goes to school without a care in the world."

"Okay, I get it. He messed up, but is that a reason to hurt yourself?" He drops his gaze to my fisted hands.

"What?" There's blood running down the sides. I open them, and sure enough, there are crescent moon-shaped cuts on my palms.

Phoenix sticks his head between the front seats. "Damn, babe. You need to calm down."

I glower at him, ready to unleash my fury when Rufio speaks. "Toby fucked up royally. Daisy has all the reason in the world to be pissed."

"Thank you," I say.

"Good job there, Rufio. I was trying to diffuse the situation, not make her more riled up," Phoenix replies.

"Daisy, I'm going to ask you something, and please don't take it the wrong way, but were you ever a hothead like Rufio?" Morpheus asks.

"Hey, fuck off. I'm not a hothead."

"You just made his point, idiot." Phoenix snorts.

"What do you think? Was I a hothead when we met?" I ask.

"Well, you were pretty sassy." Morpheus grins.

"And cocky," Rufio adds.

"I'm not sure if I should take that as a compliment or not." I cross my arms and pout.

It takes me a second to realize what I'm doing. This is not me. I'm acting like a child.

Sagging my shoulders, I reply, "To be honest, no, I don't think I was short-fused. I mean, I never accepted being pushed around, and I fought for what was right."

"But have you ever felt intense emotions like rage or despair?" Morpheus continues.

My stomach clenches painfully, and at the same time, my chest feels much tighter. "Yeah. The evening my parents were murdered."

"I'm sorry. I didn't mean to remind you of that." Morpheus glances at me with regret written on his face.

I look out the window to hide the tears that are quickly turning my vision blurry. "It's not your fault. But at least, I can take solace in the fact that I've killed one of their murderers."

"You what?" they all ask at the same time.

I look at them and catch Morpheus staring at me with his jaw hanging low. The car begins to swerve out of its lane, straight into a collision path with incoming traffic. "Watch the road!" I warn.

The tires screech as Morpheus yanks the steering wheel to the right to avoid an accident.

"Sorry," he says.

"What do you mean, you killed one of them? How?" Rufio asks.

"My father had a lightning-glass dagger in his bag. I didn't know what it was, only that it was pointy and I needed a weapon. One of the bastards was holding me by my neck, saw the weapon, and dared me to strike him." I close my eyes, reliving everything about that scene, including the pain. "So I did. I plunged the dagger into his neck. It went in like butter."

"Son of a bitch," Phoenix murmurs.

I wipe my wet cheeks and whirl in my seat. "Then Gunther Silverstone came in with his associates, and Rosie and I escaped."

"You owe the guy your life," Morpheus replies.

"I do, and I'm sure he'll remind me of that when he tries to sell me on whatever he's planning."

"You should say yes," Rufio says, surprising the shit out of me.

"Are you crazy?" Phoenix retorts loudly. "The guy kidnapped Bryce, and he knew what my fat—he knew," he finishes, his voice lower, subdued.

Damn that monster for hurting Phoenix. I wish I could have made him suffer before his demise.

"Why are you saying that, Rufio? Is it because of what you learned while in your father's company?" Morpheus asks.

Rufio's eyes connect with mine. They're more intense than ever, which in turn makes the blue even more electric.

"Yes," he replies.

"You don't remember how you came to have the gag spell in your mind, do you?" I ask.

"I have no clue. But Mr. X sure as shit knew something was up. That's why he told us not to say anything."

"I don't get why he didn't just outright tell you something awful would happen if you blabbered," Phoenix chimes in.

"I'm sure he had a valid reason," I say, but I'm not sure if I truly believe that or if it's just wishful thinking. For better or worse, Xavier is family, and I can't bear the thought of him being duplicitous to Rosie and me.

"Well, until he tells us everything he knows, I'm not putting my trust in him," Phoenix grumbles.

Still staring at Rufio, I say, "I felt it when I touched you while you were having a seizure. My power ignited, as it usually does, but I wasn't taking only your gift. I also took whatever they did to you."

"And then he stopped convulsing," Morpheus adds.

"Holy crap. Do you think you disabled the gag order completely?" Phoenix's eyes widen.

"I don't think so," Rufio replies. "Every time I even consider saying anything, my muscles spasm."

"Damn it." I cross my arms.

"Maybe Daisy didn't take enough to neutralize whatever they've done to you," Morpheus suggests.

"I wouldn't risk an attempt to neutralize it, not until I can control my powers," I reply.

The car begins to slow, and I face forward. The familiar narrow street with small shops lining both sides comes into view. Parking is usually difficult thanks to the commerce, but a van pulls out in front of us.

"Park there." I point.

Morpheus takes the spot, and immediately I notice the stares from the pedestrians nearby. His car isn't even super fancy. I can't imagine how those people would react if we were riding in Rufio's or Phoenix's cars.

"Damn, where are we?" Phoenix asks.

"Definitely not in Idol territory anymore." Morpheus leans

forward to look at the buildings. "Does your friend live here by herself?"

"Yeah. Why?"

"It doesn't seem very safe."

"It's better than the neighborhood where I used to live in Hawk City," I reply, trying not to show the pang I feel in my chest. "This is the reality for Norms and most Fringes."

"I never once stopped to consider how you guys lived," Rufio murmurs. "I didn't care."

"Me neither," Phoenix replies.

"Let's go. We're just drawing attention by sitting in the car like this." I reach for the door handle when a loud knock on the window makes me jump in my seat. A homeless man is staring at me.

"What the hell," I say.

"Daisy, wait. Your shield isn't up," Morpheus warns.

"Fuck. And I thought I'd gotten the handle of it."

"Don't beat yourself up for it. You will. Now concentrate."

The man knocks on the window again, adding fuel to my frustration. I roll down the window before I'm completely sure that I'm masking my power. "What?" I snap.

The guy's eyes widen and he scrambles backward before bolting. Shit. I guess I'm still projecting my Idol energy.

"He totally sensed that I'm an Idol," I say.

"At least you got rid of him," Phoenix replies.

"He was just a hobo. No big deal," Rufio retorts.

"It doesn't matter now anyway. But we can't go see your sister and your friend while you're like that," Morpheus says.

"I know, okay?" I bark and immediately regret my harsh response. "I'm sorry. I don't know what's wrong with me."

"It's the adjustment period. You went through a big change in a short period of time. Your feelings will normalize eventually."

"Let's pray for that. We don't need another Rufio," Phoenix declares.

"Why am I the bad guy now? Both you and Morpheus have had your share of psychotic behavior."

While the guys bicker, I close my eyes and attempt to concentrate on masking my powers. It's a little more difficult now, maybe because my emotions are all over the place. After at least five minutes, I finally open my eyes.

"How about now?" I ask Morpheus.

He nods. "You're good to go."

I exit the car and my emotions change. I get jitters, and my stomach feels heavy, almost as if there's pie made out of rocks there. What if Rosie really can't see past the Idol situation?

Stop with this nonsense, Daisy. You're acting like a coward. Have faith in your sister. She'll see reason.

I stride toward Felicity's building. The door to her apartment is crammed between a fruit stall and a Chinese deli. The intercom is old and a bit rusty, but it still works. I press the buzzer a couple of times before she answers.

"Hello, who is this?"

"It's me, Daisy."

"Oh, thank heavens, girl. I've been trying to locate you for hours. I'll buzz you in right now."

The electric sound of the door unlocking comes, and I quickly push it open. Felicity didn't give me the time to let her know I had company, but maybe it's better if she doesn't know until I'm in her apartment.

The steps on the stairway creak as we put weight on them. The walls are dirty and in need of painting, and there's a funky smell too. I've never cared much about the condition of her building. In fact, after years of living in awful locations, I thought this place was a palace in comparison. But now that I'm accompanied by Idols who have lived their entire lives surrounded by luxury, I'm embarrassed for my friend. It's stupid, and I shouldn't feel this way.

The emotion is quickly replaced by anger. Trusting the Knights or not, Mr. Silverstone is right. Things have to change.

Felicity's apartment is on the first floor. There are three other apartments on her level. She already has the door open when I reach the landing. Her blonde hair is a little messy, and the dark roots are already showing. Shit, she's going to hate me that I didn't warn her about the guys.

"Daisy, gosh, I was so worried about you." She hugs me tightly, but a curse immediately follows. "Ah, fuck. I should have known you wouldn't come alone."

I ease away from her and turn. The guys are crammed in the small hallway behind me. They've all masked their power and are trying to appear as unthreatening as possible. They didn't have to do that. Felicity knows they're Idols, but the fact that they did anyway without being asked makes my chest warmer. They did it for me.

"Yeah, I needed a ride," I reply.

She tries to comb her hair into compliance with her hand. "Well, come in, then. And please don't mind the mess."

She opens the door wider and immediately begins to straighten items. It's not even that untidy. Felicity likes to keep her apartment in order.

"Nice digs," Phoenix says, earning a backhand to his chest from Morpheus. "What did I say?'

"Where's Rosie?" I ask.

Felicity freezes for a second and then continues collecting things from the living room. "Sleeping. Poor thing didn't go to bed until five in the morning."

"What did she tell you?"

"She said she had a fight with you and that her landlord was spying on her."

I trade a meaningful glance with Morpheus. Felicity turns

around at that precise moment and catches the gesture. "That's not exactly what happened, is it?"

"I can't get into details right now. I have to speak to her."

"Of course, hon." She switches her attention to the guys. "I'm going to brew some fresh coffee. Anyone interested?"

"Got any vodka?" Phoenix replies, and I'm hoping he's joking.

Felicity turns her eyes into slits, pinching her mouth. "I drank it all last night."

That's probably true.

While she's distracted by them, I slip away and head for the only bedroom in the apartment. I spied a pillow and covers on the sofa, so I'm assuming Felicity gave her room to Rosie.

I enter without knocking. It's still dark in here thanks to the closed curtains. There's a lump on the bed, and I can only see Rosie's hair sticking out from underneath the covers. I close the door with a soft click, and Rosie turns at the sound. "Felicity? What time is it?"

"It's not Felicity. It's me." I approach the bed slowly. "We need to talk."

Rosie sits up at once, pulling the covers up to her chin. "I don't want to talk to you. Get out!"

"No, I won't. Please, Rosie. Let me explain what happened."

She shakes her head. "I don't want to hear any words coming out of your mouth. For all I know, you're not even my sister anymore."

"Okay, that's enough. You're being super unfair to me for something I had no control over. I'm your sister. Can't you see past the change in me?"

Rosie covers her face with her hands. "I've tried. But then I remember what you did yesterday. You freaking manipulated time. And then I remember those Idols who killed our parents."

I sit down on the bed next to her. "Rosie, not all Idols are bad. Remember when Bryce took us to the carnival at the beach? You had fun."

She jerks her hands down to face me. "Yeah, and then he turned you into one of them. He probably couldn't face having a Norm girlfriend, so he mutated you."

"That's not true. He saved my life."

"What do you mean?" Her eyes turn as round as saucers. At least Toby didn't rob me of the chance to tell the story myself.

"A few weeks ago, a deranged teacher tried to kill me. He threw me out the window. I would have died if Bryce hadn't shown up and healed me."

"He healed Toby too." Rosie covers her mouth. "And now Toby is a real Fringe."

"I know. But Bryce didn't know his healing ability had that side effect."

Rosie drops her gaze to the bed. "I don't want to be mad at you, or fear you, but I'm wired like that. I can't reconcile the fact that you're now one of them. It used to be you and me against the world. Now I'm all alone."

I grab her hand and squeeze it tight. She doesn't pull away, which I count as a small victory. "Nothing has changed in that aspect. It's still you and me against the world. You're my baby sister, Rosie. I love you with all my heart. Nothing will ever change that."

She watches me for the longest time without saying a word. During that time, I hold my breath, not daring to make any sudden movements.

Finally, she throws herself in my arms. "I'm sorry, Daisy. I shouldn't have reacted like that. I was terrified."

"I know, sweetie. I know. Everything will be okay. I promise you."

We stay like that for at least a minute before we break the embrace. Tears have streamed freely down Rosie's cheeks, and mine are also wet.

"What's going to happen now? Are you still going to keep attending Gifted Academy?" she asks in a small voice.

"Yes. But no one can know I'm an Idol."

"Why not? If they knew, they'd leave you alone."

A loud sigh escapes my lips. I wish I could spare Rosie the reality of my powers, but I've kept her in the dark long enough. "No, they wouldn't leave me alone, Rosie. It turns out my new powers are dangerous to Idols."

"Why? How is bending time dangerous to them?"

"That's not the only thing I can do. I can also unmake them."

She furrows her brows. "I don't understand. What do you mean by unmake?"

"I can take away an Idol's power. I can turn them into Norms."

Rosie doesn't speak for several beats as she stares at me with big eyes. "That's crazy."

"I know. If they discover what I can do to them, they'll kill me."

"One more reason for you to leave that school. You can't stay there surrounded by your enemy."

"I can't run away, Rosie."

Her expression turns from fearful to angry in a split second. "You don't want to leave because of your boyfriends."

Wait. Boyfriends?

"That's right. I know you've been hooking up with all of them." Her tone is reproachable.

Mortification makes my face warm. She's judging me big-time, and I can't stand it, but I won't go down that road with her, not when I don't know where I stand with the guys. Yesterday, I told Bryce that I loved him, and I didn't lie. But I'm also sure I'm in love with Rufio, Phoenix, and Morpheus.

"Where are we going to go? We don't have any family, friends, or money."

That's not true anymore. I have friends and Xavier. But Rosie would never accept them as such. Shit. I need to tell her about him too.

"I don't know!" She throws her hands up in the air. "This is all so bleak. I hate feeling this hopeless. I don't even have a place to live anymore."

"That's not true. You're coming to stay with me."

"Are you nuts? I can't live with you. Plus, what about my school? That place is like an hour away from here."

"You're enrolling at Gifted Academy," I say with confidence.

I don't care what I need to do to make this happen, but I'm not going to be separated from my sister again.

20

DAISY

"This is madness. You all can see it, right?" Phoenix says from the passenger seat.

Thanks to Rosie coming back to Gifted Academy with us, I decided to sit in the back with her. Rufio is driving because Morpheus is the only one who can sit next to me and not fear being unmade.

"I can't leave Rosie alone anymore. It's too dangerous. And she can't stay with Felicity either. It's not fair."

"So let's just bring her back to the academy. Because you've had it so easy there," he continues.

"Yeah, thanks to you," I retort.

"Please don't fight on my account. I can handle myself," Rosie replies.

"Sure, sure," Phoenix murmurs.

"Will you quit bitching?" Rufio interjects. "No one is going to touch Rosie, not while she's under our protection. I'm more concerned about what Daisy will have to do to convince my mother to let her enroll."

"Maybe we can finally learn what she's up to," I reply. "Isn't that why you went with your father to wherever?"

"And look how well that turned out. He can't even speak without triggering seizures," Phoenix pipes up.

"One problem at a time. I'm sure we can figure how to unblock Rufio's mind," Morpheus replies.

"I have a question. How come I can't sense your powers now?" Rosie asks me.

"We're masking it," I answer. "Just like Stephan did."

"Oh, that's right."

"Who the hell is Stephan?" Phoenix turns in his seat, his expression twisted into a scowl.

"Jeez, are you jealous?" Rosie gives him a droll stare.

"I'm not jealous," he grits out.

"Riight."

"Stop bickering, you two," I say.

"You didn't answer my question," Phoenix insists.

"Stephan Silverstone. He's Mr. Silverstone's oldest son."

"I didn't know you were chummy with his family," Rufio says accusatorily.

"I'm not chummy with anyone. I happened to meet him at a barbeque at the man's place. I also met his youngest son, if you must know all the details."

With a grunt, Phoenix faces the road again.

"Yeah, not jealous, my ass," Rosie whispers.

Both Phoenix and Rufio did sound jealous, but why? I look at Morpheus, who's been pretty quiet this whole time.

"What?" he asks.

"Nothing. You haven't said much since we left Felicity's. Do you also think me bringing Rosie to the academy is a bad idea?"

"Of course I think it's a bad idea. But considering what happened at your old place, I don't see any other option."

I don't know what I was expecting from him. Maybe reassuring words that everything will be all right. But that's not Morpheus. It's not any of them.

The conversation dries out during the rest of the ride back

to campus. By the time we cross the gates, my stomach is twisted in knots. My hands become sweaty when I think about the danger Rosie will be facing. I can't watch her 24/7.

Fuck me, I think I've made a terrible mistake. Panic sets in and I can't get air into my lungs. Maybe I should have told Rosie the truth about Xavier and asked him to find a place for her.

No, that's an even worse idea. The best way to ensure Rosie's safety is if she's with me.

"Wow, this place is fancy. I didn't pay proper attention the last time I was here," Rosie says, then looks down at her clothes. "I'm going to stick out here like a sore thumb."

"Most definitely, but not because of the clothes you're wearing," Phoenix replies.

"Then why?"

He looks over his shoulder with a smirk on his face. "You're with us. That's why."

"Seriously, what do you see in him?" she asks me. "Bryce is much nicer."

Morpheus snorts, then tries to hide it with a cough.

"Yeah, yeah, whatever. Bryce is the best. Let's go already." Rufio turns off the engine and opens the driver door. I didn't notice we had gotten to the garage already.

"What are we going to do now?" Rosie asks me once we're out of the car.

"Let's get you settled. Then I'll go talk with Principal Fallon."

The internal door to the garage opens with a loud thud, and shouts of several rowdy males echo around us. Rosie tenses on the spot, moving closer to me. The guys immediately form a protective barrier around us, but in consequence, they block my view of who's coming our way.

"Oh, look who we got here. The Magnificent Four!" someone shouts.

"Well, they're down one. Come party with us, guys," another idiot says.

"I don't think so," Rufio replies.

Unable to help myself, I walk around the guys to see what's going on. A group of five Fringe students is coming our way, and by the way they're walking like they have forgotten how to move their legs, I'd say they're drunk, or worse, high.

"Well, it's your loss. This is going to be the wildest night of all times."

They all howl, and then one of them creates a fireball and tosses it at a random car.

"Shit!" Phoenix says before he pushes me down to the floor and uses his body as a shield. The blast of the explosion comes a second later, but all I can think about is Rosie.

Immediately, the garage fills with dark smoke. I try to dislodge Phoenix from me, but he won't budge. It takes me a second to understand why. I'm sucking his power, and most likely I've rendered him immobile.

"Help!" I croak and try to push Phoenix off me.

Moments go by before someone finally pulls him off.

"Daisy, are you okay?" Rufio asks, watching me with a manic glint in his eyes.

"Yeah, I'm fine." Covering my face with my arm, I jump to my feet. "Where's Rosie?"

"I'm here. I'm fine," she says from behind me. Morpheus is holding her upright.

"Come on, let's get out of here," Rufio urges.

"What happened to the other students?" I try to find them through the thick smoke.

"I don't know. Come on." Rufio reaches for me, but I step out of the way.

He twists his face into a scowl, but I get that it's not aimed at me. Walking in the direction where we believe the exit is, we maybe take five steps forward when a strong breeze has the smoke dissipating. When the air is partially clear, we see Principal Fallon standing near the door. She's furious, no doubt, but I hope she doesn't blame us for what happened.

My gaze sweeps the rest of the garage, and soon I have my answer concerning those stupid Fringe boys. They got caught in the blast from the explosion and are now nothing but crisps.

Principal Fallon strides in our direction and stops in front of Rufio. "What have you done now?"

"Fuck you! This isn't my mess."

The slap to the face comes swiftly, and I wince as if she'd hit me. Rufio's aura becomes dark. He's going to do something stupid.

I jump in front of him, mindful not to touch him. "No, she's not worth it."

"We just got back, and those idiots were out of their minds. Then one of them caused the explosion," Morpheus chimes in.

"At this rate, they're going to shut down the school," she says more to herself than us.

Her shrewd gaze travels past us, and when she squints, I know she's spotted Rosie.

"What is she doing here?"

"She's going to stay with me," I reply.

"That's out—"

"I didn't ask for permission." I take a step forward, unmasking my powers. "She's going to stay with me, and she's going to start attending Gifted Academy. You're going to make that happen, or I'm out of here."

"And where would you go?" Principal Fallon asks, but I can see the crack in her steely countenance.

"Maybe I'll join the Knights."

"We'll talk about that later. Now get out of here and let me clean up this mess."

She doesn't need to say it twice. We hurry out of the garage, but people heard the explosion and are coming our way. If they see us, they'll immediately assume we had something to do with it.

"Everyone, move closer to me," Morpheus orders.

I'm the first one to abide, dragging Rosie with me. When Rufio and Phoenix don't move right away, I hiss, "Hurry up."

They finally get closer. Phoenix opens his mouth, but Morpheus silences him with a look. "No one make a sound."

He closes his eyes and the shadows reappear, only they're not just around his wrists anymore. Now they spread from his chest and arms, almost covering him completely. There's a gasp, and I don't know if it came from me or Rosie.

"Son of a bitch. We don't need this now," Rufio says.

Morpheus looks at him and replies, "Don't worry. I'm in control." He looks at Rosie. "Don't be afraid. Close your eyes if you have to."

She clutches my arm tighter, hiding her face against my shoulder. The shadows around Morpheus expand outward until they cover us as well. I expect to be hit by the horrible fear his power can provoke, but all the shadows do is conceal us from the crowd that's bearing our way. Silently, we inch closer to the wall and keep walking toward the elevator.

More students come out of it when it lands on the ground level, but no one is waiting to go up. We take our chance and pile in. Finally safe inside the metal box, Morpheus pulls the shadows back into him.

"Holy fucking shit. What the hell was that? Since when can you control the shadows?" Phoenix asks.

"Since Daisy broke the bracelets."

"How did you know you could use them to hide us?" I ask.

"I don't know. A hunch?"

"You made us invisible," Rosie says. "You could be a spy."

I know Rosie didn't mean her comment to be taken seriously, but I can see in Morpheus's eyes that he's intrigued by the idea.

The elevator pings, announcing we have arrived on our floor. I take Rosie to my room, but I can't stay.

"I'll be right back. I'm next door if you need anything," I tell her, half expecting her to ask to tag along.

She doesn't, though. All she does is hug me and say, "Hurry back."

Once the door clicks shut, I feel a little better. No one can break in and harm her. Well, no one besides Principal Fallon.

Great, now I'm back at worrying.

"Daisy, are you coming?" Rufio asks in front of their door. Phoenix and Morpheus are already inside.

When I don't move right away, he comes to me. I'm too lost in my head that I don't see what Rufio is up to until it's too late. He captures my face between his hands and kisses me. My head rebels against it because I know what will happen, but my heart and body succumb to the desire. I let him devour my mouth because I missed touching him. So damn much.

I grab fistfuls of his shirt and pull him closer to me. Rufio pushes me against the door and presses his body against mine. He nudges my legs apart with his, and the delicious friction quickly leaves me breathless. My entire body is tingling, and I don't care that we're making out in the middle of the hallway.

"Son of a bitch. Morpheus, help!" Phoenix says, but it sounds far away.

Another second and Rufio is being yanked away from me, leaving me cold and bereft. My pulse is drumming in my ears in sync with the beating of my heart. Morpheus and Phoenix are holding a flushed Rufio between them.

Holy crap. He can't stand on his own. I did that.

"Oh no." I press my hand against my stomach. "I didn't mean to do it."

"Relax, Daisy. You didn't take it all." Rufio gives me a crooked smile.

"Okay, Don Juan. Let's get you back inside," Morpheus replies none too happily.

My guilty heart is still stuck in my throat when I follow the guys inside, but when I see the look on Bryce's face, it drops down all the way to the floor. Something terribly wrong has happened. I can feel it in my bones.

"What is it?" I ask.

"I now know for sure why I canceled your power out last night."

"Wasn't it because we're both seventeens?"

"Yes and no. Sure, being equally matched power-wise is probably a factor, but the main reason it happened is that our powers are opposites."

"I don't follow," I reply.

"Yeah, me neither. Quit with the suspense, will ya?" Rufio says from the couch.

Bryce sighs and stares straight into my eyes. "You can unmake Idols, and apparently I can make them."

21

DAISY

Principal Fallon doesn't send for me until early the next morning. I'm not even fully awake yet when the knock on the door comes. It's crazy how I know it's her standing outside of my door and not one of the guys. I never suspected that Idols had different signatures; as a Norm, I could only guess their level on the Idol scale.

I turn around to check if the knock woke Rosie, but she's still sound asleep. Poor thing was exhausted yesterday after her ordeal. She didn't even want to talk much when I came back into the room.

I get out of bed as softly as I can and tiptoe toward the door. I'm wearing shorts and a loose T-shirt as pajamas, but I don't think Principal Fallon cares about my appearance.

I only open the door a sliver. "Really? It's not even six in the morning yet," I whisper.

"You and I have much to discuss. I'd prefer it if my sons are not aware we talked."

"That's idiotic. They know I have to talk to you about Rosie."

"Put your shoes on and walk with me," she replies as if I didn't make an asinine comment.

Clenching my jaw, I shut the door again. Not only do I put shoes on, but I also change into my uniform. I'm not going anywhere with the woman wearing sleepwear.

Principal Fallon doesn't look at me when I join her in the corridor, just walks in the opposite direction the elevators and nearest staircase are. I follow her in silence, taking the opportunity to ensure my power is concealed.

We turn left at the end of the hallway and continue until we come to a dead end.

"Did you know that my family has been in charge of Gifted Academy for three generations? This building was actually named after my grandfather."

"Peachy," I murmur.

She raises both hands in front of the wall, and a soft breeze comes out of nowhere. There aren't any windows nearby, so she must have created it. I don't know what's she up to until little hidden squares on the wall sink in and a secret passage is revealed. The wall swings forward, revealing a dark corridor beyond.

"He made sure the building had secret passages so faculty could move without being seen when the occasion called for it," she explains.

We continue down the corridor, and the motion sensor lights turn. Apprehension licks the back of my neck, a feeling that doesn't improve when the door clicks shut behind me.

"Where are we going?"

"I want to show you something."

The corridor ends in a set of narrows stairs. We don't speak a word, and the only sound bouncing off the walls is of our feet on the stone steps. The stairs seem to go down forever, and by my calculations, we must have gone underground by now. At last, we reach the bottom, only to continue our trek through another long and narrow passageway.

"Did your grandfather build secret tunnels connecting all buildings on campus?"

"Yes, he did."

"So all teachers have access to them?" I ask with a hint of alarm. I haven't forgotten that one of them tried to kill me.

"No. All faculty members who knew about the existence of these tunnels are long gone. I'm the only one with the knowledge. Well, and now you."

So not even her own sons know. And she's now sharing this secret with me. I wasn't born yesterday. She's trying to make me trust her. Fat chance of that happening. But I can play the part of the gullible idiot.

"Why are you telling me?"

The corridor we're in ends at a door, which Principal Fallon opens with a key she had in her pocket. We go up spiral stairs that wind up forever until we finally reach our final destination —a secret room filled with state-of-the-art equipment. A large desk sits in the middle, and mounted on top are three large monitors showing the security feeds on campus. I only spare a fleeting glance at them, as something way more interesting catches my eye. The entire right wall is covered from top to bottom with pictures, newspaper clippings, maps, and notes.

"What is that?"

I move closer, immediately noticing my picture and Rosie's somewhat in the center. There are also pictures of my parents, Xavier, Rufio, Bryce, Phoenix, and Morpheus, plus several connecting lines to other images and notes.

"Welcome to the war room. This wall contains every piece of information I've gathered in the last twenty-one years about our families and every other major player in this game."

I notice a picture of a stern man with the tag "Neo Gods" written below.

"Who is this?"

"My husband."

My blood runs cold. So this is the man who killed my uncle William. "You know he's a Neo God and you still married to him?"

"Oh, sweet child. Don't you know it's better to keep your enemies close? If I wasn't married to him, I wouldn't know he recruited my sons to his fucked-up organization."

Rage bubbles up to my throat. "How could you let him take Bryce and Rufio?"

"I had no choice in the matter. Rufio tied my hands when he killed Drusilla. I don't have the resources my husband does. I knew he was the only one who could help Rufio."

"Fucking fantastic. And now Rufio and Bryce are in his hands. Can't you see what you've done!"

"They haven't been indoctrinated yet. There's a test they must pass."

I narrow my eyes. "How do you know so much about the Neo Gods? Rufio and Bryce have some kind of spell that gives them seizures if they try to talk about what they saw and heard."

"I've been married to their father for over twenty years. I know how to extract information from him. He blabbers when he fucks."

Oh my God. I just puked in my mouth. Principal Fallon screwing her husband is definitely not the image I want in my head.

"Spare me the gruesome details of your sex life. How do I know you're not part of the Neo Gods?"

"If I were part of that hateful group, you wouldn't be standing here, staring defiantly at me from your higher moral ground. I don't need to read my sons' minds to know what the test is. They must kill the new weapon the Knights acquired, meaning you."

My blood runs cold. "What happens when they don't follow through with their task?"

"Most likely they'll be exterminated. Gag spell or not, they've seen too much."

I pull my hair back, yanking at the strands. "I can't let that happen."

"*We* won't let that happen. So here's my proposal to you. Help me end the menace of the Neo Gods, one Idol at a time."

There it is, the reason she brought me here. My stomach clenches painfully as I stare at the woman. "How?"

"I've compiled a list of at least twenty members. We can take them down one by one."

"Do you want me to kill them?"

"No, I want you to unmake them, turn those assholes into Norms. Let them become what they hate the most. That's what I want to see."

"That sounds dangerous. And once I turn the first one into a Norm, they'll know who I am."

"Not if you're disguised."

I turn to the wall again and consider the possibilities. Xavier said Mr. Silverstone wants equality, but as long as organizations like the Neo Gods exist, they'll fight tooth and nail to preserve the position Idols hold.

"I don't know," I mutter.

"You're worried about your sister. If you agree to help me, I'll make sure she has a place at Gifted Academy."

Damn the woman. She knows exactly what to say to manipulate me.

I spin around, facing her. "Okay. I'll help you. Who am I unmaking first? Your husband?"

"No. We're saving him for last. We'll strike far away from home."

"Where?"

"Hawk City."

22

MORPHEUS

I'm the first one up. The sun has yet to appear, but I couldn't stay in bed a minute longer, even though I'm bone-tired. There's too much to process, too much to think about. My vision of Daisy and Bryce linked together by the Infinity band is beginning to make sense. The Maker and the Unmaker, joined for all eternity. The thought is bitter.

I head for the kitchen to prepare coffee, but my head is definitely not in the task. I pour way too much water in the container and end up with something that resembles a dirty brew more than anything else. I toss everything down the drain and restart.

I'm unsettled by Bryce's revelation. Thanks to my vision, I knew he would have a special connection to Daisy, but now I'm not sure if I'm okay with it. The ugly feeling swirling in my chest is taking my head for a spin. I knew she was involved with my friends, and I didn't expect her to pick me over them, so why am I feeling this possessive now? We only kissed, nothing more.

"What are you doing up already?" Bryce asks, ending my solitude.

He had to be the one to join me while I have all these dark thoughts in my head.

"Couldn't sleep. You?"

He takes a seat by the kitchen counter and leans his elbows on the marble surface. "Me neither."

I get busy making another batch of coffee, and we don't speak for several minutes. I honestly don't know what to say to him, or maybe I'm afraid to make it obvious of how conflicted I am about Daisy.

"I don't like that Rosie is now a Gifted Academy resident," he says suddenly.

I whirl around. "Why is that?"

"She's bound to get hurt by one of the idiots who go here. We can't keep an eye on her 24/7. What if I have to heal her and she turns into an Idol as well?"

"Would that be so terrible? At least she wouldn't be defenseless anymore."

"I'm afraid that if I keep turning Norms into Idols, the secret will come out. Someone is bound to want to take advantage of that."

"And by someone, you mean your mother."

"She's one of them. But I can see the appeal to the Knights too. A Norm turned Idol would be way more inclined to join the Knights. It could triple their ranks in no time."

"Do you think Gunther Silverstone knows about you?"

"Mr. X knows about Toby. It's only a matter of time before they discover Toby is now an Idol."

"What do you think your father will do if he learns about your handy gift?" I raise an eyebrow.

The blood vanishes from Bryce's face, and his expression becomes pained.

"Are you okay?" I ask.

"No. You asked me a question about my father, and I wanted to answer, which means I can't."

"Fuck. I'm sorry, Bryce. I swear I'm going to spend every spare minute training Daisy. I believe she can take the gag spell from your mind."

"Like that would be a chore for you." He smiles wryly.

I tense on the spot. Am I that transparent? "I don't know what you're implying." I give my back to him so he can't read the truth in my expression.

"Cut it out, Morpheus. It's obvious you have feelings for her. It seems we're all destined to love the same woman."

My nostrils flare. I don't know why I'm irritated by his remark. "I'm not in love with her."

"Yeah, yeah. And water isn't wet either."

"What's all this racket this early in the morning?" Phoenix comes into the living room wearing nothing but boxer shorts and crazy bed hair.

"I'm making coffee," I answer quickly, then throw a meaningful glance in Bryce's direction. I hope he gets the message that I don't want to keep talking about Daisy.

A shiver runs down my spine, and the hairs on the back of my neck stand on end all of a sudden. I turn and stare at the door. Bryce and Phoenix do the same. A soft knock comes a second later.

Bryce is the one closest to it. He jumps out of his chair and reaches the door with two long strides. Daisy comes in silently, and immediately I know something is wrong.

"What's the matter?" Bryce asks.

"I just came down from a meeting with your mother."

"What were you doing talking to that witch at this hour?" Rufio asks, coming from his bedroom, highly alert for someone who just woke up.

"She wanted to speak to me before any of you were up." Daisy twists her hands together and purposefully avoids making eye contact with any of us. Her aura is all messed up as well, darker and restless. She's conflicted over something.

"About what?" Rufio asks.

"What do you think?" Bryce snaps at Rufio, then turns to Daisy. "Did she tell you what she wanted in return for her cooperation?" He addresses her in a much softer tone, but the tension is still present in his voice.

"Yes, but...." She looks to Rufio, biting her lower lip. Her signature action when she's in turmoil.

"She can't say in front of you," I finish the sentence for her.

"Why not? What kind of bullshit is that?" Rufio raises his voice, making Daisy wince. He needs to cut that shit out before I make him. Can't he see this situation isn't her fault?

"Because she doesn't know if she can trust us. Why do you think Mr. X didn't want to talk to us at Unearthly Desires?" Bryce poses the question.

Rufio's eyebrows meet his hairline. "Are you afraid we're going to run to our father with information? We're not working for the man, Daisy. I swear."

"I know you aren't, but if they put a gag spell in your mind, maybe they're also spying on us through you." She hugs her middle, almost as if she's trying to shield herself from all of us.

Rufio blinks fast before he replies, "Fuck. I didn't even think about that."

Dipping his chin, Bryce puts his hands on his hips and lets out a loud exhale. "Okay, we're out of here. Come on, Rufio."

"I'm so sorry." Daisy takes a step in their direction but then stops, probably remembering why she can't be close to them.

"Don't worry, darling." Bryce smiles tightly, obviously trying to hide how much this situation is bothering him, and walks out.

Rufio throws a longing glance in Daisy's direction. Unlike his brother, he's not attempting to mask his feelings at all. They don't speak for several beats until finally Rufio spins around and follows Bryce out. Moments later, Daisy continues to stare at the door.

"What did Principal Fallon want?" I ask to break the spell.

Still clutching her middle, Daisy turns to me. "She wants me to help her get rid of the Neo Gods."

"Ah, hell," Phoenix groans.

"She wants you to go against that group of lunatics by yourself, doesn't she?" I say. "They're dangerous, Daisy. She can't expect you to defeat them alone."

"You said no, right?" Phoenix asks.

I snort. Wishful thinking. Knowing her, it's easy to guess what her answer was.

"How could I say no? Principal Fallon believes they gave a challenge to Bryce and Rufio, something they must complete in order to be accepted in their ranks. Her guess is that the test is to kill the Knights' newest weapon. Only they don't know it's me. But if Bryce and Rufio don't follow through, they'll be eliminated."

I rub my face and stare at the ceiling. "Bryce and Rufio will never harm you."

"I know. That's why I had to say yes."

I go to Daisy, unable to keep my distance anymore. She throws herself into my arms and buries her face against my chest. At once, she begins to take my powers away, but since she can't unmake me, I'm unbothered by it.

Looking over her shoulder, I catch the scowl on Phoenix's face. Damn. He's jealous.

I push her back gently and say, "You're not going to do this alone. You have Phoenix and me."

"You got that right, babe," Phoenix chimes in. "What's Fallon's plan?"

"She wants me to strike key members of the organization one at a time, starting with the ones in Hawk City."

"That's where you're from. Have you ever been back since your parents died?" he asks.

Daisy steps away from me and walks to the window. "No. If I

had a choice, I'd never return. Too many awful memories there."

My heart breaks witnessing her pain. I can't begin to imagine what it must have been like being alone in the world at such a young age. "When does she want you to go?"

"She didn't pick a date yet, but soon."

"Okay. There's no time to waste, then. You need to learn to control your new powers beforehand. I'd say we skip school and get straight to it," I reply.

She whirls around. "Rosie starts school today. I can't let her face the sharks on her own. Besides, you can't miss class on my account. What about your grades?"

"I don't give a fuck about my grades anymore. I only did before to please my asshole father, and look what that got me."

"What are you moping about? At least he didn't rape you," Phoenix blurts out.

His statement feels like a punch to my stomach. I'm such a self-absorbed asshole. My suffering pales in comparison to his.

"Phoenix—" Daisy starts.

"No, Daisy. Stop." He holds up his hand. "There's no need to look at me like I'm a broken toy. I'll be fine. I don't even know why I said that. The motherfucker is dead, and that's all that matters."

Damn, Phoenix. I wish I could believe your lies.

23
____

DAISY

"Where are we going?" I ask Morpheus as we walk side by side after school.

"I don't want interruptions, and since Rosie is bunking with you, there's only one place we can go."

"The treehouse," I say.

"Yeah."

"How come no other student goes there? It's not that hard to find."

"I think that by hanging out with us, you have forgotten who we are," Morpheus replies with a twinkle in his eyes.

I roll mine. "Oh, yeah. The Magnificent Four. I totally forgot about that."

"You're the only person here who was never impressed by our status."

"True. Terrified, sure, but not impressed." I smirk.

We cross into the clearing where the treehouse is. "Who built this?" I ask.

"We did, actually. Well, not us exactly. We hired builders."

"And Principal Fallon approved it just like that?"

"She didn't know until it was a done deal. But she didn't care, as long as we didn't create problems for her."

We stop in front of the oak tree, and I take a moment to admire the beauty of its massive branches and intricate patterns on the trunk.

"Ladies first," Morpheus says with a cheeky smile.

"Ha-ha. How chivalrous. You just want to look up my skirt."

He widens his eyes, portraying the perfect picture of innocence. But he can't hide the mirth in his gaze. "I would never."

"Whatever. You go first."

Like I'd mind if he did look up my skirt, and that's the problem. My stomach is already in knots, and a shiver of anticipation runs down my back. We'll be alone again for the first time since we kissed in his car, and I'm already craving more. But I can't let my mind stray to the gutter. He's here to train me, not satiate my hunger.

The first detail I notice when I emerge from the trapdoor is the gray film of dust covering everything. "Did the cleaning person go on vacation?" I ask.

"We usually tidy the place up ourselves." Morpheus grabs a pillow from one of the bean bags and gives it a couple of smacks, releasing dust particles everywhere. It's only after a moment that he notices I'm staring at him with my mouth open.

"What?" he asks.

"You expect me to believe you guys clean this place yourselves?"

"We don't want anyone snooping around, so yeah. Why are you looking at me like that?"

I shake my head and laugh. "It's just surreal to think you would do something so menial. I thought labor work was beneath Idols."

"Most of the time, yes. Come to think of it, I'm the one who does most of the work manually. Rufio simply destroys everything he doesn't want to deal with, and Phoenix uses his telekinesis to straighten shit up like a damn fairy godmother."

The picture of Phoenix wearing a fairy godmother outfit with translucent wings and everything pops in my head. I can't help but laugh.

"What about Bryce?" I ask once I've calmed down.

"He rarely comes here."

"Well, I can help. Do you have a rag I can use to dust?"

"No, we're not wasting our time with that. Let's get down to business."

"Oh, okay." I clutch my hands together because I was totally hoping for procrastination.

"You're nervous." Morpheus stops in front of me and grabs my hand. "You don't need to be. I got you."

I stare at our joined hands because I'm afraid to stare into Morpheus's warm gaze and get lost there. With the proximity, it's impossible to ignore his intoxicating scent or how it affects my body. Damn stupid hormones.

The tingles in my fingertips are the first signs that I'm succubus-ing the crap out of Morpheus. "It's happening again," I say.

"I know. I can feel it."

"How do I stop it?"

"Close your eyes and try to give an image to your power. Pretend it's a pink string you can hold."

"Okay. And I'm going to pretend you didn't say pink."

"What's wrong with pink? It's my favorite color."

I open my eyes, expecting to catch mirth in his gaze, but Morpheus's eyes are devoid of duplicity. "Really? I thought you were being a little sexist."

"Daisy, I know what you're doing. Quit the jibber jabber and focus."

"Fine." I close my eyes again and picture Morpheus's silly pink string. I hold on to it with both hands. "I got it."

"Okay, now imagine that string is wrapped around my wrists and that the energy you feel going into your body is the movement of you pulling that string toward you."

"All right, I'm picturing it."

"Good. What I want you to do next is cut the strings around my wrists."

"With what?" I ask.

"Jeez, with whatever. Imagine a pair of scissors."

"Hey, don't get sassy with me. This is your exercise. I'm following your lead."

"I'm sorry. So, do you have the scissors?"

"Yeah."

I'm about to cut the imaginary string when a flash of memory hits my mind. The scissors and pink string disappear. I'm no longer in the treehouse with Morpheus. I'm underwater. The water is crystalline, and I can see everything clearly. I'm near a shore. With a kick of my legs, I break the surface, and a familiar island comes into view. It's the one I saw in my dream.

A loud boom behind me makes my heart jump up to my throat. I look over my shoulder and gasp when I face the storm that's quickly approaching. I can't be in the water when that thing hits. I swim as fast as I can toward the beach, knowing I have to find cover. The water is already getting rough, and the waves shove me forward when I touch the sandy bottom. I stagger onto the beach, out of breath.

Panic begins to set in when I don't see anyone around me. I scream their names from the top of my lungs, and that's when I realize this isn't me. I think I'm seeing everything through Morpheus's perspective. He keeps calling for Rufio, Bryce, and Phoenix until his young voice goes hoarse.

The wind picks up suddenly, bringing with it the ozone smell of the approaching storm. He runs toward the trees, but lightning strikes right in his path, missing him by a hair. The blast sends him flying backward, and when he falls, he hits his head on a half-buried rock. Sharp pain spreads through his skull, and his vision goes dark for a few seconds.

It finally clears when droplets of cold water hit his face. The sky has turned completely black, and rain is coming down hard. Random flashes of light illuminate the ominous clouds, followed by the terrifying booms of thunder.

Lightning begins to strike in succession on the sandy bank, getting closer and closer to him. Still dizzy from the fall, he crawls toward the trees until one bolt finally hits his back. The most excruciating pain runs through his body, rendering him paralyzed. The metallic taste of copper fills his mouth. The screams that come from deep his throat are the piercing kind.

"Daisy! Daisy!" someone calls out while my body shakes.

"Make it stop," I cry.

"Make what stop?"

"The... pain."

"Daisy, please open your eyes." I finally recognize Morpheus's voice, and that helps me get out of the nightmare in my head.

My eyes fly open suddenly, and the pain I felt a second ago goes away. My heart is beating at warp speed, and my head feels like it's filled with cotton.

Morpheus touches my face, watching me with worry. "What happened?"

"I'm not sure," I reply in a croaky voice. I guess the screaming I heard came from me.

"You froze suddenly, and then you wouldn't answer me until you started yelling."

"How did you break free from my hold?" I touch my left cheek, finding it wet.

"I'm an eighteen, remember? I can sever the connection on my own. I don't understand what went wrong."

"I-I think I took one of your memories."

His brows furrow together. "What makes you think that? And what memory?"

"Of an island."

Morpheus lets go of me and takes a step back. His face pales in an instant. "What did you see?"

"You had just arrived at a tropical island, alone and afraid. You kept calling out for Bryce, Rufio, and Phoenix. Then a terrible lightning storm broke in the sky, and you ended up getting struck."

Morpheus stares at me for several beats without blinking. "We call it the island of horrors," he finally tells me. "The guys and I wound up there after our fishing boat capsized ten years ago." He takes his jacket off first, then slips out of his uniform shirt.

"What are you doing?" I ask through a sudden dry mouth. As I suspected, Morpheus is lean and hard. His washboard abs are the stuff dreams are made of. He doesn't seem real.

"I want to show you something." He turns around, giving me the view of his equally impressive back.

"What am I supposed to be seeing?"

"Touch me between my shoulder blades."

I do as he says, and like magic, a lightning bolt tattoo appears. An electric shock comes next, and I yank my hand back. "What is that?"

Morpheus turns to me. "The mark of a very powerful deity. He's a god, but we don't know what kind. All we do know is that he recruits powerful Idols to do his bidding."

"Do Bryce, Rufio, and Phoenix have the same mark too?"

"Yup. It's invisible until a powerful Idol touches it."

"So you work for this god?" I ask.

"We did until he tried to kill you."

"What?" I squeak. "When?"

"The day you almost drowned at Echo Cove. It was his doing. He created that storm. By saving you, we defied him."

A spear of fear pierces my chest. "What does that mean?"

"It means we're on the shit list of a very powerful and wicked god."

"When you were on that island of horrors, were you struck by lightning?"

"No. That was one of the terrible things that didn't happen to me. I don't know why you saw that."

"I didn't see it. I felt it." I run a hand through my hair, getting more confused by the second. "That wasn't the first time I saw the island."

"What do you mean?"

"Soon after I came into possession of my Idol powers, I dreamed about it."

"Daisy, what did you see?"

"At first, I saw a hidden village in the middle of the jungle. There were Norms, Fringes, and Idols living together in harmony. It was like paradise. I thought it was Starlight Island."

"The legendary safe haven for Norms?" he asks.

"Yeah, though I realize now that it probably doesn't exist. Anyway, I thought I was dreaming about Starlight Island, but when I approached the village, it vanished from my sight, and soon a horrendous storm took over the sky, similar to the one I just saw in your memory."

"Lightning storms are this god's MO."

"The dream felt so real, Morpheus, almost as if I was reliving a memory."

"I think Magia has been on that island. Maybe she defied the god and hence lost her powers. It would explain why he was so keen on killing you."

"We have to figure this out. We can't have you tied to some crazy deity."

"I know." He cups my cheek. "One thing at a time."

Heat ignites in the center of my chest, spreading rapidly

down my limbs. It doesn't help that Morpheus is standing half naked in front of me either, smelling the way he does.

"We should go back to practicing," I murmur.

He moves closer, eyeing my mouth. "We should."

The awareness that I'm taking from him vanishes. "I don't think I'm stripping you of your powers anymore."

"No. I'm blocking you now."

"Why?"

"For starters, I don't want you suffering thanks to my messed-up memories. And most importantly, I want to do this."

He captures my lips in a slow and sensual kiss. I was craving another taste, but I didn't expect him to be the one to cave first. I don't think he would have if I hadn't seen one of his memories. Damn, it was a horrible experience, but if this is the reward, it's so worth it.

I flatten my palms against his taut abs, finding the skin hot to the touch. Morpheus trembles and a low growl comes from deep in his throat. The sound spurs me on. I run my fingers across his torso first, then let them travel past his belly button until they reach his waistband.

In response, Morpheus wraps his arms around my waist, pulling me closer and preventing me from moving my hands.

"Hey!" I complain between kisses, which he ignores.

Oh, like you mind that, Daisy.

We do nothing but kiss for a while, until I lose track of time. It's almost like Morpheus is in no hurry to move things to the next level. Doesn't he know how I'm burning for him?

"Morpheus," I breathe.

"Yes, Daisy." He kisses my chin and then peppers a trail of wet kisses toward my ear. I arch my back and close my eyes, savoring the sensation.

"I need more," I say.

He chuckles before his hands go south and grab my butt. "Like this?" he teases.

"No, more."

He runs his hands farther down until they disappear underneath my skirt. His fingers are hot against my skin, and when he reaches the sides of my panties, my legs almost give out from under me.

"How about now?" he whispers in my ear.

"Still not enough."

He stops kissing my neck and drops to his knees. I suck in a breath and watch him watch me through hooded eyes. His glorious curly hair is unbound and wild, a temptation for me. I thread my fingers through his strands, then trace his temple. Morpheus closes his eyes for a moment before lifting my skirt and bringing his mouth to my pussy. He licks my center through the fabric, and I have no choice but to yank his hair a little harder as I try to remain upright.

"Is that good for you, Daisy?"

Like the greedy little nympho I am, I say, "No, I need more."

He licks me again and again, teasing me mercilessly. With each stroke, he unravels me more. When I don't think he can be any crueler with his sweet torture, he pulls my panties to the side and sucks my clit into his mouth. And just like that, he obliterates me into tiny little particles of stardust. Tingles spread throughout my body as a wave of pleasure sweeps over me. I feel like I'm floating on air, or maybe soaring through the sky. I can't even make up my mind.

Morpheus keeps sucking and licking until I can't take it anymore. I pretty much collapse on top of him, thanks to my now useless legs.

Steadying me, he leans back and looks up with a shit-eating grin. "How about now?"

I want to wipe that cocky smile from his lips. "Not even close."

I push him back until his ass hits the floor, then drop to my knees and force him to lie on his back. It's my time to have some fun. I place a kiss near his belly button and then look at him from under my eyelashes. He's watching me with so much desire in his eyes that it's almost enough to send me over the edge again.

Without breaking eye contact, I unbutton his trousers and pull the fabric down. His cock is hard and straining against his boxer shorts. I could play the same move he did and lick his length through the fabric, but I'm not as patient as he is. I'm too eager, too hungry for a taste of him. I free his erection, wrapping my fingers around the base.

"Fuck, Daisy. You're killing me."

"No I'm not. Not yet anyway." I run my tongue over his head, licking and teasing just like he did me.

Morpheus groans, then reaches for my hair to grab a fistful. "More."

I chuckle, fanning hot air over his sensitive skin. "So greedy."

"No more than you. You have no idea how long I've waited for this."

"Tell me," I say before I take his cock into my mouth.

Morpheus makes an incoherent sound but doesn't answer my question, so I press. "I'm waiting."

"Honestly, I've wanted you since the first time I saw you."

I stop for a moment. "Really?"

He lifts his head, and our gazes connect. "Yeah. Beautiful enough to cause physical pain and a personality to put any Idol in their place. What's not to love?"

I sit on the balls of my feet. "You didn't love me then. The hate was pretty clear."

Morpheus leans on his elbows and stares at me intensely. "No, I didn't love you in that moment. But I do now."

My heart seems to skip a beat, only to carry on twice as fast as before. "You do?"

"Yeah," he replies in a tight voice. "You don't need to say it back."

"I know. But what if I do?"

He squints, furrowing those eyebrows again. I don't like that look.

"You couldn't possibly."

I crawl toward him like a jungle cat stalking prey. When I'm at his face's level, I stop and straddle him. My eyes lower to his high cheekbones as I caress them with the tips of my fingers. I trace a path toward the corner of his mouth, then rub my thumb over his full lips.

"You had me at tacos," I say.

He chuckles. "What?"

"The day you cooked for me, that's when I started falling, and I haven't stopped since. I love you too, Morpheus."

I capture his face between my hands and lower my mouth to his. As our tongues explore one another, a warm feeling unfurls in the pit of my stomach. I'm more than ready for this. My head feels light, and the buzzing in my ears drowns every other sound. I begin to rock back and forth, needing the friction between my legs. Morpheus grabs me by the hips, digging his fingers into my skin as he tries to help me move.

"Condom," I say between kisses. "We need protection."

"There should be some in here."

If there isn't, I'll cry.

We kiss for another minute while our hips mimic what's to come. Somehow, my panties move sideways, and the tip of Morpheus's dick slips inside.

Danger alert. We're flirting with the line of irresponsibility now.

I slide off him. "Okay, where's that condom?"

"Hold on." He jumps to his feet and heads for the cabinet in the corner of the room. "Phew. We're lucky. The last one." He grins at me, holding the foil packet between his fingers.

I stand as well so I can get rid of my clothes. I want Morpheus to see me. He freezes when I take off my jacket, doesn't even blink when I unbutton my shirt slowly. But his eyes do narrow and his lips part when I toss my bra to the side.

"Breathtaking."

I don't comment as I get rid of my skirt and panties, standing before him wearing nothing but my high stockings and shoes. His smoldering eyes drop to my feet and travel back up the length of my body slowly. It's almost a caress.

"If I wasn't so horny right now, I'd drop down on my knees and eat your pussy again." He breaches the distance between us.

"Such a filthy mouth." I reach for his cock. "What else would you like to do with me?"

Morpheus brings the foil package to his mouth and tears it with his teeth. "How about I just show you?"

Gently, he frees his cock from my grip and rolls the condom down his shaft. He breaks eye contact for a moment to gaze at the room. "Shit, I really should have planned this better. First the car and now this pigsty." He grabs the blanket that was draped over one of the beanbags and lays it on the floor.

"It doesn't matter where we are. We'll make it work." With a smile, I grab his hand and together we lie down on the makeshift bed. Morpheus grabs a few pillows, but I'm more interested in feeling his touch on my skin again than comfort, which explains why I attack him, sealing my lips over his.

In an instant, he's on board with the change of pace. More than on board, he's completely in charge. He rolls me on my back, positioning himself between my legs. This foreplay has lasted too long, and I'm done with it. I lift my knees, crossing my legs at the ankles behind his back, and then finally, he's inside.

A piece of my heart that I didn't know was missing clicks into place. All my emotions amplify and take over. My heart expands to contain the feelings that have grown exponentially, but even so, it overflows. I didn't know it was possible to love more than one person as intensely as this, but I do. I love him just like I love Bryce, Rufio, and Phoenix.

I lose control of my body completely. I cry out when Morpheus makes me come again, then again, until he finally succumbs to his own release.

If this is the reward for doing well in his class, I just became the teacher's pet.

24

——————

DAISY

The week went by in a blur. Between schoolwork, helping Rosie adjust to her new environment, and training with Morpheus, it's easy to see why it sped away like a bullet. The rumor mill is still buzzing about Drusilla's vanishing act, and not a peep has been said about Rufio's involvement in her death. His father did an outstanding job, which means he's indeed a terrible enemy.

I also managed to squeeze in sexy times with Morpheus and Bryce, the only ones I can touch without risk. We tried to keep our dates on the down-low to not piss off Rufio and Phoenix, but I can tell they know. I catch their longing glances in my direction and aggravated ones reserved for Morpheus and Bryce. This situation is not sustainable; sooner or later, someone is going to blow. I can't allow that to happen.

Nevertheless, I'm walking with an extra bounce in my step this morning, and Rosie notices.

"You've been in a good mood the entire week," she tells me.

"Have I?" I say absentmindedly, remembering the steamy evening I spent with Bryce in the treehouse, which now should be called the Love Shack, since it's where I spend time with Morpheus too.

"Yes. How much sex did you have this week?"

"Rosie!" I look around to make sure no one overheard us.

"Oh, come on. Like you care who hears about it. If you gave a rat's ass about other people's opinion, you wouldn't date four guys at the same time."

"Do I detect a judgmental tone in your voice?"

She clamps her jaw shut and doesn't answer right away. That's fine. We've reached the main building, and I definitely don't want to talk about my sex life in public.

Principal Fallon arranged for our lockers to be next to each other. Rosie opens hers first, and I see a picture of her and Toby taped to the door.

"How is everything going with you two?" I ask.

"Good. It's nice to go to the same school as him. Although, Toby is more stressed than ever with his studies, and we haven't spent that much time together."

"He's still trying to catch up for the week he missed here."

"I know."

As if we had summoned him by speaking his name, Toby joins us in the hallway. He kisses Rosie on the cheek, erasing the sourpuss expression she had a moment ago.

"Are you ready for your first assembly?" Toby asks Rosie.

She shrugs. "Is it going to be any different than the other assemblies I attended at my previous school?"

"Probably not."

We continue toward the auditorium. Bryce, Morpheus, Rufio, and Phoenix are waiting for me by the door. Immediately, my heart takes off. How is it possible to feel such intense feelings for four different guys? But I do love them with the same fervor, even though I haven't told Rufio or Phoenix that yet. Because we can't touch, I've avoided them as much as I could.

"Do you know why we have an assembly today?" I ask.

"Mom probably wants to give everyone an update about Drusilla. There's still too much talking in the hallways, and she wants it to stop," Bryce replies.

"Isn't mentioning it at an assembly only going to add more fuel to the fire?" I reply.

"Not if it's followed by more exciting news," Rufio answers.

I turn to my right and notice Rosie and Toby have already gone in. My sister hasn't quite warmed up to the guys yet. She likes Bryce the most, but that's because he saved her boyfriend. I wish she could see them beyond their Idol powers.

We sit on the last row, and a minute later, Principal Fallon takes the stage. As Bryce had guessed earlier, Drusilla is the first topic on the agenda. The narrative hasn't changed. Drusilla is still missing, but every effort is being made by the authorities to locate her. The subject makes me hella uncomfortable. I keep thinking about Drusilla's parents, their pain of not knowing what happened to their daughter. No one deserves that, but I understand it's the only solution. There's no body to be found. The only way for them to know the truth is for Rufio to confess.

"I doubt Drusilla is truly missing," a girl in front of me whispers to her friend. "I bet she's holed up in a five-star hotel with some boy toy."

"For sure," the second girl agrees.

"It would be much easier if the police thought the same," Bryce whispers in my ear. His breath fanning against my neck gives me goose bumps.

"Moving on to the next topic on the agenda," Principal Fallon continues without missing a beat, "the time has finally come to announce the name of the students selected to represent Gifted Academy in the Annual Interschool Academic Tournament, which will take place this year at Paragon Academy in Hawk City."

All my muscles seem to freeze at once. *Hawk City.* I know which names she's going to say.

"Toby Macintosh, Daisy Woods, Phoenix Westbrook, Rufio Kent, and Bryce Kent."

"She didn't call your name." I glance at Morpheus.

"She wouldn't. I'm only an average student."

I open my mouth to say I can't go without him, but then I remember Bryce and Rufio don't know the real reason my name is on that list. Principal Fallon just gave me a solid excuse to be in Hawk City.

This is really happening. I'm going to face members of the Neo Gods. I get a stomachache just thinking about it.

"But don't worry. I've made other arrangements to be in the city at the same time as you," Morpheus continues.

"Oh good. I didn't want to miss our training sessions."

"Sure, that's the reason," Phoenix mutters to himself.

"What about your sister? If we're all going, who's going to keep an eye on her?" Rufio reminds me.

Shit. I can't leave Rosie here alone. The other students haven't given her any problem so far, but I know that's because the guys have extended their protection to her. She'll be pounded mercilessly with us out of the picture.

"I'm sure my mother will allow Rosie to come with us," Bryce replies.

I smile tightly, but his comment doesn't comfort me. I'm going to Hawk City on a dangerous mission. Ideally, I'd want Rosie to be as far away from me as possible.

"Don't worry, Daisy. We'll keep Rosie safe," Phoenix says, maybe guessing my turmoil.

"Oh, come on. Hawk City isn't that bad," Rufio declares.

I refrain from commenting because I would love for them to drop the subject.

Bryce covers my hand with his and squeezes a little. "It'll be okay."

I know what's on his mind. He's concerned about what visiting the city where my parents were murdered will do to my psyche. If he only knew that's only part of what's troubling me.

"I DON'T WANT TO GO," Rosie says from her bed. Principal Fallon had an extra one delivered on Monday. My room is big enough that it fit.

"I know you don't, sweetie, but we don't have a choice." I keep sorting out the clothes I want to pack without paying much attention to her. I have more worrisome problems in my head than concerning myself with her teen woes.

"Bullshit. You could say you don't want to participate in the tournament. Principal Fallon can't force you to go."

"Actually, she can. Don't forget that we have a safe roof over our heads thanks to her."

"You did not just say that," she retorts, raising her voice. "That snake was spying on us!"

I finally look at my sister. "I have to go to Hawk City. It's high time we face our past. We can't keep running from it."

"I don't know how you can say that like it's not a big deal. Have you forgotten how bad it got in the first weeks after we lost Mom and Dad?"

My heart hurts so badly, like a dagger is twisting in my chest. "I haven't forgotten a single thing," I grit out, "but I can't let my past dictate my life. We're going, and that's final."

Rosie clutches her pillow against her chest and pouts. "At least Toby is coming with us."

"Yes, see? You're worrying about nothing. I bet you'll have fun. And you don't even have to worry about competing in some stupid academic tournament."

"True that."

Shit. I don't remember being as mercurial as Rosie when I was her age. I suppose worrying about our survival trumped teenage mood swings. I couldn't afford those.

"You'd better start packing or you'll end up not having time."

"Our flight doesn't leave until tomorrow."

I set the top I was folding down on my bed to put my hands on my hips. "And I know you. You'll wait until late at night and then start panicking that you don't have anything to wear."

"I *don't* have anything to wear."

That might actually be true and not another ridiculous whine.

"Now that we don't have to pay rent for your room, there's some money left. We can go shopping when we get there."

"I used to love going to the thrift stores with Mom," Rosie says, dropping her gaze.

The pang in my chest is sharp, almost as if I've just lost Mom and Dad. People say time heals everything, but I don't think I'll ever be able to think about them without feeling so hollow and sad. They were stolen from us when we needed them most. We'll never forget that.

I never asked Mr. Silverstone what happened that night after Rosie and I ran away. Did he kill all those Neo Gods? Maybe I should have listened to what the man had to say, but I wasn't in the right frame of mind after the confrontation with Phoenix's father.

I sit next to Rosie and throw my arm around her shoulder. "I loved going shopping with Mom too. She was always able to find the coolest stuff."

"Or see the potential in something that didn't look great at first glance."

"Yeah."

We don't speak for several minutes. My eyes prickle, but I

don't want to cry every time I think about them, so I focus on the happy memories instead.

"What do you think happens after people die, Daisy?" Rosie asks after a while. "Do you think they just cease to exist?"

I think about that island I dreamed about. The village I saw where there had no division among the races. "I'd like to believe we go somewhere better than here."

"Me too." She drops her head against my shoulder. "I miss them so damn much, but at the same time, I can barely remember what they look like or sound like anymore."

A lump the size of the moon lodges in my throat. "It doesn't matter if the details are getting fuzzy. All that matters is that we keep carrying them in our hearts."

25

DAISY

R osie and I have never traveled by plane before; that's a luxury few Norms get. It was an experience I'll never forget for sure. But thanks to some confusion during the booking of our flight, Rosie, Toby, and I sat separate from the guys, which worked out for the best since the tension among the five of us was so thick, you'd need a machete to cut it. We should have had a conversation before we came on this trip, but between classes, training, and keeping an eye on Rosie, there was no time.

Paragon Academy sent a van to pick up our group, a luxurious model with tinted windows, supple leather seats, and even a TV to keep the passengers entertained. I sit by the window, and Rosie slides in right next to me, saving me from another awkward situation with the guys. Bryce takes the seat right across from me. Rufio and Morpheus follow him, while Phoenix sits next to Toby. This is the best seating arrangement we could have considering our situation; Rosie still can't relax around any of them, despite my reassurance that Bryce, Rufio, Phoenix, and Morpheus are not the bad guys.

To avoid the intense stares they're giving me, I look out

the window, but I don't find solace in the view. Seeing the familiar landscape of Hawk City brings a sharp pang in my chest that makes it harder to breathe. I knew coming back here would be difficult, but I didn't expect it to be this painful.

The sun is setting, and the sky is tinged in a beautiful combination of orange and pink hues, something rare for Hawk City. It's almost like the gods themselves are going out of their way to make me suffer.

A derisive laugh sounds in my head. *That could very well be possible.* The god from the island controls storms; he could be responsible for this sunset too.

We don't head downtown, and soon the buildings disappear from view. But unlike Gifted Academy, which is in the boonies, Paragon Academy is right smack in the city. The prestigious school is situated in one of the most upscale neighborhoods where the houses are centuries-old red bricks and the brass on the doors shines under the sun. Most streets are lined with tall trees, and there's no littering in sight. It's a far cry from where I used to live. Only the crème de la crème lives here. That fact makes me even more apprehensive to set foot in Paragon Academy. If the students of Gifted Academy are bad, I can't imagine what the kids here are like.

The van stops in front of a four-story stone building that takes up almost an entire block. Its gothic architecture tells me it's been here for centuries. It was probably one of the first structures built in the city. Staring at it, it's almost like I'm transported to a different era—or a horror movie. The clustered columns, large expanses of glass, and intricate sculptures are astonishing, though.

"Wow," I exclaim.

"Wow? Shouldn't you be saying 'yikes'?" Phoenix jokes.

"I second that. I hope the inside looks better than the outside. This building is super creepy," Rosie chimes in.

"It's a little better but not by much." Bryce, who's sitting across from me, opens the door.

"So you've been here before?" I ask as I follow him out.

"Yeah, a couple of years ago for a stuffy social function with my mother."

Standing in front of the impressive building, I look up and spot gargoyle statues perched on the roof. My jaw drops. I don't care what anyone says, I love it.

"Careful now. You might swallow a fly if you keep your mouth open like that," a male voice says.

I turn in his direction. Stephan Silverstone and his brother, Soren, are standing in front of the school gate.

"Stephan, what are you doing here?" Toby goes to his friend and they hug.

From the corner of my eye, I catch the guys staring at Stephan and Soren in a not-so-friendly way. I shouldn't be surprised that they would extend their animosity to Mr. Silverstone's sons as well.

"The headmaster called in a favor. He needed a substitute teacher, and I had time to do it." Stephan turns to my sister with a huge smile on his face. "Good to see you, Rosie."

"Hi," she replies shyly.

Soren's expression remains serious as he watches the exchange of pleasantries. I only saw him briefly at the barbecue, but it seems to me his personality is the total opposite of his brother's.

With his easygoing smile still in place, Stephan turns to me. "Daisy, I was so happy to hear you were coming to Hawk City. You're going to love the tournament. I can't wait to show you around school."

At once, Bryce and Morpheus move closer to me while Rufio and Phoenix take a step forward. I don't even need to look in their direction to sense the threatening aura they're emanating.

"I'm glad to be here," I reply.

Bryce clears his throat. "Can we move this inside the court-yard at least?"

Stephan's expression changes in the blink of an eye from open and warm to serious and irritated. "Of course."

"What about our bags?" Rosie asks.

"Someone will bring them up to your rooms," Soren replies.

The courtyard beyond the wrought iron gate is beautiful with small trees placed strategically, wood benches, and a fountain. A set of stairs leads to the main building, which has three different entries.

"The doors straight ahead will take you to the academic section where all classes are held. Dormitories are split by gender, boys to the left and girls to the right," Stephan explains.

Shit. I knew I wouldn't share a room with the guys, but I wasn't counting on being that far away from them. How am I going to keep practicing with Morpheus? Despite our intense training sessions, I haven't made much progress. I still can't stop taking his powers.

"What's on the agenda for today?" Bryce asks.

"You're the last group of out-of-towners to arrive. There's an official mixer at seven in the auditorium," Stephan replies.

"So we can do whatever we want after that?" Rufio asks.

"Yeah, but there's an unofficial party at Casper's Nightclub. A big group is going. You should come too." Stephan glances at me with a much friendlier expression. I'm sure none of the guys missed it.

"I don't know. I think everyone is pretty beaten," Bryce replies before I can say anything.

I'm not in the least bit tired, and I'm curious about the Silverstone brothers. Maybe I can learn more about the Knights without actually having an official meeting with their father.

"I'd like to go," I say.

"Really?" Morpheus arches his brow.

"Yup. I haven't done anything fun in like *forever*."

"Is that an Idol club?" Rosie asks.

"Well, it's not a club exclusive to Idols, but most of the patrons are Idols. Don't worry, though. No one will have an issue with you and Daisy."

Crap on toast, I didn't even consider that. That's life outside the gilded hallways of Gifted Academy. The division is more glaring in Saturn's Bay, but just because there's more mingling of Norms, Fringes, and Idols in Hawk City, it doesn't mean there's true integration. There weren't any Idols living in our old neighborhood, for instance.

"I think I'm going to pass," Rosie replies.

"What? You're just going to hide in your room during your entire stay?" Phoenix asks, truly surprised.

Rosie's spine goes taut, and I can tell she's about to offer an angry retort when Toby turns to her. "Let's go out on a date. There are plenty of amazing Norm restaurants in town."

My sister rewards Toby with a big smile. It seems only he can cheer her up these days. But he's still masking his new powers around her. She doesn't know he's an Idol too. He needs to come clean soon.

"Okay, that sounds lovely."

"Great. Now that that's settled, let me take you to your rooms." Stephan veers toward the right and Soren to the left, but Bryce halts Stephan.

"Do you mind taking us to our room?" he asks. "I'd like a word with you." His tone is pleasant, but there's no mistaking the veiled animosity.

Stephan trades a glance with his brother first. The younger man shrugs.

"I don't mind taking the girls to their accommodations."

And so we part ways. I don't know if Bryce truly wants to talk to Stephan or if he simply didn't want the guy around me. Maybe he thought Stephan was too friendly. But why would he be jealous? Does he think that because I'm involved with the four of them, I'm going to keep adding to my harem? If I add another penis to this equation, I'll overload on the testosterone.

Soren walks ahead of us without saying much, unless I ask him a random question here and there. I give up trying to strike up a conversation after a few minutes and focus on my surroundings instead. Like Gifted Academy, Paragon Academy is an example of old-money glamor. From marble floors to wood-paneled walls, it's a far cry from the public school Rosie and I used to attend. Since it's Saturday, we don't see that many people roaming the entry foyer of the girls' dorm, which resembles a luxurious hotel lobby with gold-plated signs indicating where everything is.

We take the elevator to the third floor, and once there, we cross paths with a few students. The girls don't try to hide their surprise at seeing two Norms in their domain.

"Which school are you from?" a girl with straight black hair and sharp bangs asks.

"Gifted Academy," I reply.

Her almond-shaped eyes become rounder. "Oh, you're *that* Norm."

"*That* Norm?" I bristle. "What does that mean?"

She gives me the fakest smile. "Oh, nothing. Just FYI, our school has strict rules about curfew, so if you're planning on extracurricular activities, you'd better do it off campus."

I narrow my eyes to slits, immediately catching the double meaning of her words. Her friends giggle, which just solidifies my suspicion.

"Oh, and another thing. They don't sell condoms in the little shop downstairs, so I hope you brought your own. We don't need you spreading your Norm diseases here. Welcome to Paragon Academy!" she adds with an extra cheer to her tone.

Fucking bitch. I curl my hands into fists, a second away from knocking the grin off her face, but Rosie grabs my arm.

"Don't. They aren't worth the trouble."

She's right, but the anger is still running wildly in my veins. The stupid bitches carry on in the opposite direction, still laughing at my expense.

"Don't mind them. They're brainless bimbos," Soren chimes in.

"They're probably jealous that you have four boyfriends," Rosie mutters.

I throw her a glare and then nod at Soren, who's walking ahead of us. She mouths, "What?" like she's clueless as to why I'm staring daggers at her. I might be dating four guys, but I don't want the entire world to know.

The thought is sobering and takes me aback. *Why do I want to keep it a secret? What am I afraid of?*

Soren stops in front of room 225 and unlocks it using a card key. I wonder if the doors here are protected against intrusion like the ones at Gifted Academy are.

"Here we are." He holds the door and lets us in first.

I was expecting a small room with two beds and a bathroom attached. What we get is a proper apartment with a small living room, kitchen, and separate bedrooms.

"Wow, this is nice." Rosie drops her backpack on the couch and heads for the window.

"Only the best for visiting students. Not that the regular dorm rooms are bad. Here are your keys." He hands them to me. "And this is the schedule for the weekend and the following week, plus a map of the rest of campus and all other information you might need for your stay." He taps the folder that was already on the kitchen counter.

"You're not going to show us around?" I ask.

He looks startled. "I don't think we have time for a tour before the mixer. You probably want to freshen up."

"Excuse me, I need to use the restroom." Rosie makes a beeline for it, leaving me alone with Soren.

This is my chance to grill him for information.

"How's your father?" I ask.

Soren glances at the bathroom door before moving closer. "My father is fine. He sends his regards, and also a message."

I hold my breath. "I'm listening."

"Whatever you're planning to do in Hawk City, don't."

Literal chills go down my spine. "I don't know what you mean. I came for the tournament."

Soren's lips curls into wry smile. "No you didn't. Hawk City is not Saturn's Bay, Daisy. The players here are much more powerful and dangerous. It's in your best interest to keep your head down and not draw attention to yourself. People are looking for you."

My heart begins to beat at a rapid pace, and my mouth becomes dry. "Are you talking about the Neo Gods?"

He narrows his eyes for a moment, almost as if he's surprised I know about the Idol supremacist group. "Them and others. Be careful."

What the hell does he mean by others?

Rosie walks out of the bathroom, forcing my conversation with Soren to an abrupt end.

"Well, like I said, this is all the information you'll need," Soren continues without missing a beat. "I'll see you later at the mixer."

"See you later, Soren," Rosie replies. When he's gone, she turns to me. "What's the matter? Your face has gone ashen."

"Really? It must have been the trip. I think I'm going to lie down for a little bit."

I head for one of the bedrooms and pretend to take a nap, but it's only for Rosie's benefit. I can't rest when Soren left me hanging like that. Who else could be looking for me besides the Neo Gods?

26

BRYCE

"I don't like that fucker," Rufio says over the loud music in the club.

"Yeah, I heard you the first time, brother," I reply absentmindedly while I observe the scene.

The mixer was a snooze fest, so we got out of there as soon as we could and headed to the nightclub. The headmaster of Paragon Academy runs a much tighter ship than Mom does back home. Maybe because the guy is actually interested in doing his job instead of plotting the end of the world.

My eyes immediately find Daisy, who's talking to Morpheus near the bar. Anyone looking in their direction can tell they're involved. And the idiot tried to deny he was in love with her. Shit, he looks at her the same way we all do.

A few days ago, Daisy told me she had slept with him. At first, I was so jealous, I almost blew up all the lights in the treehouse. It took me a moment to calm down. I'm still a little confused as to why I reacted so strongly. Daisy never made it a secret that she was interested in the four of us, and the guys and I never really said anything about exclusivity. Daisy is the type of woman we can't keep to ourselves. If I have to share her with my best friends and my brother, I can deal with it. Not that there isn't a competition going on between Morpheus and me. Without Daisy knowing, we're keeping tabs on who can give her more orgasms.

"Ugh, look at them," Rufio groans. "I swear he's not training her hard enough so he can keep hogging her."

"Come on. Morpheus would never do that." I take a sip of my drink.

"You don't care because you're not in the freeze zone. I'm going out of my mind that I can't touch her."

"You can say that again. Here, I scored us some pick-me-uppers." Phoenix hands Rufio a vial of Silver-voltage.

"Really? Your solution to blue balls is getting high?" I glower at the duo. "Have you forgotten what's at stake here? We need to keep our minds sharp at all times."

"Bite me, Bryce. Nothing is going to happen. Besides, Daisy isn't lacking in the knight-in-shining armor department. Did you see how that Stephan douche was eating her up with his eyes?" Rufio retorts.

"Will you quit with the Stephan thing?" I snap.

I also noticed that the guy was overfriendly, but Daisy didn't spare him a second glance. Sure, I asked him to show us to our room instead of his brother, but I also wanted to feel him out. I didn't ask point blank if he was part of the Knights, but all the subtle nudges I gave him about the organization went unnoticed. Or he simply didn't want to take the bait. But if my mother knows Rufio and I are tied to the Neo Gods, it's possible the Knights do too. Then Stephan wouldn't say anything useful to me.

Morpheus turns to the bar, and that's when Daisy switches her attention to me. Our gazes connect, despite the space between us, and she smiles.

Next to me, Rufio groans again. "Fuck this shit. I can't take it anymore."

"Where are you going?" I watch him push people out of his way, heading in the opposite direction.

"Hey, wait up." Phoenix follows him.

Damn it. I can't let him and Phoenix loose in the club in their current foul mood. I don't trust either of them to behave. But my path is blocked by an attractive blonde girl. She's almost as tall as me with sharp features and a dazzling smile. She could be a model with her looks. Who knows, maybe she is.

"Hi there. I'm Amanda."

"Whatever. If you exc—" I start to walk around her.

She puts a hand over my chest, stopping me, and then she leans closer. "Dance with me."

Her touch feels strange, and when she steps back from my personal space, I catch the same strange glint in her eyes that I noticed in my mother's assistant. I'm on high alert in an instant.

"Sure," I reply, my curiosity piqued.

She grabs my hand and steers me toward the dance floor. I spare a glance in Daisy's direction. Her incredulous scowl tells me I'm going to pay for this later, but I have to know what this Amanda chick is up to.

The girl leads me to the middle of the dance floor, which is jam packed. Our bodies are pushed close together by the crowd. Amanda laughs as she throws her arms around my neck.

"What's the matter, Bryce? You seem tense."

"How do you know my name?"

"I know everything there is to know about you." She leans in again and puts her lips near my ear. "I also know that you're running out of time. My boss gave you a task, and he's not a patient man."

Fuck. I knew it. She's a Neo God, which means Miss Walker, my mother's assistant, is also working for that odious organization.

"It's only been a week. He can't expect me to locate the Knights' weapon in such a short period of time."

"Oh yeah he can. You have three days to eliminate that threat. Maybe you need extra motivation."

"What do you mean by that?"

"I saw the way you were looking at that disgusting Norm girl. You said you were done playing with her, but my guess is that's far from the truth."

My blood turns to ice in my veins, and my heart squeezes tightly, gripped by fear. I should have been more careful. It was naïve of me to not count on being spied on by the Neo Gods. Fuck. I can't let them get near Daisy.

"I don't blame you, really. She's a hot piece of ass." Amanda grins broadly.

"She's nothing to me," I grit out.

"Really? So you wouldn't mind if I took her for a spin."

I narrow my eyes, trying my best to not unleash my fury on the woman. "You're not her type."

"It doesn't matter, does it? We can take whatever we want." She grabs my ass and squeezes it to make a point. "Remember, Bryce. Three days or the Norm is toast."

Amanda kisses me on the lips, making my skin crawl before she sashays away. I wipe my mouth, disgusted by the whole thing.

Three fucking days. How am I going to get out of this mess?

~

MORPHEUS

"Who was that girl?" Daisy asks, still staring at the spot where Bryce disappeared into the crowd with the bimbo.

"I have no idea," I reply. I could try to mollify Daisy, but

Bryce wouldn't simply take off with a random woman like that. Something isn't right. "Let's go after them."

Daisy takes the lead, but I have to grab her hand and pull her back.

"What?" She looks over her shoulder.

"You're slipping. I saw glimpses of your power just now."

Her beautiful eyes widen. "Shit. I didn't even notice my barrier was crumbling."

"It's back up now. But you have to be more careful." I run my hand down her arm.

"Yeah, sure." She whirls around like I didn't say anything. Boy, jealous Daisy is a one-track-minded person.

She elbows people out of the way, careless of the fact that, for all intents and purposes, people believe she's a Norm. And Norms don't get to push Idols around. Several nasty glances are thrown in her direction, which means I have to unleash some of my fearmancer abilities. But not everyone in the club is in their right mind, and some are so high, they don't even see me behind Daisy.

"Hey, watch it, skank Norm." One guy grabs Daisy's arm.

"Get your paws off her." Phoenix appears out of nowhere, flanked by Rufio.

With one quick glance at their auras, I know they've taken Silver-voltage. Un-fucking-believable. A pair of morons.

"Make me, assh—"

Rufio grabs the guy's arm and yanks him off Daisy. But that's not all he's doing. Rufio's eyes are glowing bright blue, which means he's using his destructive powers. Son of a bitch.

"Aargh. What the fuck! Let go of me," the guy begs.

"Rufio, stop it!" Daisy pleads, but she won't touch him. Maybe she ought to, just a little, because we're about to have another Drusilla incident if Rufio doesn't cool off.

I push Daisy out of the way so I can get to Rufio. He's so out of it that he's gonna end up dusting the guy. There's no way his father will be able to take care of so many witnesses.

Suddenly, Bryce is there. With a motion of his arm, he sends Rufio's victim flying backward, knocking several people out of the way.

The music stops briefly, and all we can hear are the murmurs of the crowd. Bryce turns to the DJ's booth, and the music restarts. I have no doubt that wasn't the DJ's doing.

"Come on. Let's get out of here." I grab Daisy's hand and steer her toward the edge of the dance floor.

Once we're out of the most crowded part of the club. Stephan and Soren meet us. "What the hell happened?" Stephan asks.

"Nothing," Rufio snaps, getting free of Bryce, who has holding him by the back of his collar.

"Hey, I don't care if you're in a bad mood," Stephan retorts. "All your ridiculous attitude is doing is drawing attention to Daisy."

"Why do you care? She's not your problem," he replies angrily.

"So I'm a problem now?" She stares him down with her hands on her hips.

"Daisy, I'm sorry. That's not what I meant." Rufio takes a step toward her, but she pulls away.

"No. You can't, Rufio."

"This is maddening." He makes a jerky movement with his hand, and half the bottles on display at the bar behind us crumble to dust.

There are a few yells in the crowd, but thanks to the loud music, it's muffled.

"For fuck's sake! Cut that shit out. I don't care what your problem is, you need to calm down." Stephan moves closer to Rufio.

Phoenix cuts him off, getting into his personal space. "Who the fuck do you think you are to tell us what to do?"

Curse all the gods. It seems Rufio and Phoenix decided to take a trip to Stupidville today.

I try to pull Phoenix away from Stephan, but it's like trying to move a mountain. I really don't want to use fear to make him stop acting like an ass.

"Phoenix, cut it out! You and Rufio are acting like two cavemen," Daisy shouts.

"Sorry, babe. But I have to show this douchecanoe that no one messes with my girl."

"*Your* girl?" Soren snorts. "She was all over your friend's business earlier."

Daisy switches her ire to him. "Don't you start with me too."

His eyebrows shoot to the heavens. "What? You know you were."

"Shut up, asshole," Rufio retorts.

Daisy pinches the bridge of her nose. "Ugh. I can't deal with this shit right now. Do you want to fight like a bunch of idiots? Go ahead, get yourselves kicked out of the club. I don't care." She whirls around and strides away.

"Hey, where are you going?" I run after her.

"Don't follow me, Morpheus. I'm going to the restroom."

I stop in my tracks, letting her take the lead but having every intention of following at a distance. She's not safe in the club alone. If someone attacks, she'll be forced to reveal herself.

But my idea goes to shit when I sense the situation behind me is only getting worse.

"I don't want to fight you, Westbrook. Don't push me," Stephan grits out while Phoenix is holding him by his shirt.

Now I'm the one who's pissed off. I march toward the duo, and without a second thought, I strike both of them with a whip made out of shadows. They break apart with a gasp, both bending forward and clutching their arms where I hit them.

Stephan turns to me, grimacing. "What the hell was that? My arm is freezing cold."

"That was just a warning shot. Now back off."

"Tell that to your friend," Stephan replies with a grunt.

"Come on, Phoenix. Let's go." Bryce starts to steer him away from the Silverstone brothers.

Rufio glances in my direction. "Where's Daisy?"

Ah, fuck.

27

DAISY

oing to the restroom was just an excuse to put some distance between me and that idiotic scene. I could feel my control slipping away. I was seconds from revealing my power to a whole bunch of Idols. I'm careful not to shove anyone this time. It was stupid of me to act like I was in a Norm club where I can hold my own. Technically, I can now hold my own here too, but I can't actually do it. This is so frustrating.

I stop when I catch sight of the line to the women's restroom. Fuck that shit. I'm not getting in that. I don't even have to pee. But I'm not ready to face the guys yet, so I head in the direction of the exit sign I spotted earlier. I don't realize it's actually an employee exit until I find myself in a dark alley. Since I burst out the door, I'm too slow to stop it from shutting behind me. I try to open it again, but of course, it locks from the inside. That's just my luck. Now I have to walk around the building to the front of the club again.

But you know what? I'm in no hurry to return. I'm sure Bryce and Morpheus are capable of controlling Rufio and Phoenix.

A gust of wind blows down the alleyway, giving me shivers. I hug myself, but it doesn't do much against the chilly air. Living in Saturn's Bay for so long, I forgot that other states in the country actually have all four seasons. I'm lucky it isn't colder.

It's okay, though. A bit of fresh air will help me clear my mind. I take a couple of deep breaths, letting my lungs expand to the max. I wish I could say it's helping, but the irritation still refuses to leave my system. I can't believe Rufio and Phoenix were acting like two spoiled children. It was almost like they blamed me for this situation. Do they believe I'm not learning to control my powers on purpose?

Guys are so fucking stupid. And now I have four. What was I thinking?

My peace is disturbed by a strangled scream down the alley, followed by male laughter. More than one. Shit. Someone is in trouble. I take off toward the noise. The sounds grow louder, and when I turn the corner, I find three guys circling a young girl like she's prey. She's sprawled on the ground, searching for something in front of her with her hands.

"What's the matter, sweetheart? Can't find your cane?"

She jerks her head toward them but misses the exact spot where they're standing. Son of a bitch. The girl is blind. Those fucking assholes.

"Leave her alone!" I step forward before I even scan their auras.

The trio spins around, and their wicked grins widen. "My, my, look at what we have here. Another stray Norm."

"It's our lucky night, guys." The man closest to me laughs.

I raise my hands and brace for their attack. They aren't Norms, but thankfully they're only mid-level Fringes. I can take them.

"I don't think so."

"Oh, we got one with spunk. It'll be that much sweeter when we break her."

The guy in the middle makes a sharp movement with his arm, and the puddle of dirty water in front of him turns into a whip. He attempts to strike me with it, but my time-bending powers kick in unbidden. Time slows to a crawl, allowing me to move out of the way. The trick only lasts a split second, though.

"What the hell! How did she do that?" the elemental Fringe asks.

I rein in my powers once more, hoping they didn't have time to notice I'm an Idol. I'm so focused on them that I lose track of the girl on the ground. She's back on her feet, and holy cow, she's not a Norm at all.

"All right, assholes. You wanted a good time, I'll give you a good time." She moves her arms, and golden, glowing chains shoot out from them. One has a huge barb at the end and the other has a spiked ball. The chain with the barb pierces the Fringe to my left on his chest. Blood splatters from the hit, covering his entire shirt and face. The chain with the spiked ball hits the guy to my right on the back of his head, smashing his skull. Both men drop like potato sacks on the filthy ground, lifeless. There's only one Fringe left.

He looks at his fallen companions and drops to his knees. "Please don't kill me."

The blind girl's chains retract from their victims and circle the last Fringe like cobras waiting to strike.

"You're a wretched stain on this Earth. You preyed on me when you thought I was weak. I'm not going to kill you. I'm going to obliterate you."

The circle of chains closes around the man, squeezing him like a boa constrictor. I should try to stop the Idol, but I don't want to. Those Fringes remind me of the gangbangers who hurt Felicity. In another second, the chains turn the man into a blob of flesh, blood, and broken bones. Gruesome but satisfying.

The chains retract, their glow dimming until they disappear inside the girl's leather jacket.

She glances in my general direction. "You're still here."

"Yes."

"Most people would have run away by now."

"I'm not most people."

"Clearly. You tried to save me. I've never met anyone who would risk their lives to help a stranger in need."

"I'm sorry you've only come across assholes."

She grins at me. "Me too."

"Daisy!" Bryce's voice booms not far from us.

She cocks her head to the side, lifting an eyebrow. "Is that you?"

"Yes."

She picks up the cane from the ground as if she could actually see where it was. "I'd better go, then." With a power leap, she reaches the railing of the fire escape ladder of the building near her.

"Wait. You don't need to run away."

Still dangling from the railing, she replies, "I'm not running away." With a swing of her legs, she pulls herself up and then speeds up the ladder, blending in with the darkness save for her lavender-colored hair.

"Daisy! There you are." Bryce pulls me into his arms, crushing me against his chest. "I was so worried about you."

"I'm okay."

"Son of a bitch. What the hell happened here?" Rufio asks.

I break free from Bryce's bear hug and face not only him but also Phoenix, Morpheus, Stephan, and Soren.

"Are you okay?" Morpheus moves closer.

"They didn't hurt you, did they?" Phoenix whirls me around and gives me a once-over. For some reason, his touch doesn't ignite my powers, but I step away from him just the same.

"No, they didn't hurt me."

Stephan approaches the corpse of the guy who had his head bashed in. He stares at if for a couple of seconds with a narrowed gaze, then looks at the remains of the other two Fringes.

"We need to get out of here." He glances at us. "Now."

"Why? Do you know who did that?" Bryce asks.

My gaze connects with Stephan's. His eyes are intense, and he's projecting a wild energy now. Even when he was about to come to blows with Phoenix, he didn't seem so rattled.

"No, I don't. But we can't get caught anywhere near here."

No one argues with that. We sprint away from the gruesome scene, heading for the main street. When we reach the front of the club, Stephan walks in the middle of the road and almost gets run over by the cab he's trying to flag. Without missing a beat, he opens the back door for us.

"Get in. All of you."

"What about you and Soren?" I ask.

"Don't worry about us. Head back to Paragon Academy, and don't stop until you get there."

"What's the matter with you Idol kids?" the cab driver complains as soon as I slide in the car. "That asshole could have seriously damaged my car."

"Sorry," I mumble.

Morpheus is the one who sits next to me. He leans closer and whispers in my ear. "Is he a long-lost relative?"

"What? Why?"

"No reason."

It takes me a moment to understand what Morpheus meant. The cab driver is a Norm, and he was just complaining to Idols. I thought I was the only crazy fool to do that. The guy continues his tirade even after we're all in the car and well on the way to Paragon Academy.

"Hey, buddy. Do you have a death wish or something?" Phoenix grumbles from the front seat.

"What? Am I supposed to cower in fear because you're Idols?" He snorts. "The time of Idols' coercion is coming to an end."

"Is that so?" Rufio butts in.

Oh, brother. We can't have them starting trouble again.

"Ugh!" I groan. "Can everyone shut up? You too, grumpy driver."

The man whistles. "That's what I'm talking about."

Nobody says another word during the rest of the ride, but as soon as the driver drops us off in front of the school's building, the guys form a circle around me.

"What happened in that alley, Daisy?" Bryce asks first.

"What were you doing there in the first place? Were you trying to give us a heart attack?" Rufio asks angrily.

I scoff. "Yes, jerkface, that's exactly what I was doing. God, you're so infuriating sometimes."

Bryce rolls his eyes. "Ignore my brother. But seriously, what were you doing there alone?"

"I wasn't there on purpose, okay? After the scene you caused in the club, I needed fresh air to clear my head. I ended up taking the wrong exit door and got locked out. I was planning to circle around the building when I heard someone in distress. I had to check it out."

"Was it a trap?" Morpheus asks.

"No, it wasn't a trap. There were three mid-level Fringes attacking a girl. I couldn't just walk away. I used my time bending gift."

"Who killed them?" Bryce keeps staring me in an intense way, making me feel like I'm a criminal or something.

"The girl did. It turned out she wasn't a blind Norm as I had originally thought. She was an Idol, a powerful one. I didn't get a chance to do a proper reading of her aura, though. I was too stunned by what I saw her do to those men."

"Son of a bitch." Bryce runs a hand through his hair. "If you dropped your shield, she knows that you're... you know."

"It doesn't matter. I think she's truly blind. She doesn't know what I look like."

"I've never heard of a blind Idol before, or of any Idol having any kind of disability." Phoenix rubs his chin.

"Maybe she was just pretending to be blind to lure Daisy into showing her powers," Rufio replies.

"Shh. We shouldn't be having this conversation out in the open." Morpheus glowers at him. "Let's go back to our room."

I should have known that a curfew and separate dorm buildings wouldn't keep us apart for much longer. Sneaking into the guys' building is child's play with Morpheus's ability to conceal us under his shadows.

They were also given an apartment, but one with four bedrooms instead of two like mine.

"Is Toby not staying with you?"

"Nope. He's bunking with Soren," Rufio replies with disgust.

I refrain from commenting. It won't do any good anyway.

Bryce grabs my hand and makes me take a seat on the couch. He crouches in front of me and stares deep into my eyes. "Did you use your other abilities in front of that blind Idol?"

So, we're going right back at the grilling.

"No. All I did was time bend. It was a reflex. I didn't do it on purpose."

"Okay, that's good. She doesn't know you, and it's possible you won't cross paths with her again."

Phoenix snorts. "I don't want to rain on your parade, but that's wishful thinking."

Bryce looks over his shoulder. "You're not helping."

"I'm not going to sugarcoat things. Everything has gone to hell, and I'm fucking angry," he yells.

"This isn't about the Idol in the alley or even about your dislike of Stephan and Soren. This is about me, isn't it?" I reply.

Phoenix stares at me with a pained expression, and I know we can't keep going like we have been.

"I think it's time we all have a talk," I say, surprised that I was able to keep my voice steady. I'm awfully nervous of all a sudden.

"About what?" Rufio asks gruffly.

"About our situation. This." I wave my hand to encompass all of them. "Ever since I became an Idol, I've sensed a shift in our dynamics. You and Phoenix are mad at me."

"We're not mad at you." Phoenix furrows his eyebrows. "At least I'm not. I'm frustrated. You know how I feel about you. I can't stand not being able to be with you like those two can." He points at Bryce and Morpheus.

"I'm not angry with you either, Daisy," Rufio says, "but I'm jealous as hell."

"I don't want you to feel that way. I care about all of you equally. You don't think I'm torn up for not being able to even hold hands without taking your powers away?" I choke out.

Bryce unfurls from his crouch and moves to the window. "I confess that I've been feeling more possessive of you than before."

"Me too," Morpheus admits.

My stomach clenches painfully. I'm afraid where this conversation is going. "Why?"

"I don't know. But the feeling is festering in my chest. It's almost unnatural," Morpheus replies.

"For me too." Bryce turns to me.

"Hold up." Phoenix raises his hand. "You guys have no reason to feel jealous. You aren't the ones forbidden to touch Daisy."

"Exactly," Rufio agrees.

Morpheus's eyebrows arch suddenly. "Fuck me. I can't believe I didn't figure this out sooner."

"Figure what out?" I ask.

He laughs without humor, pulling his curls back. "That son of a bitch. I know why we're all acting like cavemen, competing for your affection. It's him. The island god. He couldn't stop you from getting Magia's powers back, so he's trying to destroy the trust in our inner circle by making us irrationally jealous of you."

"So, are you saying you don't actually have a problem with sharing me?" I ask, still not believing I'm having this conversation. Surreal doesn't begin to cover.

"We didn't before," Rufio replies.

"Have you ever done anything like this?"

"What? Share a girl?" Phoenix smirks, making me regret the question. Now I'm the one suffering from retroactive jealousy.

"You know what? Never mind. I don't want to know." I cross my arms.

"I've never loved anyone before, if that makes you feel better." The mirth vanishes from his eyes, and it's replaced by longing.

My heart does a cartwheel. *Did he just say he loves me?*

"Oh." I look at him like an idiot.

"Yeah, yeah. He loves you, Bryce loves you, we all love you." Rufio throws his hands up in the air. "So now, pretty please, learn how to master your powers already, because I don't know how much longer I can go without touching you. It physically hurts."

All those love declarations flying left and right has set my face into flames. It's one thing to hear it when I'm alone with each one of them, but like this, it's too much.

I jump from the couch. "I'd better get back to my room."

"Daisy, I was kidding about the mastering of your powers

bit. I know you're trying as hard as you can." Rufio stares at me with regret in his eyes.

"No. It's not that. I'm tired, and I also don't want Rosie to worry about me."

"I'll walk with you." Morpheus follows me to the door.

I'd like to be able to decline his offer, but I don't want to get in trouble with the host school for breaking their rules. I can't forget that I'm here in Hawk City for a reason, which is to unmake as many Neo Gods as possible.

28

———

DAISY

When I wake up the next morning, my mind is still whirling nonstop, replaying last night's events. By the time I made it back to the apartment, Rosie was already in her room, for which I was glad. I didn't want her to guess why I was the happiest person on Earth and also the weariest. I have four incredible guys as my boyfriends, and they all confessed their feelings to me last night. But at the same time, I could lose them in the blink of an eye. And I'm so over losing people I love.

It's hard to pretend everything is fine in front of Rosie. I swore to myself I'd be honest about what's going on in my life, but I don't have it in me to tell her about the brutal scene I witnessed, or that I'll have to face some nasty piece-of-shit Idol very soon. I can't help but want to protect her from my harsh reality.

My head is pounding when we make it down to the cafeteria. Sleep eluded me big-time, and I need caffeine stat. My entire life I believed Idols didn't suffer from maladies such as headaches like this. I didn't even know Idols got sick until Nurse Ellen set me straight.

"How was your date with Toby last night?" I ask.

"It was lovely. He took me to an Italian restaurant near the Museum of Modern Art. It was super romantic."

"Great. I'm glad you had a good time." I smile, but it feels forced. I'm happy for my sister, but there's too much worry in my heart. It's keeping me from experiencing joy to the fullest.

"I did. Even when the cab drove us near our old neighborhood, I didn't let that damper my mood."

"You really like Toby, don't you, Rosie?"

"Yeah. I've never felt anything like this before." She dips her chin, trying to hide the blush that's spreading on her cheeks.

"Well, you're only fifteen."

"So? You had way more boyfriends than me at my age."

"Ugh. Don't remind me. They were all losers."

She snorts. "I'll say."

Being a Sunday, most of the regular students aren't present. But the majority of the visitors are here, if I were to guess by the number of tables taken. I met most of them yesterday at the mixer but didn't really spend too much time getting to know them. Not like they were interested in talking to the poor Norm student either.

Breakfast is served in a buffet style, and the delicious smell of bacon and freshly brewed coffee wafts to my nose.

"There's Toby." Rosie waves at him.

I follow her line of sight. Toby is sitting at a table with Stephan and Soren. Great.

I search the rest of the room, but the guys aren't here yet. Rosie is already moving toward Toby's table, so I have no choice but to follow her.

He stands to greet Rosie with a kiss on the lips. They're cute together and Toby makes her happy, but sometimes I mind that he's a little older. Of course, I'm being a hypocrite; I was dating guys way older than Toby when I was fifteen. I act like a mother once in a while, and I think she resents me for it.

"Good morning," I say.

"Good morning, Daisy. Did you get home okay?" Stephan asks casually, only I know his question is loaded.

"Yeah. But now I'm in desperate need of coffee."

I also make a plate of eggs and bacon for Rosie and me while I'm at the buffet. This is me feeling guilty for all the secrets I'm keeping from her. When I return, Bryce, Rufio, Phoenix, and Morpheus are all sitting at the table, and immediately the crazy butterflies awake and start wreaking havoc in my belly. I hope that after last night's conversation, they'll stop the jealousy act around Stephan. They'd better behave, or I'll cut all of them out of my bed.

Like you could follow through with that, Daisy.

I square my shoulders and force my facial expression into neutral. It's a pretty hard task when the foursome turns to watch me return to the table. If it's hard not to hyperventilate when I'm under the smothering look of one of them, it's impossible when I'm facing all four. I drop my eyes to the tray as I sit in between Rosie and Morpheus.

"Morning, Daisy. Did you sleep well?" he asks.

With my eyes still glued to the plate of food, I reply, "Uh-huh."

"My mattress was so comfy. I slept like a baby." Rosie reaches for the plate I made for her.

A long silence follows, so I lift my gaze to gauge the atmosphere. The last time we saw the Silverstone brothers, they helped us escape the murder scene. But I don't know if that will diffuse the tension between them and my guys.

Yup, it's still there, though not as nuclear as last night. Either way, I can't deal with any of it while caffeine deficient. I bring the hot brew to my lips but freeze when I spot a familiar face coming into the room.

"You have got to be kidding me," I mutter.

"What is it?" Rosie asks.

Stephan looks over his shoulder and then curses.

"Do you know that girl, Daisy?" Rosie asks.

"I think I saw her last night," I reply vaguely, regretting my big mouth.

"Who is she?" Toby turns to Stephan, since he cursed under his breath.

"Andromeda Belfor. She's a senior, although she only joined Paragon a few months ago. She was homeschooled before."

"Why?" Rosie furrows her eyebrows.

"Because she's blind," I say, but it's mostly a guess.

"Yup. Her parents didn't want her to be bullied because of her condition." Soren snorts. "They really don't know their daughter very well."

"I don't follow," Toby replies.

"Don't worry, buddy. If you're lucky, you won't have to interact with her at all." Stephan forces a smile.

Andromeda walks into the cafeteria with the help of her cane, drawing the attention of the crowd. She reaches the buffet table without a problem, grabs a cup of coffee and a muffin, and then picks an empty table to sit down.

"She's not very social, is she?" Phoenix reaches over Morpheus to steal a piece of bacon from my plate. I glare at him, and he winks in return while taking a bite of the stolen morsel. God, I miss that mouth on me.

Holy crap, I did not just think that. *Focus, Daisy. Focus. The Idol who murdered those three Fringes last night is only a few feet away from you.*

"Not really," Stephan grumbles.

Something tells me there's more to his reply than he's letting on, and I'm not sure if it's only because Andromeda is a total badass. I scan her again, but she's toning down her powers big-time. She felt way more powerful yesterday.

As if reading my mind, Morpheus asks, "What level is she? I can't get a clear read on her."

Stephan and Soren trade a glance, but it's Stephan who answers. "She's an eighteen."

No one speaks for several beats, but everyone at the table is staring at the girl now.

As if sensing our collective stare, she turns to us, and then she flips us off.

"What the hell? How did she know we were looking?" Phoenix asks.

"Who the fuck knows? That girl is a psycho," Soren replies. "I'd give her a wide berth if I were you."

Stephan doesn't say a word, but the clench of his jaw tells me he's not happy about his brother's comment. I really need to find a time alone with him to ask about Andromeda. I bet he knew she was responsible for the massacre last night.

My brand-new phone vibrates in my pocket. I just received a message. Since everyone in my inner circle is presently at the table, I'm afraid to open the message. It must be from Principal Fallon, which means information about my target. Suddenly, my appetite is gone, and the coffee I just drank sits funny in my belly. I push my chair back and stand.

"I have to use the restroom."

I hurry out of the cafeteria before Rosie or any of the guys decides to join me. The hallway is empty, but even so, I head for the nearest restroom to read the message. I only dare to open it once I'm locked in one of the bathroom stalls.

The message is from an unknown number. She warned me that'd be the case. With my heart stuck in my throat, I read the text. My target is the owner of an upscale Italian restaurant who has a taste for schoolgirls. I feel sick, and bile pools in my mouth. I'm supposed to slip out of school tomorrow and carry on with my mission, which means seduce the perv and get alone time with him. I don't know if I can do this.

The sound of someone coming in tells me my time is up. I flush the toilet just to keep up with the pretense and walk out.

Ah, hell. Andromeda is the girl who came in, and judging by her body posture—leaning against the sink with legs crossed at the ankles—she was waiting for me.

"Hi, Daisy. Fancy seeing you here." She smirks. "But of course, I can't really *see* you."

"How did you know I was here?"

"When you're born blind, you learn to see through other means. I recognized your signature—that is, your *Idol* signature."

Oh shit. Did I fuck up and let my guard down?

As if reading my mind, she says, "Don't worry. Your shield is still in place. Those idiots outside can't tell you're one of them."

"How come you can?" I cross my arms over my chest.

She tilts her head to the side. "I'm special."

And cocky.

"What do you want?"

The girl shrugs. "I just thought I'd introduce myself properly. My name is Andromeda, which I guess Mr. Pain In My Ass already told you. But you can call me Andy."

"Are you referring to Stephan?"

"Who else?"

"That's it? You just cornered me in the girls' restroom to introduce yourself?"

"Yeah. What? You thought I came here to be nasty to you?"

"It crossed my mind. I haven't had good experiences with the girls in my school."

"I'm sorry you've only come across assholes." She throws my own comment back at me and smirks.

I can't help but return the grin. The girl is powerful, and bloodthirsty as hell, but I'm not threatened by her. Maybe she is different than the rest.

"Uh-oh. I'm afraid our tête-à-tête is coming to an end in three, two, one." She points at the door.

It bursts open and Stephan fills the frame, looking worried

as shit. He glances at Andromeda first, then at me.

"What's up, Stephan?" I ask.

Before he can reply, Andromeda says, "I know you spend way too much time styling your hair, dude, but this is the girls' bathroom."

He narrows his eyes to slits, clenching his jaw. "Is everything all right here?"

"Yup. Everything is dandy." She turns to the mirror and runs her fingers through her long, lavender-colored hair. It's peculiar that she acts like she can actually see her reflection.

"I wasn't asking you," Stephan replies harshly.

"Everything is fine." I walk toward him but stop to glance at the strange girl. "It was nice to meet you, Andy."

"Same. We'll talk more during the week." She winks at me.

Once out in the hallway, Stephan whirls on me. "What did she say to you? Did she threaten you?"

"No. Nothing of the sort. She was nice."

"Come on, Daisy. You can tell me."

"I am telling you. She was nice."

Stephan keeps staring at me like he's having a hard time believing my words. Then he shakes his head. "Damn. Only you could make friends with that fiend."

"You don't like her?"

"No, I can't say I do. Would you appreciate someone straight out of the bowels of Hell?"

I pegged Stephan to be a super easygoing guy, so for him to make such a statement, things between him and Andromeda must be pretty intense. I wish I had truly come to Paragon Academy for some silly tournament. I'd have loved to get to know her more, but instead, I have to seduce a fucking perv tomorrow.

I promised Morpheus and Phoenix I'd keep them in the loop, but if they know what the plan is, they'll never let me see it through. There's no way I can tell them.

29

DAISY

I tried my best to act normally after breakfast on Sunday. Stephan, mercifully, didn't tell the guys about my meeting with Andromeda in the restroom. That would have caused another ruckus for sure. For all intents and purposes, the guys still believe she has no idea that I was the Idol she met in the alley. I'll tell them when we get back home. My gut is telling me I don't have to worry about her, and my instincts have saved me from pretty unsavory situations in the past. I won't stop trusting them now.

We all spent the day together playing tourists in Hawk City, and when we came back to Paragon Academy, I managed to sneak in an hour to practice with Morpheus. And that's all we did. Nothing else. I made the decision to cease all hookups until I can learn to control my powers. It's not fair to Rufio and Phoenix that I can't be with them. Plus, with the possibility that the island god is messing with their feelings, it's best not give them reason to feel jealous.

Keeping busy the whole day helped control my nerves, but alone in my bed at night, I let the fear sneak into my heart again. Suffice it to say, I didn't sleep more than a few hours, and

I'm a wreck this morning. Rosie and I went grocery shopping yesterday, so we have breakfast in our apartment. Neither of us wants to mingle with the students here.

By the time we head down to the school building, the hallways are packed. Two Norm girls alone in a sea of Idols are sure to garner extra attention. But aside from curious glances, not one really pays much attention to us. Huh, maybe Idols in Hawk City are a little more accepting. That cab driver from last Saturday sure had a sharp tongue. Norms in Saturn's Bay aren't that bold around Idols. I was the exception. Maybe his courage steamed from the fact that Idols here are not as quick to go postal on Norm ass.

A derisive laugh sounds in my head. I'm delusional. On that same evening, I witnessed Andromeda kill three Fringes without a second thought. And Soren warned me that the Idol players in Hawk City are way more ruthless and dangerous.

The loud chatter around us is making me even more anxious. I clutch my backpack straps tighter, worrying about how I'm going to slip out without anyone seeing. If I could tell Morpheus about my plan, he'd be able to conceal me, but I'm still determined to not say a word. Principal Fallon guaranteed that the Idol on my list would be alone and I'd have no problem carrying out my mission. I can only hope that's true.

We meet the guys in front of a small auditorium where the first round of the tournament will take place. It's advanced math, which means I'm with Rufio and Phoenix on this one. Bryce and Toby are taking part in different rounds this morning. Rosie, being the good girlfriend she is, decides to watch Toby. And since Morpheus isn't here for the tournament, he also has some other place to be; Paragon Academy has one of the best art programs in the country, and Morpheus is eager to speak with the teacher.

I just go through the motions, so dazed that I don't even remember taking my seat on the stage. I'm distracted during the questions and don't answer any. I keep glancing at the clock mounted on the wall. I have to get out of here soon or I'll miss my window of opportunity. My target goes to his office downtown around ten and stays there until eleven, and it's already nine. I still have to put my disguise on—a dark wig, brown contact lenses, and a different school uniform, which are already in my bag together with the lightning-glass dagger I brought. I'll have to improvise.

"How much longer until this round is over?" I whisper to Rufio, who's standing to my left.

"Another half hour. Is there something wrong? You haven't said a word since we got here."

"To be honest, I'm not feeling well. I don't think the croissant I had for breakfast was a good idea. I feel queasy."

"Do you think you need to throw up?" He sounds worried, and it makes me feel guilty as hell. I'm lying through my teeth to him.

"Yeah, I do."

He raises his hand, catching the moderator's attention. "Sir, my teammate is not feeling well. May she be excused to use the restroom?"

The man with bushy eyebrows dips his chin and peers at me from above his glasses. "You can't wait?"

"No," I reply.

"Okay. You may be excused, but I'm not going to stop the tournament on account of there being one less person on your team. Therefore, you'd better hurry up."

"What's the matter with Daisy?" Phoenix asks.

"Upset stomach." I stand from my seat.

I catch Rufio motioning to do the same, which would totally ruin my plan, and I panic. Fuck. Of course he would want to accompany me to the restroom.

"Mr. Kent? Where do you think you're going?" the moderator asks.

"She's not well. I was—"

"I think Miss Woods can walk to the bathroom by herself."

"Yes I can." I throw an apologetic glance at Rufio over my shoulder and then hurry to the door.

The coast is clear in the hallway. All students are presently in classrooms. I make a dash to the stairs, bypassing this floor's restroom. I head for the guest one on the ground floor. It has a window from which I can climb out. I checked yesterday.

Ten minutes later, I'm off school grounds and running toward a parallel street so I can hail a cab without being seen. My wig itches like crazy, and the contacts are super uncomfortable. I just hope they'll be enough to conceal my true identity.

Out on the street, I try to find a cab, but I had forgotten how hectic the city is and how scarce taxis are during busy week hours. It doesn't help that free cabs aren't stopping for me either. Shit. Of course they'd give priority to an Idol, even if the drivers are Norms like me. I wish I didn't have to do it, but I lower the barrier on my power. A minute later, a cab stops for me.

"Where to, miss?" he asks in a thick Hawkian accent.

I give him the address, sagging against the seat. Thankfully, this guy isn't one of those chatty ones. I stare at the window, but I see nothing. Everything is a blur. If anyone would have told me I'd be back in Hawk City to exact revenge against some of the most dangerous Idols in the country, I'd have laughed on their faces.

Fifteen minutes later, the driver stops in front of an upscale building downtown and announces we have arrived. I pay for the fare in cash—don't want to leave a trail—and step out. I don't move from the spot for a moment, giving myself a couple of minutes to steady my nerves. I reach inside my pocket, curling my fingers around the handle of the dagger. The weapon wouldn't have fit if I hadn't made a small hole in my pocket.

I loosen the tie around my neck and undo the top buttons of my shirt. The guy likes sexy schoolgirls, so I have to play the part. The final touch is to dampen my powers enough to pass for a Fringe, since that's the type the perv prefers.

At the reception desk, I give the guy my target's name. The man looks me up and down with an expression that says he knows exactly why I'm here. "Do you have an appointment?"

"I'm from St. Jude's All-Girls School. and I was hoping to interview Mr. Cornwall for a school paper article," I reply innocently.

"Okay, but you didn't answer my question about having an appointment."

"I was told I didn't need one." I bite my lower lip, hoping I can use sex to convince this buffoon to let me through.

He simply rolls his eyes. "Ah, heck. I don't get paid enough to play gatekeeper. Go on. His office is on the twenty-fifth floor."

"Thank you, sir."

I speed walk to the elevators, making sure to keep my chin down so I'm not caught on any security camera straight-on. I keep my gaze down on the ride up as well, especially since I'm surrounded by businessmen and I really don't want anyone remember seeing me there.

I'm the last one out of the elevator, and on this floor, there's only one office door at the end of the corridor. Before I lose my nerve and bolt, I force my legs to move toward the tempered glass double doors with gold lettering on top.

They're unlocked and lead to a reception area with a massive desk. An older woman with white hair and thick glasses looks up from her laptop.

"May I help you?"

"I'm here to see Mr. Cornwall."

She asks if I have an appointment, and I give her the same excuse I did downstairs. With a scowl, she buzzes her boss and lets him know he has a visitor. I'm not surprised when he says I can come in, nor when he tells his assistant to take an early lunch break. Fuck. He knows exactly why I'm here.

The woman gives me a haughty look as she leaves, but I don't hold her stare.

My heart is beating a staccato rhythm when I enter the man's office. It's a big space with tall windows that garner breathtaking views of the city. But my eyes are riveted on the fat and bald man sitting behind a glass desk. He leans against his fancy leather chair and rubs his chin.

"So, you're here for an interview, huh?"

"Yes."

"And from which school did you say you were from again?"

"St. Jude's All-Girls."

"Hmm. I wasn't expecting a visit from one of you girls this week, but I suppose for you, I can make an exception." He smiles in a leery way, making my skin crawl. "Come closer, darling. Let me take a good look at you."

I walk to his desk, but that's not what he meant when he said closer.

"No, no. Over here." He swivels his chair to the right and waits for me to walk around the barrier between us.

I do so slowly, trying to appear seductive. I don't want him to notice how disgusted I am. When I stop in front of him, I'm hit by a bolt of panic and freeze. *What if I can't unmake him? What if he overpowers me?*

"Ah, yeah, you're a beauty." He places his grubby hands on my legs and then goes under my skirt.

This is it, Daisy. Now it's your chance.

I hold his wrists, stopping him from exploring further. Immediately, my powers ignite and I start to take his.

"What the hell is this?" His eyes round.

"Nothing, darling. This is just foreplay."

His eyebrows arch as he takes a good look at me. "You're an Idol. You're the Unmaker."

"That's ri—"

My reply is cut short when the man electrocutes me. I let go of him, staggering backward. Fuck. That didn't happen when I faced Phoenix's father.

"You little bitch." He sends another discharge in my direction, but I manage to move out of the way, colliding with a chair.

The impact with the piece of furniture brings me to my knees, leaving me vulnerable to another bolt. It hits me right in the middle of my back, making my muscles spasm uncontrollably. I fall on my face, unable to move at all. I can't even reach for the dagger in my pocket. Why did I think this would be easy?

The man approaches, though I can only see his expensive leather shoes. He stops at a safe distance from me.

"Did you think you could come into my office and unmake me, little Knight whore?" He hits me again with his energy blast, and the pain almost makes me faint. I have to make him stop.

If I try to reach for my weapon, he'll stop me. I don't know how to slow down time at will—when it happened before, it was an accident—but I have to try, because this is my only chance of getting out of here alive. I lift my arm and think about freezing the man, but he throws something on me before I can, a net that immediately blocks my connection to my Idol powers.

Hell. This must have lightning glass in it. The realization is dark and bitter.

"So, you're the Knights' weapon, huh? To be honest, I'm kind of disappointed. It was almost too ea—"

A gurgling sound stops the man's tirade. I lift my chin with difficulty and see the glowing chain that's embedded to his chest. Slowly, a circle of blood stains his pristine white shirt. He drops to his knees with mouth agape and eyes round with surprise. The chain gets yanked from his body, tearing his chest apart in a bloody mess. He falls forward with a loud thud, too close to me.

My muscles are slowly recovering from the electric shocks, and I try to break free from under the net. Andromeda stops next to her victim's corpse and tsks. "Lived as a pig, died as a pig."

"A little help here," I say.

She leans forward and pulls the net from me, tossing it to the side. "Let's go. Security will be here in no time."

I jump to my feet and attempt to fix my wig. "Did you follow me?"

"Yeah. I caught your signature as you ran to the ground floor. I was curious to see where you were going in such a hurry." She shrugs and then walks toward the door.

I don't ask any more questions until we leave Mr. Cornwall's office behind and race down the stairs. Andromeda takes the lead, running faster than me. I don't know how she can be so agile when she can't see. She doesn't slow down until we're out on the street and a block away from the building, though it's me who stops first.

"Wait. Are you planning to run back to Paragon Academy on foot?" I ask, out of breath.

She whirls around and faces me. Her gaze is vacant, but even so, I have the impression she's scrutinizing me.

"I'm not going back there now. But you should. And don't forget to lose the wig."

"How do you know I'm wearing a wig? Are you truly blind?" I narrow my eyes.

"As a bat." She smiles wryly.

"Thank you for saving my ass back there."

"I was just returning the favor."

"Aren't you going to ask what I was doing with that man?"

"Hey, I'm not one to judge other people's kinks. If fat and

disgusting makes you hot and bothered, I'd say go for it. But I know that's not what you were doing there."

"Maybe I like fat and disgusting. You don't know." I cross my arms.

"Sure you do. Don't worry, Daisy. I'm not telling your boyfriends about your side job as an avenger. I just have one favor to ask in return."

"What is it?"

"Please don't tell Stephan that I helped you."

"I wasn't planning to. But why not?"

Andromeda shakes her head. "I have my reasons." She grins. "Well, I'd better get going. See you later, alligator." She salutes me with two fingers and then crosses the street, unbothered by the incoming traffic.

What a crazy girl.

30

PHOENIX

When Daisy hadn't returned from the restroom after ten minutes, Rufio and I said sayonara to the moderators and went to look for her. She wasn't in the restroom and she didn't answer her phone, so we decided to split up to look for her. She's been gone for nearly an hour now, and I'm about to lose my mind.

She's definitely not on campus. We looked for her signature everywhere. I'm pacing in the courtyard, waiting for the others to join me and also berating myself for being so stupid. With everything that's happened in the past week, we shouldn't let our guards down. People are looking for Daisy to either use or destroy her, and we simply let her wander off in a strange school by herself.

I stop short when tingles run down my neck and my heart skips a beat. I look over my shoulder, and there she is, crossing through the gates of the school. I don't stop to think, just cross the distance between us and crush her against my chest.

"You're all right." I kiss the top of her head.

"Phoenix. What are you doing?" Her complaint is muffled

since her face is pressed against me, but almost immediately my energy levels begin to drop and I feel faint.

"You scared the shit out of me. Where the hell have you been?"

"Please let go, my love. I'm hurting you."

My love. It's the first time she used the term with me, and if her gift wasn't sapping my strength, my legs would still turn to mush. I don't move, though. Her powers have paralyzed me like before.

"Phoenix!" She shoves me back, breaking free from my hold.

I'm stunned for a moment, but when I recover, I notice something is terribly wrong with Daisy. There's panic and fear in her gaze mixed with guilt. It breaks my heart that I can't comfort her the only way I know how. And that's when the light bulb flashes above my head.

I'm such an idiot. There's another way.

"You need to come with me." I head for the street.

"Where are we going?"

"I'll let you know in a second. Please, Daisy. Don't make me beg."

She shakes her head almost imperceptibly. "I never want you to do that."

We walk off Paragon's property side by side, but leaving a safe gap between our bodies. I'm not planning to go far.

"So where are we going?" she asks.

I don't answer because she'll see as soon as we round the next corner. One of the most upscale five-star hotels in Hawk City is only a few yards away.

"You can't be serious." She halts and turns to me. "Phoenix, I miss you too, and this situation is driving me insane. But you saw what just happened a minute ago. I'm a menace to you."

"I know. But we can still be together without touching." I tap my forehead with my index finger.

Daisy widens her eyes a bit. "Oh."

"Come on."

I'm afraid she'll say no, and in the seconds I wait for her response, it seems I've swallowed a thousand needles.

"Okay," she finally replies, and a wave of relief washes over me.

"Thank you."

She rewards me with a dazzling smile, something I haven't seen in a while. It shoots straight to my chest, making my heart flutter like a hummingbird.

My phone vibrates in my pocket, jarring me back to the real world. I answer on the second ring without taking my eyes off her, afraid she'll vanish.

"Westbrook," I say to whoever's calling. I didn't even check the number.

"Phoenix, where the hell are you? I told you to wait for us," Rufio barks in my ear.

"Sorry, Rufio. Something came up. Don't worry about Daisy. She's with me."

"Where are you?"

"Nearby. We'll be back in an hour."

"The hell you will. You need to come back right now."

I pull my phone away from my ear before I go deaf.

"Can I talk to him?" Daisy stretches her hand out to me.

"Sure. Hold on, Daisy wants to talk to you."

She takes the phone from me, careful to not brush her fingers with mine. "Hey. Yeah, I'm okay."

"Where have you been?" Rufio asks so loudly I can hear him from where I stand.

"I'll explain later. I need to do something with Phoenix first. We'll be back soon. Don't worry about me."

There's more grumbling from Rufio's side, but in the end, he relents. Only Daisy could tame that Tasmanian devil.

"All good?" I ask.

She smiles. "Yeah. I'm all yours for an hour."

"Babe, that's the best news I've heard this whole week."

DAISY

Getting a room without reservation wasn't hard, not when Phoenix pushed his diamond-member credit card toward the receptionist. In true fashion, he splurged, getting us a presidential suite.

"Phoenix, you shouldn't have. We can't stay long."

"It's the least that motherfucker can do from the grave. I've earned it."

It breaks my heart whenever he speaks about his father. And it also makes me angry as hell. But I try not to show anything but love for him.

"Forget him," I say.

He grins, but unfortunately his amusement doesn't reach his eyes. "Let's check out our love nest."

My stomach clenches a little with the awakening of the stupid butterflies. They don't care that I'm prohibited from doing more than staring at the gorgeous guy in front of me. He walks ahead and whistles in appreciation as he stares at the king-size bed.

"Does this remind you of anything?" He turns to me with a cocky grin on his lips.

I narrow my eyes to slits as the memory comes to me. "This is the hotel room from the first vision you sent me."

"Yeah." His smile widens.

"You made me orgasm in front of everybody." I cross my arms and glower at him.

Phoenix's smile wilts to nothing. "Ah, damn. I did. I'm such an idiot for reminding you of that."

I turn to the panoramic wall-to-wall window. We're on the top floor, so the room has the most incredible view of Hawk City. But so did the office of that pig Mr. Cornwall.

Thinking about him makes me sick to my stomach. The fact that he put his hands on me feels like a stain on my soul. I quickly forget the incident with Phoenix. It didn't happen that long ago, but it feels like eons have passed since then.

"Daisy, darling, what's the matter? Are you mad at me?"

I shake my head in an attempt to dispel the dark memories from my mind, but it's almost impossible.

If it weren't for Andromeda, I'd be dead.

"No, I'm not mad at you." I dip my chin.

"Then what's going on? Does your mood have to do with where you were today?"

Closing my eyes, I suck in a sharp breath. "Yes."

"Babe, talk to me." His voice is tight.

"I snuck out during the tournament because I had a job to do."

"Did you go after a Neo God, Daisy? Without telling us?"

I whirl around, hating to see the look of betrayal and worry etched on his face.

"You wouldn't have let me go if you knew."

"I would have come with you."

"I had to do it alone."

"Why? To prove you could do it?" He takes a step forward, curling his hands into fists.

"No, I just... had to. Please don't make me tell you why."

Understanding, or at least partial understanding, crosses his face.

"What happened?" he asks in a much lower voice.

"He fought back. I almost didn't make it."

He presses a fist against his forehead. "Damn everything to hell!"

"I'm sorry." I glance down, wriggling my fingers together.

"No, Daisy, don't apologize. This whole situation is not your fault. I'm fucking angry at Principal Fallon for risking your life like that."

"It has to be done. We need to free Bryce and Rufio from the Neo Gods' grasp."

"I know." He sighs. "Shit, you have no idea how much I want to hold you right now."

"I do. It's probably just as much as I want to hold you."

We don't speak for several beats until I finally take a seat on the edge of the bed and close my eyes. "Come to me."

Phoenix lips are on mine in an instant, fiery and electrifying. His scorching tongue delves in my mouth, mingling with mine in a manic frenzy. I throw my hands around his shoulders and bring him closer. There's no tingling in my fingers, no stealing of his powers.

I ease off to peer into his eyes. "This is a vision, isn't it?"

"Yes."

I trace his forehead with the tips of my fingers, then his nose, his lips. "You feel real."

"You do too. God, I missed you so fucking much." He kisses me again, pushing me down on the bed.

My legs part to accommodate Phoenix's massive frame between them. He leans his forearms against the mattress on each side of me, effectively caging me in, while his hips press against mine. The bulge of his erection rubs right where I so desperately need it, but we're wearing way too many clothes.

In the blink of an eye, they're gone.

"That was neat." I laugh against his lips.

"Yeah. And you know what else is great?" He kisses my neck before sucking hard.

"What?" I arch my back and raise my knees, hooking my legs at the ankles behind him.

"No need for a condom." He slides into my wet heat, filling

me completely. I know this is only his imagination, but it's almost like the real thing.

"Oh, fuck," I cry out. "This feels amazing."

He pulls back, almost all the way out, only to slam back inside of me again. "Damn it, babe. Even in my vision your pussy is divine."

"Maybe you're just willing it so," I murmur, already losing control of my body.

"No, this is the real deal." He prevents my reply with a long and glorious kiss while unraveling me with each thrust.

My bones turn to fire, my brain is scattering into tiny pieces, and any coherent thought is impossible. I don't know where I end and Phoenix begins. He's all I can feel. He's everywhere.

"Phoenix, am I doing any of this?" I murmur against his lips.

"Yeah, babe. This is as much my vision as it is yours."

I squeeze my internal walls against his cock, making him grunt. "You're devilish."

"It's only fair that I make you lose control too."

"Oh yeah? You want me to lose control? You got it, babe."

He flips us over using nothing but his telekinesis so he's lying on his back and I'm on top. Without missing a beat, I rotate my hips while he squeezes them tightly.

"Is this what you want?" I sit straighter, straddling him.

With narrowed, lust-infused eyes, he reaches for my breasts, squeezing them together. "Fuck yeah. I love your tits."

To make his point, he sits up halfway and captures one of my nipples in his mouth. I move faster, spurred on by his tongue on my body. The tension keeps building down below, and I don't know how much longer I can continue without falling apart.

Phoenix lets go of my nipple with a soft pop and looks into my eyes. "Go ahead, babe. Let go."

"I don't want to. Not yet." I kiss him hard, loving how soft his lips are, a stark contrast to his body.

He grabs a handful of my hair and pulls back. "Don't worry, my love. We can come as much and as often as we want. There are no rules here. Let's do it together."

I nod, unable to utter a single word as a wave of desire crashes over me.

Then I'm gone, gone, gone.

31

RUFIO

"I can't believe you just caved." Bryce stares at me with indignation. "Daisy disappeared for over an hour and you couldn't even get their location?"

"Phoenix said they were nearby." I run a hand through my hair, frustrated at myself for not doing just that. Why the hell didn't I even get an address from her?

"It doesn't matter. Daisy's presence in Hawk City is by design. Our mother wanted her here."

"To do what exactly?" I ask.

"Who the fuck knows. Nothing that will take Daisy's safety into account." Bryce walks out the gate of Paragon Academy. "I'm going after her."

"What are you going to do, sniff around until you get her scent like a damn hound dog?"

"Something like that," he grits out.

The sound of tires screeching nearby stops us in our tracks. A black van just squealed up to the curb next to us. The passenger door opens, and a tall man with white hair and an eye patch steps out.

He opens the sliding door and barks, "Get in!"

"Like fuck we will," I say, bringing my hands up.

"Do not cause a scene. You either come willingly or your Norm whore gets hurt."

"What's the meaning of this? We had two more days." Bryce steps in front of me.

"Things have changed. Get in. Now!"

Bryce turns to me, and in his gaze I read fear. He told me about the Neo Gods' ultimatum, that we had three more days to find and kill the Knights' weapon or they'd punish us through Daisy.

"Let's see what they want," he says.

Once inside the van, we find blindfolds. "Not this again," I grumble.

"Put it on." The blond guy takes the front passenger seat.

Anger is running rampant through my veins, but the fear that something will happen to Daisy makes me compliant.

The ride is short, no more than ten minutes. I know we entered a garage when the sound of the busy traffic is muffled and the noise of tires screeching echoes outside. We're instructed to keep our blindfolds on as we get out of the car too.

When a beefy hand curls around my forearm, I try to jerk free. "I can walk on my own."

"Shut up and keep walking." I recognize the blond dude's voice. So he's the one who's holding me. Motherfucker. He'll be the first of the lot who I'll turn into dust when I get rid of this damn gag order in my mind.

We enter an elevator. Without sight, I focus on getting a read on the number of jackasses around us. There's Bryce, keeping his signature subdued. I don't know why he's bothering to mask his powers. The Neo Gods know he's a level seventeen. Aside from Bryce, I get readings from three other guys, the asshole still clutching my arm and two others.

The elevator pings, announcing we've arrived at our floor. I'm pushed forward none too gently, and I can't help but let my powers leak out a little. The asshole holding me drops my arm with a curse.

"You little piec—"

"Delta, not now," my father's voice sounds ahead.

Son of a bitch. What the hell is he doing in Hawk City? I yank my blindfold off and glare at the man.

"This is getting old, *Father*." I toss the piece of fabric to the side.

We're now in an empty office space under construction. Plastic curtains section off parts of the room, and pieces of equipment are spread out randomly. My father is standing at the panoramic window, and next to him are a young man and woman who could be mistaken for fashion models. Tall, skinny, and mean-looking.

"Hi, Bryce. Nice to see you again," the woman says.

I look at my brother. When did he meet that chick?

"Amanda. Too bad I can't say the same," he replies.

Her lips curl in a cruel grin. "I'd be hurt if I cared."

"Why did you bring us here?" I ask.

"Because you fucked up." My father takes a step forward. "One of our members was murdered earlier today, and we have reason to believe he was killed by the Knights' weapon."

The small hairs on the back of my neck stand on end. Daisy snuck off campus earlier. That's where she went. *Son of a bitch.*

"What makes you say that?" Bryce asks.

"The Knights acquire their precious weapon, and a few days later, one of the highest-ranking members of our organization is killed. That's not a coincidence."

"But you have no proof that the person who killed him is the one," I argue.

"It doesn't matter. The killer is here in Hawk City. Find her." Dad's response leaves no room for argument.

"*Her?* How do you know it's a woman?" Bryce asks.

"The idiot got caught on tape. She was wearing a bad wig but was careful to keep her gaze down," Amanda replies.

"Why do you want us to find this chick? We're not officially members yet. We haven't passed the test," I argue.

My father narrows his eyes and moves closer to us. "Because I know she *is* your test. You have until tomorrow to find her."

~

BRYCE

The meeting with our father didn't last long. I'm not sure why he brought that chick Amanda and the other dude who didn't make sound. He sure as hell didn't take his eyes off us, though. Like the other Neo Gods we've met, he was toning his power down big-time, so I couldn't get a good read of his level.

My chest feels heavy as fuck when the Delta guy drops us off in front of Paragon Academy. During the ride, I weighed all my options, which aren't many. One thing's for sure: we have to get rid of the gag spell controlling our minds. And I only know one person who can.

Wordlessly, I stride toward the school building, but Rufio grabs my arm and whirls me around before I can enter.

"What are we going to do?" he asks.

"Right now, I'm going to find Stephan."

My brother's eyebrows shoot to the heavens. "Why? He can't help us."

"Actually, he can."

He said he has a job here as a substitute teacher, so I head toward where the faculty offices are. After asking for directions, we find him as he was about to leave. He glances in our direction and furrows his brows in an instant.

"What's the matter?" he asks.

"I need your help with something."

"All right." He pushes the door to the office open. "Come in."

The place is nothing like I expected it to be. It's the barest faculty offices I've ever been in. There's nothing besides a desk and a few chairs.

"Damn, you really went for the minimalist look," Rufio says.

"I don't fuss over trivialities. So, what I can do for you?" Stephan asks my brother.

"I need to borrow one of your special cords that nullify Idol powers."

Stephan squints. "I don't know what you're talking about."

"Cut the crap, man. The Knights kidnapped me and kept me trapped for an entire weekend, and I couldn't use my gift. You know exactly what I'm talking about."

Stephan keeps staring at me with his jaw clenched tight for several beats before asking, "What are you planning to do with that?"

"I can't tell. *Literally.*" I emphasize the word, hoping he catches my drift.

With a narrowing of his eyes, he replies, "I'll see what can do."

"I'm not asking to borrow a fucking pair of rollerblades, dude. This is a life-or-death situation."

"Do you think I have it just lying around?" he retorts. "I need to make a few phone calls. I'll get back to you within an hour."

Judging by his stance, this is the best answer I'm gonna get from him.

If only the safety of the love of my life wasn't on the line.

32

DAISY

I blink my eyes open, out of breath and boneless. Rays of afternoon sunshine breach the wide windows, bathing everything with a soft orange hue. There's a warm feeling deep in my chest and a perceptible throbbing between my legs, yet I know I'm no longer in Phoenix's vision.

He groans from a place nearby, prompting me to sit up in bed. He's sprawled on the chair opposite me, legs spread wide and a hand covering his crotch. But the look on his face, the hunger in his eyes, sets me ablaze once more.

"Hi," I croak.

"Babe, please don't look at me like that." He sits up straighter, adjusting the visible bulge in his pants.

"Sorry. That was amazing."

"I know. I wish it didn't happen only in our minds."

"Soon, I promise. I'll learn to control my powers."

The sound of a cell phone ringtone comes from the living room.

Phoenix sighs. "It seems our time is up. I can't believe Rufio let me have this time alone with you."

Yeah, I can't believe it either. Not because I don't think he's capable of selfless gestures, but Rufio is hurting so much with this forced separation. Then there's the island god, messing with his feelings. Now that the guys aren't at each other's throats, what other nasty surprises does he have in store for us?

Phoenix stands and walks out of the room. I do the same but veer toward the luxurious bathroom that's three times the size of my room at Gifted Academy. I take a good look in the mirror. My face is flushed and a little sweaty. It looks like I've been fucked for real, not only in my imagination. My nipples harden on the spot as desire curls around the base of my spine.

Shit. I have to control myself. Staying in a permanent state of arousal won't help me. I need to focus, figure out what I'm going to do about my deal with Principal Fallon and how I'm going to help Bryce and Rufio break free from the Neo Gods' clutches.

I turn on the faucet and throw cold water on my face. It doesn't completely douse the fire in my veins, but it helps.

"Babe?" Phoenix calls from the bedroom. "We need to go."

"Coming." I comb my hair with my fingers and take a deep, steadying breath.

When I leave the bathroom, I find Phoenix burning a hole in the carpet with the way he's pacing back and forth.

"What's the matter?"

"Morpheus called. The gruesome murder of a prominent Idol figure has hit the news."

Cold dread runs down my back. "Do the police have any leads?"

"That I don't know. Did you cover your tracks, Daisy?"

"Yes. I wore a wig and a different school uniform. I tried to keep my gaze down so my face wouldn't be caught by the security cameras."

"Good. You said the Neo God fought back, right? So how did you escape?"

I nibble on my lower lip because I know Phoenix won't like my answer. "Andromeda helped me."

"What? That psycho blind chick?"

"Yes, she followed me and saved my ass. She's not a psycho, though."

Phoenix rubs his face and resumes pacing. "We don't even know which side she's on."

"I think we can rule out that she works for the Neo Gods. She killed that pig without mercy."

"One more reason for me to be suspicious of her. A rogue player can be just as dangerous as the most nefarious organization. Especially an Idol as powerful as she is." He stops pacing abruptly and whirls around, facing me with arched eyebrows. "She knows you're an Idol."

"Yeah, she knew from before."

"Fuck. Do you realize how dangerous that is?"

I close my eyes, feeling like the stupidest girl on the planet. "I'm sorry. I screwed up, okay?"

"You know what? I'm telling the guys to come meet us here. We need to figure out our next move, and it's best if we don't do it on Paragon Academy grounds."

"Yeah, you're right. I'm going to call Rosie and let her know I'll be gone for a while. What are we going to do about Toby? He's also a brand-new Idol with the power to read minds. And if I have more than one ability, he probably does or will develop another too."

"One problem at a time, babe. First, we have to make sure you're not linked to that murder."

MORPHEUS ARRIVES before Bryce and Rufio do. He's rattled, that much I can tell. The first thing he does when he steps foot in our presidential suit is engulf me in a bear hug.

"Daisy, I'm so glad you're okay. You shouldn't have gone on that mission alone. We had a deal."

"I know. I'm sorry. It won't happen again," I reply, meaning every word. I do not want to have a repeat of what happened this morning. I blindly trusted Principal Fallon's instructions, and that almost got me killed.

"My vote is for you to stop working with Fallon ASAP. The Neo Gods know you're coming for them now. They'll take precautions. If it was difficult today when you caught them by surprise, imagine if they're prepared for you," Phoenix says.

I can't argue with his logic, but how am I going to help Bryce and Rufio, then? I'm so torn about what to do. Maybe I should tell Xavier about Principal Fallon's plan. He's my uncle, after all, and he's the only adult in this game who seems to truly care about me.

"Where are Bryce and Rufio?" Phoenix asks Morpheus.

"I haven't seen them since we split up to look for Daisy."

"What part of 'we need to meet urgently' didn't they get?" Phoenix throws his hands up in the air.

"They'll be here," I say.

No sooner have the words leave my mouth than a knock comes at the door.

"Finally." Phoenix strides across the room.

We don't need to ask who's outside. If I can pick up Bryce's and Rufio's distinct signatures, so can Phoenix and Morpheus.

As soon as they enter, both of their intense gazes sweep over me, scrutinizing.

"I'm in one piece, as you can see," I say quickly before either of them decides to chastise me for taking off in secret.

"I'm not going to give you a tongue lashing, Daisy. I'm sure Morpheus and Phoenix already beat me to the punch," Bryce replies.

Rufio grumbles next to him, folding his arms. "Pretty reckless, if you ask me."

"I know." I notice the bag in Bryce's hand. "What's that?"

He pulls out a roll of dark cord. "This is what the Knights used to neutralize my powers. You're going to tie me up and remove the Neo Gods' gagging spell from my mind."

I shake my head automatically. "I can't. That's too dangerous."

"Daisy is right, Bryce. With your powers neutralized, you won't be able to stop her from unmaking you in the process," Morpheus chimes in.

"It's a risk we'll have to take. I can't have the Neo Gods' leash around my neck forever. It's the only way."

My chest feels tight. I understand his point of view, and I can relate. I walked into an extremely dangerous situation with the same motivation behind it.

"Morpheus, are you able to actually see me taking powers away?"

"Probably, yeah."

"You're really going to do this?" Rufio asks, wide-eyed.

My eyes lock with Bryce's again. "I hate this, but if you're sure that's what you want...."

"Yes, love. I'm sure."

"Okay, I'll do it with one condition." I look at Morpheus. "If you see I'm about to unmake Bryce, I want you to stop me."

"Of course."

"Let's get this started, then." Bryce sits in a chair with arms and then hands the cord to Rufio. "Make sure the knots are tight enough so I can't break free."

"You got it."

Phoenix helps Rufio with the task, and a few minutes later, Bryce is securely tied. I stop in front of him, fighting the jitters and trying to ignore the big ball of dread that's settled in my stomach. My palms are sweating thanks to the nervousness, and my mouth is unbearably dry.

"Don't be nervous, Daisy. I know you can do this," Bryce says with a smile.

I stare deep into his golden eyes, allowing myself a moment to drown in them. I love him so much. I won't be able to forgive myself if I hurt him. But I also can't live with the knowledge that there's a trap in his mind.

I take deep, steadying breaths before I place my hands on each side of his head. Immediately, I sense his energy whooshing from his body into mine, and this time there's no resistance. Bryce grunts and I almost yank my hands away, but it's like I'm glued to him. I understand now that my power, once ignited, takes control and it won't be satisfied until the Idol under my mercy has been sucked dry. The Neo God reacted fast before I could get a good hold on him. It's the only explanation for why he caught me by surprise.

The longer Bryce's essence rushes into me, the more I crave it. It's like a drug, and I'm flying high. If I stay at this rate, I'll take everything from him within a few minutes. *No! I won't be a puppet, a mere vehicle for this strange and powerful ability.* I have to retake control of my body, just like Morpheus was able to do it with his shadows.

I ignore the euphoria that's coursing through my veins and focus on the most awful memory I have of the Neo Gods. A vivid image of the blond monster who killed my father takes center stage in my mind. He represents Bryce's gag spell. I don't try to pull him into me, though. I imagine my fists turning into spiked balls, just like Andromeda's chain, and with them, I punch him repeatedly until he becomes nothing but a pound of flesh.

Strong arms circle around me, and a soothing voice whispers in my ear. "It's okay, Daisy. You can let go now. Let it go."

The fury races out of my body at once, turning my muscles into jelly. Morpheus finally manages to pull me away from Bryce, and I fall into his arms.

I blink my eyes open and find Bryce's head hanging low. *Oh no.* "Bryce!"

Rufio lifts his chin while Phoenix is busy untying him from the chair.

"Did I unmake him?"

Bryce's eyelids flutter, and then he slowly opens his eyes. "You didn't unmake me, my love. And also, the gagging spell is gone."

33

DAISY

"For real?" I ask, disbelieving that I was able to remove the block in Bryce's mind.

"Yes, for real." He smiles broadly before he stands up with Phoenix and Rufio's help. "I'd kiss you right now if I was stronger."

"Yeah, let's not push your luck, Romeo," Morpheus grumbles.

"I can walk on my own." Bryce pushes Phoenix and Rufio away.

Phoenix steps back with a wicked grin on his lips. "Fine. If you fall, I *will* laugh."

I turn to Rufio, who's staring at the Knights' special cord on the floor.

"I can try to remove your gag too," I say.

He pierces me with his intense stare, the one that makes me weak in the knees. I have to lock my legs tight to remain upright.

"Only if you're up for it," he replies.

"I'm good. I don't want those assholes to have any leverage over you."

A different emotion flashes in his electric blue eyes. A shadow of worry, if I were to guess.

"So, we're tying Rufio up?" Phoenix claps his hands. "All right."

Rufio takes the same seat as Bryce did, and this time Morpheus and Phoenix do the honors of tying him up while Bryce rests on the couch. While I wait, I scan his essence. His power is still intact inside his core, but his aura is less bright than before. Guilt sneaks into my heart despite knowing what I did was necessary. With the guilt comes restlessness too. When will I finally learn to control this terrible power? I wonder if Magia was ever able to, or if this is the type of gift that can't be tamed.

"Are you ready, Daisy?" Morpheus asks, bringing me back to the present.

"Yes. As ready as I'll ever be."

I take position in front of Rufio, and once again I'm taken over by jitters and fear. I follow the same steps as I did before by taking deep breaths and getting into the zone. Before I touch Rufio, I close my eyes and bring the image of the hateful Idol who killed my father to the forefront of my mind again. I'll be ready to obliterate the gag spell from the get-go. When my fingers make contact with Rufio's forehead, an electric current shoots straight up to my arms, locking my muscles. It's painful, and it didn't happen the previous times I've touched him. Grinding my teeth, I attempt to ride the pain silently, but a grunt escapes my lips.

"Daisy?" Morpheus concerned voice sounds far away.

I can't even answer him. This is not okay.

I open my eyes with difficulty, and finally a loud gasp comes from me. I'm no longer in the hotel room with the guys but in a dark jungle—the same jungle I saw in my dream.

"Hello?" I call out.

There's nothing but the rustling of leaves being caressed by the soft breeze until a faint cackle echoes in the distance. My breath catches as shivers run down my spine. I spin around, trying to pinpoint where the awful sound is coming from. Suddenly, the pitch-black sky lights up with a flash of lightning. The wind picks up speed, howling in a menacing way. My long hair is caught in the turbulence, flapping wildly in front my eyes. It almost feels like I'm about to face a tornado.

When another bolt strikes through the sky, a see a tall mass of swirling black smoke fast approaching me. Wisps of electricity are trapped within its massive form, flashing brightly as if they were miniature lightning bolts, which allows me to see the shape of the phenomenon.

My muscles tense, ready to run away, when a face appears in the dark smoke. Electric green eyes shine with malice while black lips are curled in an ugly grin.

The island god.

"You thought you could simply regain your powers and defy me?" He approaches, smothering me with his malignant presence. My tongue is thick in my mouth. Even if I wanted to scream, I wouldn't be able to.

"Tsk, tsk. You're more foolish than I thought, Magia. And now you and everyone you hold dear will pay."

Fear spears my chest. He's going to take his revenge against Bryce, Morpheus, Rufio, and Phoenix.

"No," I grit out with difficulty. "I won't allow you to continue torturing them. Your reign of terror is about to end."

The god throws his head back and laughs, giving me goose bumps. "Thousands of years have passed and yet you're still the same arrogant bitch who thought you could change the world. When will you learn, Magia?"

"My name is not Magia. I'm Daisy, and I will fight against evil until my last breath."

He narrows his eyes while the sky explodes in a shower of frightening lightning and booming thunder. My body is shaking, an involuntary reaction, but I lift my chin in defiance and brace for what's to come.

"I didn't kill you when you betrayed me and begged Gaia to take your powers away. But I won't make the same mistake again."

Tendrils of dark smoke shoot forward, curling around my body in a merciless vise. It has substance and it's crushing me. When the pain becomes too much, I scream, but I can still hear the vile laughter of the island god mocking my torture.

I can't die like this, trapped in a nightmare, so I focus on the power I inherited from Magia and attempt to weaken the god's powers.

"You're pathetic. Your powers don't work on me. I'm the force that moves the world, primordial, absolute. I'm the beginning, the middle, and the end."

"You... are... vile," I grit out.

"Yes, and many other things. But you'll never know. Goodbye, *Daisy*."

The shadows cover my face, sending me into an infinite void where nothing but an endless darkness exists. I lose the feeling of my body, of my mind, until I'm nothing.

MORPHEUS

Daisy has been screaming for over ten minutes, and we still can't pull her away from Rufio. We untied him as soon as we noticed something was wrong.

"She won't let go. We need to try something extreme," Phoenix says.

"Extreme like what?" I shout.

"You're the most powerful one here," Rufio replies.

"You want me to use fear to make her let go?" My voice rises to a shrill while my heartbeat doubles in speed.

"I don't think that'll work," Bryce replies. "But your shadows might."

"I can't strike her with them."

"No, but you can strike me," Rufio replies with a determined glint in his eyes.

Daisy lets out another piercing scream before she goes utterly quiet. She's still poised in front of Rufio like a statue.

"We're running out of time. Do it now, Morpheus!" Bryce urges.

"I'm sorry, Rufio."

With a brusque movement of my arm, I send a whip of dark smoke in his direction. It strikes him straight in his chest, sending him and the chair backward. Daisy remains in her spot thanks to Phoenix and Bryce, who are holding her. Immediately, she collapses in their arms as if she were a rag doll.

Phoenix steps back so Bryce can sweep her off her feet. He lies on the bed and tries to shake her awake.

"Daisy, my love. Open your eyes."

She doesn't respond, and if it weren't for the rise and fall of her chest, I'd believe her to be dead.

Rufio moves closer. "How is she?"

"Unresponsive."

Something dark leaks from Daisy's hand, an oily substance that stains the light fabric of the couch. I touch it, smearing the tips of my fingers with it. It's cold to the touch. When I bring to it my nose to take a whiff, I'm hit with a sense of familiarity.

"What is that?" Rufio asks.

"I don't know, but I think I've seen this before. It feels familiar."

Phoenix turns to Rufio. "What did you sense when Daisy was attached to you? Did she start to take your powers?"

"No, nothing like that. In fact, the moment she touched me,

it felt like she vanished from the room, not physically but her essence."

"I can't get a good read on her aura. It comes and goes," I say. "Bryce, can you heal her?"

"I'll try. But without knowing what ails her, it could be more difficult."

He kneels next to her, placing one hand in the middle of her chest and the other over her forehead. Scrunching his eyebrows together, he closes his eyes and doesn't move for a good minute. Time seems to slow down, and the longer Bryce remains with his eyes closed without moving a muscle, the more fearful I become.

Finally, he pulls his hands back and opens his eyes. "I gave her everything I have."

"Daisy." I touch her legs, shaking a little. Her skin is ice cold, but that's not the only thing I sense. My spine goes rigid in an instant. "Son of a bitch."

"What is it?" they all ask at the same time.

"Our wonderful boss, the island god, has been near Daisy. I sensed his presence just now, lingering on her skin."

"That motherfucker!" Rufio yells, kicking the chair nearby into the distance. For once, he didn't pulverize the furniture.

"What the hell did he do to her?" Phoenix looks at me, wide-eyed.

"I don't know. But we need to find someone to help us," I reply.

"There's only one person we can turn to right now." Bryce rubs his face before pulling his cell phone out.

"Who are you calling?" Rufio asks.

"Stephan."

34

RUFIO

I can't help but think that what happened to Daisy is my fault. If the island god attacked her, he did so through me. He didn't use Bryce to do it, which means I wasn't strong enough to deter him.

"How long until that douchecanoe gets here?" I ask Bryce.

"He's on his way. A few minutes tops."

No sooner does Bryce reply than a knock sounds at the door.

"For all his faults, at least he's fast." Phoenix strides across the room, but when he opens the door, it's not Stephan waiting outside. "What the—"

"Move out of the way, pretty face." Andromeda, the blind psycho chick, uses her cane to push Phoenix aside.

"What the hell are you doing here?" I take a step forward, ready to deal with her, blindness or not.

"Oh bite my heinie, emo boy. I'm here to help."

Emo boy? Who the fuck does she think she is? And how does she know Phoenix is good-looking?

"Did Stephan send you?" Bryce asks.

"Of course not." She moves forward with enough confidence that makes me suspect she's not entirely blind. When she goes straight toward the couch where Daisy is lying down, my suspicion doubles.

Morpheus blocks her way, projecting his darkest aura. Even I can sense the terrible fear he's about to unleash on the girl if she doesn't back off.

"Oh come on now. Not you too," she whines.

"You're not getting any closer to Daisy until you tell us who you're working for."

"I could indulge in your pathetic need for male reassurance, but unfortunately, Daisy doesn't have the time. So you either let me help her, or she'll be lost forever."

"Do you know what happened to her?" Phoenix asks.

"Not the details, but I can guess she's in a very dark place."

A myriad of questions runs through my head. How did she find us, and how does she know what's wrong with Daisy?

"How can you help her?" I ask instead of drilling her with questions that she most likely won't answer. "My brother and Morpheus have failed."

She smirks in my general direction. "Dude, I'm at a whole different level than you guys."

"You're only a level higher than me," Bryce retorts.

She rolls her light gray eyes. "Allegedly. Now, can you get out of the way so I can help her?"

Still staring at Andromeda through slits, Morpheus steps aside.

"You're still too close. I need space to work. Shoo." She opens her arms wide, motioning for us to retreat even farther.

Phoenix leans closer and whispers, "How does she know we're too close?"

"My eyes are sightless, but that doesn't mean I can't see," she replies without looking in our direction. "And really? Do you think I can't hear you whispering? Even if I weren't an Idol, I'd have enhanced senses, you know, with being blind and all."

"Enough talk. Are you going to help Daisy or not?" I ask.

Without another word, she turns to her. Andromeda's body begins to glow from within, a soft and warm yellow light. Then her golden chains sprout from her wrists, creating a towering circle around her and Daisy, who arches her back and lets out a painful scream.

I tense on the spot, ready to stop Andromeda, when she yells, "Don't come any closer unless you want to die."

A hand on my arm keeps me in place. I'm surprised to see it's Morpheus who's holding me. "Let her do her thing."

"Do you trust her now? What if she's hurting Daisy?"

"She isn't," he replies simply before switching his attention to the scene.

Daisy is now thrashing on the couch, but Andromeda maintains her chains in the same position. The only thing that changes is how the glowing from her weapons intensifies. It becomes so bright that I can't see Daisy and Andromeda anymore.

Another minute passes before finally I can't hear Daisy's screams. The light begins to fade, and the rattling of Andromeda's chains diminishes. When she pulls them into herself, Daisy is awake and staring at the ceiling.

Bryce is the first to get to her, pushing Andromeda out of the way without care. She staggers back and then curses under her breath. "Stupid, ungrateful boys."

"What happened?" Daisy asks as she tries to sit up.

Bryce takes her hand and helps her up. "You went into a trance of sorts. We couldn't get you to wake up."

She closes her eyes briefly, pinching the bridge of her nose. "The island god took me back to his domain. He tried to kill me."

"Where did you go?" I ask.

"At first, I was on the island of horrors, and then... I don't know. It was all dark. I couldn't even feel my body or my mind. It was almost like I had ceased to exist."

"You were trapped in another dimension—the Eternal Void, to be precise. If you had stayed there a little longer, I wouldn't have been able to find you," Andromeda chimes in.

Daisy looks up, almost if she's just noticing the girl's presence. "I guess I have to thank you again."

She shrugs, but before she can reply, Phoenix butts in. "How did Daisy get there in the first place?"

"I don't know, but only a primordial deity would be strong enough to send her there," Andromeda replies.

I trade a worried glance with Morpheus. We've always known the island god was a powerful being, but we had no idea he was a primordial god.

Fuck. We're so screwed.

"Bryce! Open up!" Stephan's loud voice, followed by his pounding on the door, interrupts the moment. Shit. I'd already forgotten my brother called him.

"Great. Mr. Pain In My Ass is here." Andromeda folds her arms and pinches her lips together.

Phoenix doesn't bother walking to the door this time. With a flick of his wrist, he opens it. Stephan and Soren barge in, ready for battle. When the older brother notices Andromeda's presence, his expression turns into a scowl.

"What are you doing here?"

"I'm being social. I thought you'd be happy." She smirks.

Soren walks around his brother and stops short when he sees Daisy is no longer in a coma. "What was the emergency?"

"It's all good now. Andromeda was able to help Daisy," Morpheus replies.

"You did?" Soren turns to the girl.

"Yes, I did. You should all be thanking me. If I hadn't sensed a great disturbance in the vicinity, Daisy would have most likely perished. Next time, just call me."

"Cocky much?" Phoenix raises an eyebrow.

"No, realistic. You should know the Silverstone brothers are always a day late and a dollar short."

"You know what? Fuck off, Andromeda. You think that just because you're blind, you can throw insults left and right. You're nothing but a pampered brat seeking attention," Soren rebuffs.

In the blink of an eye, her chains shoot out. Soren moves so fast, he becomes nothing but a blur, and the chains end up striking the far wall.

"Andy, that's enough!" Stephan grabs her arm and Andromeda tenses, but she doesn't break free from his hold.

Phoenix whistles. "Damn. Talk about poking the beast with a short stick."

"I'm not a beast," she grits out.

He raises both hands in a sign of peace, forgetting she can't see his gesture. "It was just an expression. Relax."

"How were you able to find me?" Daisy asks Andromeda.

"Through my chains. They can track anything, anywhere."

"Can they also assist in your visual handicap?" Phoenix asks, staring at her chains, which are still imbedded in the wall.

"Yes." She retracts them, leaving two gaping holes behind. If Soren hadn't moved out of the way as fast as he did, that would have been him. I've never seen anyone move that fast, which means his main gift must be supersonic speed.

Stephan steps away from her and turns to Bryce. "Now can you explain what the hell you were doing here and why you needed those special cords?" He points at the coil on the floor.

"No offense, but should we be discussing this in front of her?" I point at Andromeda.

"You don't need to worry about me, emo boy. I'm not affiliated with any of your enemies"—she turns to Stephan—"or wannabe allies."

The guy clenches his jaw tightly, and by the way his energy

field changes in nature, my guess is that Andromeda struck a nerve.

"You can speak freely in front of her. Despite her acerbic personality, Andromeda can be trusted," he replies.

She flips him off, which is a better reaction than trying to skewer him to the wall.

Bryce hesitates, and my guess is he's not concerned about Andromeda. Stephan and Soren are the sons of the Knight who kidnapped him and plotted to have Daisy's powers restored. I can't blame him for not completely trusting the duo.

"It's okay, Bryce. You can tell them." Daisy touches his arm, and immediately my brother's tense posture melts.

With a deep sigh, he replies, "Last week, my father took Rufio and me to the headquarters of the Neo Gods."

His statement drops like a bomb in the room, and for a few seconds, no one speaks.

"Son of a bitch." Stephan rubs his face and then looks at Andromeda's destruction of the wall. "We've been trying to find their hideout for years, but all clues we acquired led to a dead end."

"Don't get your hopes up, buddy. Our father made us wear blindfolds," I reply, and that's as much as I can say on the matter. I can feel the gag spell squeezing my brain already.

"Your mother said you were most likely given a test," Daisy says.

Bryce takes her hand in his. "Yes. They know the Knights have acquired a new weapon. They want us to kill you."

Daisy's face becomes as white as a sheet. "I suspected as much. What are we going to do?"

Even from where I stand, Bryce's conflict is clear in his eyes. He drops his chin and stares at Daisy's lap for a couple of beats. "We're in an impossible situation. We have until tomorrow to find and kill the weapon. If we don't comply, the Neo Gods are coming after you."

Andromeda snorts. "Oh, the irony."

Daisy squares her shoulders. "Let them come. I'll be ready for them."

"I don't want to rain on your parade, sunshine, but you couldn't handle that fat asshole without my help. How are you planning to face a horde of Neo Gods?"

"She wouldn't be facing them alone," I say.

Bryce shakes his head. "No, it's too risky. We need more time to prepare. We're dealing with high-level Idols here."

"So how do you propose we appease your father and his friends?" Stephan asks.

"I have an idea, but it requires us forgetting our morals."

"Bryce, we can't resort to anything illegal now. It's thanks to the incident with Drusilla that you fell under the Neo Gods' clutches," Daisy retorts.

I wince, even though I know she didn't mean to lay the blame for what happened on me. It was my fault, nonetheless. I was the idiot who didn't see Drusilla's trap.

"That ship has sailed, girlie. Unless murder doesn't qualify as a crime in your vocabulary." Andromeda picks her nails as if the topic of conversation wasn't a life-or-death situation.

"What do you have in mind?" Soren asks.

Bryce looks up, his eyes cold and calculating. "Do you know where we can hire an assassin?"

DAISY

With great effort, I convince the guys to let me walk to my dorm room alone with Andromeda. She's already saved me twice—three times if I count the evening I met her—but they still don't trust her completely.

We don't talk much. I'm preoccupied with the aftermath of my actions, more so than my almost deadly encounter with the island god.

The elevator pings, and she announces, "This is me. I'll *see* you later, Daisy."

"Bye."

As soon as the doors shut again, my phone rings. It's a surprise that I can get connection inside the metal box. I fish it out of my jacket pocket, and when I see it's an anonymous call, my blood freezes.

"Hello?"

"Do you have any idea the mess you've made?" Principal Fallon asks. Her voice is low and hard, which is worse than if she were shouting. Yeah, she's pissed, but so am I.

"The mess *I've* made? You said the job would be simple. You never mentioned the guy was strong enough to overpower me," I grit out.

"I said simple, never that it would be easy. I guess I overestimated you. It's my fault you were underprepared. The important thing is that the pig is dead and you weren't caught."

There are so many things that I want to say to her, but of all the people who want something from me, Principal Fallon is the one I trust the least.

"I thought you didn't want him to die."

"That wasn't the plan. But a dead Neo God is one less asshole to worry about."

She doesn't want to know how I was able to get out of that tower or if I'm okay. She's a fucking bitch. I'm about to tell her that I'm done being her lackey, but then I remember Bryce's plan. He wants me to keep pretending to be working for his mother.

"You said there would be other targets here in Hawk City."

"Yes. Unfortunately, thanks to your pitiful performance, the Neo Gods are on high alert now. A few of the targets I had planned for you are no longer in the city."

"So are you saying my work here is done?"

"No. There's one more Neo God that I want you to take out of commission. Getting to him will be more complicated."

"Why?"

"Because he's the chief of Idol police in Hawk City."

Son of a bitch.

"Are you crazy? How am I supposed to get near the guy?"

"You'll need to get caught by the cops."

I don't say anything for a couple of beats, too busy trying to control the fury that's spreading like wildfire through my veins. She truly doesn't give a fuck about me.

I arrive on my floor but remain in the elevator. I don't want anyone to overhear this conversation.

"You must be out of your mind," I grit out.

"It's the only way, Daisy. You *do* want to free Bryce and Rufio from the Neo Gods' clutches, don't you?"

Damn. The woman doesn't even attempt to mask her manipulative ways. The desire to tell her to fuck off is immense, but I can't burn this bridge yet. She has information we want. For now, I'll play the game.

"Of course I do. What do we need to do?"

"I'll send you instructions soon. In the meantime, try to stay out of trouble."

"Yes, ma'am. I have to go now." I end the call before she can say anything else.

Thanks to her, I'm more anxious than before. Going after another Neo God was already bad enough, but this new mission is suicidal. Bryce won't change his mind about his plan, though. That much I know.

I see nothing as I make my way down the corridor. I have to tell Bryce I got a new target, but I'm hesitant to do so right away. I'm still lost in my turmoil when I open the door to the apartment.

"Where have you been?" Rosie demands when I walk in.

"I needed some time alone with Phoenix," I reply, avoiding her gaze.

"You left me alone to hook up with your boyfriend?" Her voice rises to a shriek.

Great. I so don't want to deal with Rosie's antics right now.

"I didn't leave you alone. Are you going to tell me you didn't spend all this time with Toby?"

Her cheeks become bright red, and she avoids my gaze. That's what I thought. I do feel guilty for abandoning her, but it wasn't like I had a choice.

"Yeah, we did. But still. I thought we would spend more time together here, and so far I've barely seen you."

Guilt sneaks into my heart. It's not Rosie's fault that I'm in such a mess.

"I know. I'm sorry. Let's go out tonight, just the two of us."

She nibbles on her lower lip and seems to ponder my suggestion. "Where would we go?"

"We could catch a movie or have dinner at a hole-in-the-wall restaurant."

"Only if we go to a place where Idols won't be around. I've had an overload of them to last me a lifetime."

So stupid Toby hasn't told her yet about his status upgrade. Can't he see that the longer he waits, the worse it'll be for him?

She cocks her head to the side. "What's the matter?"

Shit. I didn't know I was making a face. "Nothing." I shake my head. "We can go to Station 33 Mall. No Idol will be caught dead there."

Rosie's eyes light up. "We always had the best time there. Do you think the old arcade still exists?"

"Why don't you look it up online while I take shower?"

Rosie claps her hands together and lets out a squeak. "I hope it is. How many hours did we spend playing Battle of the Giant Gorilla?"

My lips curl into a genuine smile. "Countless."

"Do you think Solaine still works there?"

"I don't know, Rosie. It's been ten years. She might have moved on to a better job." The moment the words leave my mouth, I hear the falsehood in them. Norms don't usually move on to better jobs.

Rosie's smile wilts a fraction. She turns to the window, almost as if she wants to hide her disappointment. Solaine was a teen girl who worked at the old arcade every day after school. She adored Rosie and used to give her free tokens all the time. I do hope she left that job, maybe even to go to college.

"All right, let me get ready so we can go," I say.

Once in the shower, I don't need to pretend everything is fine for Rosie's sake. The magnitude of what I went through today hits me hard. The only reason I don't bawl my eyes out is because I'm tired of crying. I was almost killed twice in the span of a few hours, and I know this is only the beginning. Staying strong is the only way I can survive what's to come. But I'm done with doom for the day. I'll have a good time with Rosie tonight, no matter what.

The most difficult part of the plan is to convince the guys to let me go out with Rosie alone. It would be easier if we just snuck out, but I can't do that to them twice in a day. Ugh, and if I tell them I got a call from Fallon, my chances of convincing them goes from hard to impossible. I'd better text Bryce when I'm on my way to the mall.

When I get out of the shower, Rosie points at my cell. "Tell your boyfriends to stop blowing up your phone. Don't they know clinginess is an unattractive trait?"

"Who's been calling me?" I ask.

She gives me a droll stare. "Duh, all of them."

I grab my phone, worried that I have another disaster to deal with. When I read the text messages, my shoulders sag forward. "Rosie, did you already tell Toby about our plans for tonight?"

"Yes. Was I not supposed to?" She arches both eyebrows.

"It's not that. But now I know why the guys are hounding me."

"Tell them to stop being such whiny babes. It's not like you're defenseless. You're an Idol, for crying out loud."

"Well, I don't think they'll ever stop worrying about me."

And they have reason to, but I can't tell Rosie that.

"Are you ready?" I ask her.

"Yup. And guess what? The old arcade is still there."

"Awesome." I force a smile. I wish my enthusiasm was real, but the prospect of convincing my boyfriends to let me go out in Hawk City alone is akin to a visit to the dentist.

I click on the newest message on my phone, the one from

Rufio, and reply that I'll meet them in the front courtyard in five minutes.

When Rosie and I step out of the elevator at ground level, I can sense them before I get a visual. They each have their signature essences, but right now their rattled moods are almost identical. Damn. This is going to be a battle of wills.

As we reach the courtyard, they turn as one in my direction with matching scowls. My mood plummets to below zero. Winning this argument will be like shoving shit uphill with a fork.

In a surprising move, Rosie steps in front of me and declares, "Don't even think about pooping on my parade. Daisy and I are going out alone tonight, and I don't want to hear a peep of complaining."

Rufio rolls his eyes. "Yeah, right. Nice try, baby shark."

"I'm serious." Rosie curls her hands into fists.

I glance at Bryce, who seems amused by Rosie's bravery display. He turns his attention to me and asks, "Do you think it's a good idea to saunter off alone in Hawk City today of all days?"

I open my mouth to reply, but Rosie beats me to the punch. "I don't see the big deal. Why can't we have a girls' night out without you guys losing your minds over it?"

"Daisy knows why," Morpheus replies, leveling me with a stern expression.

Crap on toast. The guys are right to be worried, but if I cave, I'll never hear the end of it from Rosie.

"What's going on here?" Andromeda asks, coming into the courtyard out of nowhere. The girl has a penchant for stepping in when we least expect her. I wonder if she's a spy.

"Oh, not you again," Rufio grumbles.

"Bite me, emo boy," she fires back. "So what's the deal? Are we hitting the town or what?"

I look at her with a question in my gaze, forgetting for a moment that she can't really see my expression.

"Wait, are you going out with them?" Phoenix asks.

Rosie turns to me with eyebrows furrowed and pinched lips. I don't need to read minds to know she thinks I invited Andromeda to tag along. I'm not sure when she thinks I had the time to do so. My phone was sitting right next to her when I hit the shower.

"Yup." Andromeda winks in my general direction. Maybe she overheard the dilemma and is just trying to help.

"Do you feel better now that it's not only Rosie and me?" I make a point to look each one of the guys in the eye.

Toby scratches the back of this neck and glances at Rosie. "I thought you wanted a break from Idols."

"I did." Rosie glowers at me.

"I can pretend to be a Norm." Andromeda smiles innocently.

"I suppose I do feel a little better that Andromeda is tagging along," Bryce replies. "Where are you going?"

"To Station 33 Mall. It's mainly a Norm hangout with the occasional low-level Fringes," I reply.

"You aren't seriously considering letting them go?" Rufio retorts.

"Letting me go? Did I miss the part when I suddenly became your property?" I throw him a death glare.

"Preach, sister," Andromeda chimes in.

Rufio has the decency to show some remorse in his gaze. "I didn't mean it like that."

"Going to a Norm hangout is probably the safest place for Daisy right now," Morpheus adds.

Rufio throws his hands up in the air. "I give up."

"That's the only smart course of action for you." Andromeda laughs, earning an irate glance from him.

Bryce stops in front of me, circling my waist with his arms. "Please be careful, Daisy. I can't go through that torment again."

"What torment?" Rosie asks.

Shit, of course Rosie would pick up on his comment.

"Ignore my brother. He has a flair for the dramatic." Rufio waves his hand dismissively.

I grin in his direction, and then reply to Bryce. "I'll be careful. Besides, you know how ruthless Andromeda is."

He peers in the girl's direction. "Yeah, I know, which doesn't comfort me. She could very well be working for the enemy."

"Right. I'm working for the enemy. Good grief." She shakes her head and then begins to twirl her cane between her fingers.

"You don't need to worry about her. Seriously. I'm a pretty good judge of character, and my danger alarm hasn't been triggered by her."

"Well, keep your cell phone on you at all times." He kisses me briefly on the lips and steps back.

"I will. Promise."

I glance at Rufio, but he's sulking and not looking in my direction. Morpheus and Phoenix are both staring at me wearing matching worried countenances. I would say a proper goodbye to both if we weren't out in the open; I'm still not completely comfortable showing to the world that I'm in love with four guys.

"Let's go, then, before some kind of disaster strikes." Andromeda veers toward the street. "You're a chaos magnet, after all."

I really wish I could offer a retort to that, but truer words have never been spoken.

36

BRYCE

"So, are you guys planning to do anything tonight?" Toby asks.

We've never hung out before, and I can tell he's unsure of what his place is. I wish I could tell him to get lost—we really shouldn't be adding to our party if we want to avoid detection—but I don't know how to do so without sounding like an ass.

"Daisy told us you can read minds now," Rufio says bluntly. "Can you do that now?"

His face goes from white to bright red in zero point five seconds. "Not really. I'm not very good at it, to be honest."

I scan him again, confirming what my mother was already able to assess. Toby is indeed an Idol, but barely. He's between levels ten and eleven.

"You've learned to tone down your powers fast."

"Yeah. Principal Fallon taught me."

That's news to me, and not the good kind.

"When did you spend time with my mother?" I ask.

"Right before our trip. We only had enough time for me to

learn the power-masking trick, but she promised to teach me how to use my new abilities."

Of course she would take an interest in Toby. An Idol with the ability to read minds is the perfect asset to her shady agenda. Fuck, we really need to set him straight about her.

"Listen, Toby. I wouldn't be too quick to trust her. We can show you how to use your abilities."

His brows furrow. "Why would you say that about your own mother?"

"You know nothing, dude," Phoenix chimes in.

Toby narrows his gaze and crosses his arms. "Don't treat me like I'm a kid."

"We aren't. And to prove that, you're coming with us tonight," I say.

"Wait a second," Phoenix interrupts. "We're planning on following the girls, right?"

"No, we're not," I reply calmly.

"Are you out of your mind? We shouldn't let Daisy out of our sight. What if the island god returns?"

"She's with Andromeda, the only one who was able to help her before," Morpheus replies.

"Island god? What are you talking about?" Toby asks.

My phone vibrates in my pocket. It's a message from Daisy. I knew this was coming, but I can't help the anger that sweeps over me when I read her text.

"What now?" Rufio asks.

"Mommy dearest gave Daisy another target, so you know what that means."

"Are you sure you want to do that?" Morpheus watches me intently.

"Yes. It's the only way."

"This could very well blow up in our faces," Phoenix remarks.

Hell. I thought we were over this second-guessing bullshit.

It took almost an hour to convince everyone to get on board with the plan.

"I'm totally lost now. Can someone explain what's going on?" Toby looks left and right, no doubt trying to guess the answer from our facial expressions—or read our minds.

"Why are you all trying to backpedal? Even the Silverstone brothers agreed to help," I retort. "They were the first ones to agree."

"And you're not even a little bit concerned about that part? How do they even know who to contact in the first place?" Rufio replies.

I pinch the bridge of my nose and count to ten. "Probably because they've been fighting the Neo Gods for much longer than we have. Let's not forget we just opened our eyes to the real world."

Rufio stares at me without blinking for several beats. Then with a grunt, he says, "Fine. Call Stephan already."

TO AVOID DRAWING ATTENTION, we agree to meet Stephan and Soren far away from Paragon Academy. We're at a pub right smack in the middle of the touristy part of town. We didn't talk much during the cab ride, but we've been waiting for the Silverstone brothers for over fifteen minutes now, so we used that time to fill Toby in on what we plan to do. I'm positively surprised how well he took everything for a Norm who just suddenly became an Idol.

I'm about to call Stephan again when I spot him and his brother making their way through the crowd.

"Fuck. About time," Rufio blurts out.

"Sorry, princess. Arranging the meeting you requested wasn't that easy." Stephan returns the glower.

"What, you don't have mobsters on speed dial?" Phoenix grins.

Soren narrows his gaze, and I can sense he's about to fall for Phoenix's goading, so I speak before he can. "But it has been arranged, right?"

"Yeah, but we can't meet this guy with an entourage. It's only going to be you and me."

"Fuck that," Rufio retorts angrily. "We're all going."

"He's right, Rufio. It's best if only the two of us go meet this person. A large group would only draw attention," I reply.

"I still think this plan is foolhardy. You're risking your neck for Neo God recruits, and we don't even know if it'll work out," Soren pipes up.

"We're not Neo God recruits. Not by choice anyway," I grit out.

"I can come too and no one will know I'm there," Morpheus chimes in.

"You can become invisible?" Soren's eyes widen.

"In a way. I'm a master of shadows."

"Okay, that's settled, then. We leave now and will be back in an hour," Stephan announces. "Please try to behave while we're gone." He looks pointedly at his brother.

"I can behave as long as they do." Soren stares at Rufio and Phoenix.

"Don't worry. I'll make sure everyone gets along," Toby replies.

MORPHEUS

I do think Bryce's plan is crazy with a mega low rate of success. But I also know we're out of options. The Neo Gods have us by the balls. We don't have any illusions that we're way out of our depth dealing with them, but protecting Daisy is our main priority. We'll risk everything to keep her safe.

This isn't my first visit to Hawk City, but like most Idols, I've only stuck to the most prominent neighborhoods such as the one where Paragon Academy is located. They're all a far cry from the place we're at, a seedy area even powerful Idols should avoid.

It's not the landscape that lets someone know they've ventured into an entirely different world but the ominous vibe in the air that clings to you in the most oppressive way. A foul energy seems to crawl out from every crack in the asphalt. It's almost like pure evil lives here. It's no wonder the small hairs on the back of my neck are standing on end.

The sun set a long time ago, and the few people in the streets scurry by as if afraid to be caught out in the open for too long.

I've been concealing all of us since we left the pub at Marvel Square. The Neo Gods must be following Bryce and Rufio, and we definitely don't want them to know where we're going. For that reason, we took public transportation instead of a cab. Stephan wanted me to stop concealing them once we got near our final destination, but I shot down that idea hard. I'm not taking any chances.

Without saying another word, he takes us to an unsavory bar where the neon sign's letters are only half lit and graffiti takes up most of the front wall. One scribble catches my attention. It says "death to all Norms," and below it is a symbol I don't recognize. Could it be the Neo Gods' insignia?

Stephan avoids the front door, veering toward the narrow alleyway between the buildings.

"Okay. We're here now. You need to make us visible again," he says.

I peer over my shoulder to make sure we haven't been followed. I don't see anyone on the main street, but it's impossible to tell if we're being spied on from a top window from one of the buildings. I release them from my shadows, though, since I don't have a choice.

Inside the bar is smoky and dim. At once, I'm blasted with the collective animosity wave the patrons are emanating. They spare a fleeting glance in Bryce and Stephan's direction before returning to their drinks. I scan the room thoroughly, taking inventory of the assortment of individuals we're dealing with here. It's a good mix of low-level Idols and high-level Fringes. No one who comes near us is in power, but we're most certainly outnumbered. If this turns sour, we can't fight them all.

For that reason, I check all exit points. There's the door we came in, and to the right of the bar, I see another door with a faded "Exit" sign above it. I'm banking there's also a back door used by the employees to get rid of the trash.

Stephan heads for the pool table area where a group of mean-looking Idols is playing. A mountain man is about to take a shot when Stephan steps closer. The Idol lifts his gaze away from the ball for a split second, resulting in a bad shot. His demeanor changes completely, and I can guess who he's going to blame for his lack of concentration.

I prepare to intervene, but the lights above the table begin to flicker as crackles of energy surround Bryce's body. The aggressiveness from the big guy recedes, but now everyone in the vicinity is staring at the duo. So much for conducting this meeting without drawing attention. Wishful thinking on my part. When do things ever go easy for us?

Stephan seems to have missed Bryce's little demonstration, or at least he's pretending to be oblivious. Without missing a beat, he continues his trek to a lonely booth at the end of the room where the only source of illumination is coming from the pinball machine nearby. But I don't need light to see the woman sitting there. She's an Idol, level thirteen if she's not tuning her power down.

Stephan slides onto the booth seat across from the mysterious woman, and Bryce follows suit. I remain closer to the pool table area to make sure my essence is concealed. According to Stephan, this is no ordinary Idol. She's one of the most dangerous criminals in Hawk City. No one can reach that status without some serious ability to scan for threats.

"I didn't expect to see two teens when I got the call," she says.

"The money is the same no matter the source. We heard that if we want someone to disappear without a trace, you're the one for the job," Stephan replies.

"You heard correctly. Did you bring the agreed amount?"

Stephan slides a manila envelope across the table, which disappears under a gloved hand.

"A picture of the target is also in there."

The assassin fishes out a piece of paper, and immediately I sense a change in her demeanor. My muscles tense while I gather my shadows around my hands and wrists.

"Are you out of your mind?" the woman whisper-shouts.

"What's the matter? You can't handle the job?" Bryce asks.

"I can handle any job. But this is... suicide."

A commotion behind me draws my attention. I turn to the source, finding all the guys who were playing pool a second ago gathered in front of one of the TVs mounted on the wall. I'd dismiss it as nonsense, but then I catch sight of a big structure on fire. My blood runs cold when I read the caption.

It's Station 33 Mall.

Daisy is there.

37

DAISY

I'm nervous during the ride to the mall. I texted Bryce that I got a new target as I had promised I would. Now he's probably busy putting his plan in motion. I hate that it involves hiring an assassin to do the job Principal Fallon gave me. It's all a setup. The assassin will attempt to kill my target, and Bryce and Rufio will show up and kill her instead. Then they'll tell the Neo Gods the assassin was the Knights' new weapon. Basically, Bryce and Rufio are hiring a decoy.

Rosie is still sulking when we arrive at the mall despite Andromeda's many attempts to lighten the mood. I know I just met the girl, but I'll miss her when I return to Saturn's Bay. She's actually been pretty interesting and fun.

She insists on paying for the ride, which only adds to Rosie's aggravation.

"Does she think we're a charity case or something?" Rosie whispers to me, but I know she doesn't care if Andromeda overhears.

"Please, Rosie. Try to be nice. She's not like the other Idols," I say.

"I know your name is Rose, but you don't need to be so

prickly." Andromeda grins innocently, but all she does is ruffle my sister's feathers.

"I'm not prickly. I don't like Idols, and with reason." She puts her hands on her hips to emphasize her point.

"Really? Then why the hell are you dating one?" Andromeda raises an eyebrow.

Ah, crap.

"Toby is not an Idol," Rosie replies through clenched teeth.

Andromeda opens her mouth, but I cut her off. "Let's go into the mall already. It's getting late, and I don't want to miss all the fun inside."

"I see what you're doing, Daisy. This is to be continued," Andromeda replies.

In the blink of an eye, she masks her powers, so now no one can tell she's not a Norm. Rosie glances fleetingly in my direction, enough for me to see the storm of bad emotions shining in her eyes. Great. I've barely managed to make up with her after I became an Idol, and now I'm back on her bad side.

I try to push my problems to the side as I pass through the sliding doors into the place where Rosie and I spent much time of our childhood. We couldn't afford to buy anything from the stores, but there was the old arcade and the cinema, plus it was fun to simply people watch. It was also much safer to play inside the mall than venture out in the few public parks in the Norm side of town. I'm not sure if things have gotten worse, but ten years ago, Fringe gangs used to terrorize some Norm neighborhoods, including ours.

Rosie is walking a little ahead of us with her arms crossed. Andromeda is next to me, using her cane to guide her.

"I'm sorry I created a rift between you and your sister. I was just trying to help you sneak out without your boyfriends."

"I know. And I appreciate it. I used to be like her."

"Let me guess. You hated Idols with a passion."

"Yeah. Our parents were murdered by Neo Gods. We escaped thanks to Mr. Silverstone."

"Stephan's father," she adds.

"Yup. What's the deal between you and him, if you don't mind me asking?"

"No deal. He's my advisor, and he thinks it gives him the right to control my life."

"He told us you just recently joined Paragon Academy. You were homeschooled, right?"

"Yup. My parents are super protective of me because, you know, my blindness."

"Do they know what you can do with your chains?"

"Not really. I don't want to terrify them. Don't get me wrong, they know about my chains, but I keep my powers contained around them. They have no idea I'm an eighteen."

Her confession reminds me of Morpheus's story. His father was also terrified of him.

Rosie stops in front of the old arcade. It's called 1001 Games, the biggest false advertisement on Earth. I'd be surprised if the arcade has more than fifty different games.

"What is this place?" Andromeda furrows her brows. "I'm picking up a lot of different wave frequencies."

"It's the old arcade. We used to spend countless hours here when we were kids."

"I didn't realize you lived in Hawk City."

"Yeah."

Rosie looks over her shoulder, moving her long straight hair like a whip. "Are you done chatting? I'd like to spend some time with you too."

"Go on. You're already in the doghouse thanks to me," Andromeda says.

I walk ahead, joining Rosie as we enter the establishment. The smell of old carpet and stale popcorn is familiar and welcoming. It brings back a myriad of feelings, and I'm surprised at how overwhelmed I am by them. I have to clench my jaw hard to maintain my composure. We head for the ticketing counter, and I'm glad to see it's not Solaine working behind it. As much as I'd love to see her, I'd be mega depressed if she was still working here after all these years.

A friendly, tanned teen smiles at us. His name tag says Cory. "Welcome to 1001 Games. How can I help you?"

"We'd like ten tokens each, please," I reply.

"Gladly. You're in luck. We just got Battle of the Giant Gorilla back. It was out of commission for a while."

"Awesome. It's our favorite game," Rosie replies excitedly.

Her change in attitude makes me feel like the trip here won't be a complete disaster after all. If she could just get past her Idol hatred and give Andromeda a chance.

Andromeda approaches the desk, and I notice an instant change in Cory's demeanor.

"Oh, I'm sorry. We don't have any games suited for the visually impaired."

"Don't worry about it, kid. I'll manage." She slides a fifty-dollar bill across the counter. "This should cover it."

Before he can take Andromeda's money, I push her hand away. "No way. You're not paying for this too. This is my treat."

Andromeda turns to me, staring with her unseeing eyes. She blinks a couple of times before shrugging. "Okay. Fine by me."

"Can I ask you a question?" Rosie addresses Cory.

"Sure," the kid replies.

"Does Solaine still work here?"

His face turns ashen in the blink of an eye. "Ah shit, you knew her?"

"Yeah, she used to give me free tokens all the time," Rosie replies. "What happened to her?"

"She died two years ago."

I can't breathe or utter a single word for a couple of beats as

I process the news. Then comes the acute pain in my chest, like a dagger, burrowing its way in.

"How did she die?" I ask, fighting the choke in my voice.

"The local police said it was a robbery gone wrong, but we all know it was this new Fringe gang who think they're something akin to gods."

"Why would Fringes have the notion that they're gods?" Andromeda asks.

"I don't know. Maybe because they're high level and most of the folks who live in this area are Norms." Cory's eyes flash with anger. At least it's not fear. Angry people have the will to fight against oppression; scared people don't.

I shake my head, trying to dispel the sadness. "Can we have our tokens, please?"

"Yeah, sure. Here you go."

I sense someone staring at me so intently that it's burning a hole through my face. With tokens in hand, I confirm Rosie is the one glowering at me.

"I can't believe you still want to play after you heard that awful news."

"What do you want me to do, Rosie? Sit down with my head in my hands and cry?"

"It's like you don't even care that she died. Is that because you're no longer one of us?" she retorts angrily.

Worried, I glance at Cory, but he didn't seem to notice Rosie's outburst. I grab her arm and drag her away from him. "Shh. Do you want to blow our cover?"

She lifts both hands in a mocking gesture. "Oh, I'm sorry. Far be it from me to ruin your charade."

"Let's play some Battle of the Giant Gorilla and forget about it, okay?" I plead, not wanting to keep feeding her anger.

No sooner do I say that than a loud explosion somewhere in the mall rattles the floor and machines near us. A second later, the panicked screams of several people trickle down to us, but they get muffled by another explosion, and another.

"What the hell is going on?" I ask, temporarily paralyzed by fear.

"Come on! We have to get out of here," Andromeda shouts.

The urgency in her tone propels me into action. I take Rosie's hand, and together we follow Andromeda toward the arcade's exit. But when I notice Cory's feet sticking out from the side of the counter, I stop.

"Wait."

Andromeda glances over her shoulder. "What is it?"

"We can't leave Cory behind." I backtrack toward the counter and find Cory sitting on the floor, holding his knees together. "Come on. You can't stay here." I offer him my hand, which he mercifully doesn't hesitate to take.

The four of us run toward the arcade's exit, but thick smoke has spread throughout the main atrium. Thanks to my enhanced Idol senses, I can discern different sounds. There are the voices of several people who are either asking for help or crying, but there's also the crackling of fire and the dry twig-snapping noise of circuitry as it dies. Even with my Idol vision, I can't see much ahead of us, but it's incredibly hot, which means fire is coming toward us.

"We can't go out through the main mall exit," I say.

Andromeda forgets about hiding her powers, releasing her golden chains.

"Holy crap! You're an Idol," Cory exclaims.

We all ignore his outburst and pay attention to what Andromeda is doing. Her chains creep forward like a snake slithering on the floor. She remains as still as a statue, but I notice her eyes are also glowing gold now.

"What is she doing?" Rosie asks.

"I don't know."

"We definitely can't go out the way we came in," Andromeda replies. "We have to find an alternative exit point."

"Does the arcade have a back door?" I ask Cory.

"Y-Yes. It opens to a corridor that leads to the service exit."

"Let's go, then." I grab Rosie's hand and turn toward the back of the arcade.

"What if that exit is also blocked, Daisy?" Rosie asks fearfully.

"Then we'll find another way out." I look her in the eye. "We're getting out of here, Rosie. I promise."

Cory almost takes the back door off its hinges as he slams against it. I let Andromeda go after him first, then push Rosie forward. There's smoke in the corridor to my right, but it's not as bad as in the front of the store.

"Which way?" I ask.

Before Cory can reply, an explosion to our right sends us flying backward, only we don't hit the floor hard. Instead, we float on air, moving in slow motion. As it had happened before, my time-bending gift kicked in without me willing it so. For that reason, I can see clearly the fireball that's coming our way, but time bending or not, I can't stop it from hitting us.

Andromeda's chains fly forward at lightning speed while we're still trapped in slow motion. They aren't affected by my power, it seems. They form a protective barrier in front of us, blocking us from the fire. We finally hit the floor softly, and time resumes to normal. Andromeda holds her chains in place for another minute, and for the first time, I notice her struggle with the task. Her face is twisted into a grimace, and her jaw is locked tight. It becomes unbearably hot as the raging fire tries to break through her chains.

Shit. Will she be able to hold the barrier long enough?

"What are you fools waiting for? Run," she grits out.

I jump to my feet, pulling Rosie with me. Cory spares

Andromeda one fleeting glance before bolting in the opposite direction. I hesitate, not wanting to leave Andromeda behind.

Rosie tugs my hand. "Come on. We have to get out of here."

"Listen to your sister," Andromeda pants. "Go now. I can't hold the chains up for much longer."

"No. I won't leave you behind." I turn to Rosie. "You go. Don't stop until you're out of the building."

Rosie's eyes grow as round as saucers. "I can't leave you."

A loud grunt escapes Andromeda's lips before her chains drop to the floor, listless. Without a second thought, I throw my hands forward, willing time to stop again. Maybe I can delay the flames long enough for us to run out of their reach.

There's no need, though. The fire has died, leaving behind a scorched mess.

"Shit! That was close," Andromeda says, leaping to her feet.

"Let's go before there's another explosion."

"How fast can you run?" she asks me.

"I don't know."

"Probably faster than your sister."

I get what she's saying. Being Idols, we can reach the exit much faster than Rosie.

"Jump on my back," I tell Rosie.

For once, she doesn't argue with me. Even with the added weight, I run like the wind, keeping pace with Andromeda. Her chains are out, and my guess is she's using them to guide her to the exit. In less than a minute, we reach the mall's side door.

Outside, the world is in chaos. It's a cacophony of sirens, helicopters flying over us, trucks, and distressed people. I search the crowd, trying to find Cory, but it's dark and busy. It was a straight shoot down the corridor, so he must have found the way out.

Firefighters immediately usher us out of the danger zone, asking if we're hurt. In a daze, I glance at the mall. We exited through the left side, but I can see the other end of the building has collapsed and is in flames. Shit. We got lucky.

My thoughts are premature, though. Whoever orchestrated this attack wanted to level the mall. Andromeda's chains react a second before another huge blasts rocks the ground we stand on. Instinctively, I use my time-bending gift as well, so when the explosion would have knocked everyone down, now it turns into a dark cloud of smoke and debris that expands at a crawl.

"Everyone move back!" a firefighter shouts.

I lose sight of Rosie for a minute, too focused on managing my powers. This is all new to me, and I have to concentrate.

"What should we do?" I ask Andromeda when the cloud of destruction gets near us.

"Retreat slowly."

I'm not sure how long it takes for us to reach a safe distance from the blast, but when we do, my muscles are shaking and I feel drained. Dizziness takes a hold of me. I'm about to collapse to the ground when strong arms wrap around me.

Without glancing back, I know it's Bryce holding me tight.

"You're okay. Thank heavens you're okay," he whispers in my ear.

I sense Morpheus's presence but not Rufio's or Phoenix's. I'm about to ask where they are when my stomach bottoms out.

I can't see Rosie anywhere.

She's gone.

38

RUFIO

My heart has been stuck in my throat since I saw the news. Phoenix and I couldn't get out of that pub fast enough. Knowing traffic near the mall would be completely blocked, we didn't even try to catch a cab. Instead, we bolted down the busy street, running as fast as our legs would take us.

Soren and Toby catch up with us, and then without a word, Soren blazes past us, becoming nothing but a blur. He's gone in the blink of an eye. I've never envied another Idol's ability until now. Getting to Daisy as fast as I can is paramount to me.

The closer we get to the mall; the crazier the traffic becomes. I hear different sirens in the distance, followed by the sound of helicopters flying over our heads. I wonder if the Neo Gods are behind the attack at the mall. Who else would want to kill a bunch of Norms in one fell swoop?

When the streets are blocked by a mob of people running in the opposite direction, we have no choice but to jump over cars and buses. It takes a herculean effort on my part not to obliterate everything in my path. The only reason I rein in my destructive nature is the knowledge that Daisy would hate me if

I hurt anyone. But if there's even one scratch on her, I won't hold back. I will destroy every single person responsible for it, collateral damage be damned.

"Guys, wait!" Toby yells. "I think I see Rosie."

He doesn't wait for us before he changes course. Without missing a beat, we follow him. It takes me a second to get a visual on the blonde girl who's being pushed by the crowd. It's indeed Rosie, but there's no sign of Daisy anywhere.

"Rosie!" Toby yells.

She looks in his direction and raises her arm, but someone shoves her to the side, knocking her down. She disappears from view. Shit, the mob will crush her.

Suddenly, the sea of people surrounding her parts as if being pushed by a great force. I'm not sure if it's Phoenix or Toby doing it. After all, we still don't know if the former Norm can do more than read minds.

Toby jumps off the car, landing into a crouch next to his girlfriend. He pulls her into his arms, crushing her into a bear hug. For the second time today, I envy him.

Phoenix gets to the couple first, and without missing a beat, he pulls them apart.

"Where is Daisy?" he asks.

"I-I don't know," Rosie stammers. "I got separated from her when our side of the mall exploded. She and Andromeda tried to contain the blast."

Fear spears my chest. "Are you saying she's using her gifts in public?"

"Yeah. She was trying to save people," Rosie replies with a glare in my direction.

"We can't worry about that now. Let's find her," Phoenix replies.

"Come on, Rosie. I'll take you to safety." Toby lifts the girl into his arms, and then he leaps on top of a nearby car.

She gasps. "You're an Idol."

Phoenix is already on the move, going toward the towering inferno that used to be the mall. I run after him, missing Toby's reply.

Without slowing down, I search for Daisy in the crowd with my eyes and my extra senses. It takes me a minute to find her signature, and my guess is Phoenix has also caught on to it, because we both veer left. I finally get a visual of her. She's in Bryce's arms. Thank fuck. Morpheus, Stephan, Soren, and Andromeda are also there.

Pushing my legs to the max, I run ahead of Phoenix. When I leap near Daisy and Bryce, I push my brother off her and pull her into my arms, ignoring the danger of such an action.

"You're okay," I murmur against her neck.

She hugs me back, making me dizzy in an instant. "It was close, but we managed."

"Rufio, you ne—" Morpheus starts.

"Not now," I cut him off, then capture Daisy's face between my hands and kiss her like the world is about to end.

For a blissful moment, she returns my passion beat by beat, but then she tenses. I feel her resistance, but I can't let go.

"For fuck's sake," Andromeda murmurs a second before my body is ensnared by an energy field and I'm yanked from Daisy's arms.

I stagger back, and maybe I'd have fallen on my ass if it weren't for the glowing chains coiled around my body.

"Are you out of your mind?" Bryce glowers at me.

I'm ready to offer him an angry retort when terrified screams erupt in the distance. Andromeda's chains release me, and for a split second, I believe my legs are going to give out from under me. Morpheus wraps his fingers around my forearm, steadying me.

"Are you all right?" he asks.

"Yeah," I lie. The world around me is spinning, and it feels like all my energy has drained from me.

I test my powers. My chest warms as my essence churns. Daisy didn't take it all. Tingles run down my arms, and when I lift my hands, dark sparks appear on the tips of my fingers.

A wave of people trying to get away from the newest threat pushes us forward, and we're soon surrounded by chaos. I catch Phoenix's stare, reading in his eyes his intention to use telekinesis to stop those people from crushing us.

"You can't use your powers against them!" Daisy yells over the cacophony, guessing where his train of thought was.

"We have to get out of here or we'll be crushed," Morpheus interjects.

In the blink of an eye, Stephan soars skyward, taking Andromeda with him. Son of a bitch. The motherfucker can fly, and he chose to save the blind girl over his own brother.

"Wow, your brother is a piece of work," I tell Soren.

"Shut your mouth. You don't know what he's doing."

"Looks like he's running away," I retort.

Soren's expression twists into a scowl, but I don't get to hear his response as a dark whip coils around his neck and drags him back. In the mob, I see who has the end of the whip. It's the good-looking Neo God chick Bryce and I met yesterday.

My suspicions are finally confirmed. They're behind this.

"Let him go!" Bryce steps forward, but he's quickly trapped by another whip. I can't see who's holding the leash this time, but I sense more Idols approaching us.

This is a fucking trap.

I attempt to use my powers against the girl choking the life out of Soren, but a terrible pain in my head renders me powerless. The gag spell also prevents me from attacking them. Hell and damn.

"You can't fight them. Get Daisy out of here," Morpheus urges.

"No, I won't leave you guys," she rebuffs. "I can help."

We all know she can, but there's a slim chance the Neo

Gods don't know about her yet. We're not about to let her reveal her powers to them.

I grab her hand and steer her away from the Neo Gods. "Come on, Daisy. Don't fight us on this."

With the contact, I become weak again, but I fight against the lethargy. I won't fail Daisy now. Instead of thinking about the draining of my powers, I focus on getting us out of the crushing crowd. I can't use my powers against these people, but I can shove and elbow my way through.

We finally reach a side street away from the epicenter, and by that time, I'm already seeing dark spots across my vision.

Daisy pulls her hand from mine and stares wide-eyed at me.

"Rufio, I'm so sorry."

I lean against the building nearest me and close my eyes for a second. "I'll be okay. I just need a minute."

Only I don't get a minute. I hear feet shuffling down the alleyway, followed by the shattering of glass. All my senses are on high alert as I scan the dark street. Immediately, I pick up a familiar signature. Toby.

He shuffles into the dim light, revealing his awful condition. Bleeding and bruised, he's holding his torso as if he's in great pain.

"Toby!" Daisy runs to him.

I expand my search, trying to locate Daisy's sister. The last time I saw the girl, she was with Toby. No sign of her anywhere now, which isn't surprising considering the state Toby is in.

"What happened to you?" she asks.

"We... were... ambushed," he replies.

"We?"

I amble forward, and with each step, my strength returns. I'm going to need it, because I know exactly what Toby's answer will be.

"Rosie and me. They took her, Daisy. Even with my new Idol powers, I couldn't stop them," Toby whimpers.

"Who took my sister?" Daisy shrieks.

The answer is on the tip of my tongue, but I can't reply thanks to the Neo Gods' hold on my mind.

"We did," a sinister male voice replies from the shadows where Toby came from.

Ah, shit. It's Delta, my father's henchman.

Daisy gasps, drawing my attention to her.

"You," she murmurs.

Delta curls his lips into an ugly grin. "We meet again, dirty brat."

I scramble through my brain, trying to figure out when the hell Daisy and Delta met. The answer smacks me right in the forehead. I should have guessed sooner.

Delta was part of the Neo Gods' assassins sent to kill Daisy's family.

Son of a bitch.

39

DAISY

I thought countless times about what I would do if I came face-to-face with the man who killed my father. Now that the moment has come, I'm speechless, frozen in terror. I'm staring at death's face, and I can't do anything.

"Why did you take her?" Rufio takes a step forward, trembling from head to toe. His face is twisted into a grimace, almost as if he's in pain.

"Because you've shown your true colors. You betrayed the order, and now you'll pay."

The monster pulls a gun from inside his leather jacket and aims it at Rufio.

"No!" I jump in front of him, but it's not a bullet that shoots from the barrel. It's a net. It covers my entire body, and when I land on the dirty ground, I'm trapped. The Neo God I tried to kill used something similar, a net that annuls Idol powers, making me helpless.

"Daisy!" Rufio shouts. "You son of a bitch." He pulls his arm back, but another net covers him. My father's killer didn't come alone.

Rufio falls to his knees, trapped like me. Toby is captured

next, though it wasn't like he could put much of a fight, beaten up like that. The alleyway brightens thanks to the headlights of a vehicle approaching us. It gives me a clear view of the man who killed my father. I don't recognize his companions, but it doesn't matter. I'm memorizing their faces now.

Finally, I'm beginning to understand the force that drives Principal Fallon. She's right. The Neo Gods must be exterminated until there are none left.

Tires screech nearby as the vehicle comes to a sudden stop. The sound of boots on the ground makes me even more tense. I yank at the net, but the more I struggle, the more tangled I become. Rough hands lift me and then toss me inside a black van with tinted windows. I fall on my right side, banging my head against the van's wall. My yelp is muffled by Rufio's and Toby's grunts as they're tossed inside just as roughly as me. I keep fighting against the net only to quickly realize there's no escaping it.

"It's no use, vermin. You're not going anywhere," the assassin says before shutting the van's sliding door.

"Are you okay, Daisy?" Rufio asks, trying to scooch closer to me.

"I'm not hurt, but I'm far from okay. That man killed my father."

"I... figured," Rufio grits out.

"You still can't say anything about the Neo Gods, can you?"

"No."

"I'm sorry I failed you," I murmur.

"You didn't fail me. I'm the one who couldn't protect you from... *them*."

Toby moans, reminding me that he's hurt.

"Hey, are you okay there, dude?" Rufio asks him.

"No. I feel like I've been hit by a bulldozer. I didn't know Idols could get so hurt like this."

"What did they do to you?" I ask.

"They trapped me with a special cord and beat the shit out of me."

"How did you escape the first time?" Rufio probes.

"I don't know. But if anyone failed here, it was me," he replies in a soft voice. "I thought being an Idol would make a world of difference, but I couldn't protect Rosie, the most important person in my life."

"They want—" Rufio stops suddenly and groans. Shit. He's trying to tell us what the Neo Gods' plans are, but he can't.

"They want me," I complete his sentence. "They're using Rosie as bait."

"Why would they want you?" Toby asks.

I don't answer in case there's a slim chance they know I'm not a newly turned Idol. A sudden thought occurs to me, though.

"Toby, were you masking your powers when the Neo Gods attacked?" I whisper.

"No."

Principal Fallon said the Neo Gods knew the Knights had acquired a new weapon, so how come they didn't suspect Toby was it? Unless they weren't aware Toby used to be a Norm. He did pretend to be a Fringe at Gifted Academy.

"Why?" he asks when I don't reply.

"No reason." I don't want to answer his question, not when our captors are most likely listening to our conversation.

The ride doesn't take long, and soon we're dragged out of the van. We're in an underground garage, but I don't get to see much of our surroundings before one of the Neo Gods throws me over his shoulder. I'm upside down and can't really move my head much as he carries me along.

We enter an elevator, and judging by the duration of the trip, we're at one of the highest floors when it stops. Once out of the elevator, my captor doesn't take more than a few steps before he throws me to the floor like I'm nothing but a garbage bag. I hit my shoulder when I fall, and the impact sends white-hot pain down my arm and up my neck. But I suffer in silence. I won't give these monsters the satisfaction.

With my mobility compromised, I can't take in my surroundings. When a pair of expensive leather shoes approaches me, all I can do is brace for violence.

"I can't believe you were hiding in plain sight. I have to give it to my wife. She's a clever bitch."

"Where's my sister?" I ask.

The net is suddenly removed from me, and in an instant, my powers return at full capacity. My muscles flex as I prepare to leap to my feet, but gloved hands grab me by the arms and lift me up. I don't waste any time, though. I unleash all my destructive powers on the Neo God holding me, hoping it's the one who killed my father.

"Tsk, tsk," the tall man in front of me says. "We know who you are, darling. Your unmaking tricks won't work on us."

"Dad, leave Daisy alone!" Rufio screams from his prone position on the floor.

Dad? I look closely at the man in front of me, trying to find any resemblance between him and his sons. It takes me a while, but then I see Rufio in his father's arrogant chin and eyebrows. Bryce has his nose and mouth. But the main difference between father and sons is in their eyes. I see nothing but pure hatred and coldness shining in the Neo God's gaze.

His nostrils flare as he gazes at Rufio on the floor. Then he signals to one of his cohorts, who removes the net from Rufio and roughly yanks him up.

"You disgust me," his father sneers.

"I can say the same about you," Rufio spits back, glowering at the man.

"Tie him up."

I fight against the Neo God holding me, but it's like trying to break free from steel chains. "What are you going to do to him?"

"Me? I'm not going to do anything." His eyes shine with malice, turning my stomach into knots. "You, on the other hand, will make a demonstration."

"What?" I squeak.

"My son betrayed me when he chose you over his own kind. I can't think of a more fitting punishment than turning him into the vermin he was desperately trying to protect."

My chest feels tight, and my mouth is as dry as a desert. "I'm not going to hurt him."

The man shakes his head and chuckles. "I didn't think you'd cooperate, so I acquired leverage. Bring her in."

Two beefy Neo Gods enter the empty office space, dragging Rosie bound and gagged between them. Her green eyes are round and dark with fear.

"Rosie!" I attempt to reach her, but my captor pulls me back.

She tries to say something, but nothing reaches me besides muffled sounds. Seeing my sister in that condition snaps something inside of me. Uncontrollable fury spreads like wildfire, filling me with the strength of a thousand gods. I can't unmake the Idol holding me, but I can bend time. Everyone practically stops moving while I maintain normal speed, which allows me to stomp on the Neo God's instep, pushing him off me, and reach Rosie before anyone can react.

I punch the first of Rosie's captors in the nose, then dispatch the second Neo God with a kick to the groin. Rosie falls into my arms, and somehow I lose control of my gift. Time returns to normal speed for everyone else.

Shit.

With Rosie still attached to me, I whirl around and freeze.

Rufio's father has a lightning-glass dagger pressed against

my love's neck. "Nice move, freak, but one more step and he's gone."

"Don't worry about me, Daisy. Get out of here," Rufio grits out, which prompts his father to pull his hair back and press the blade in hard enough to draw blood.

My fury is still bouncing inside of me, but I can't unleash it now. I won't risk Rufio's life.

"Don't hurt him," I reply.

"Let go of your sister and do as I say," he commands.

Rosie curls her hands around my shirt and protests through her gag. I turn to her, hoping she can forgive me for not saving her. "I'm sorry," I whisper.

Her eyes are brighter and filled with tears, but I don't read resentment there. She nods and then steps away from me. At once, the men I punched and kicked grab her again, moving her out of my reach.

When I face Rufio, he's being tied to a folding chair. The cords the Neo Gods are using are similar to the one Bryce got from the Knights. Both factions possess the same Idol-annulling materials, but so far, only the Neo Gods seem to have the numbers. Maybe that's why Principal Fallon wanted me to strike the top members of the nefarious organization in a covert operation. If the Knights are outnumbered, only stealth could win this war. But unfortunately, I fucked it up.

"I'm losing my patience, Daisy Rodale," Rufio's father says with venom. "Get your ass moving. Now!"

I amble toward Rufio, unable to hold back the tears. Breathing is impossible when the terrible weight of failure and regret is crushing my chest.

"Don't cry, Daisy. It'll be okay," Rufio says.

"I can't do this," I murmur.

"Yes you can."

Rosie's whimper draws my attention. I look over my

shoulder and see Toby is now free from the net but also being held at knifepoint.

"He'll kill your sister and Toby if you don't do it," Rufio argues.

He's right, but when I raise my hands, they're heavy like lead. I capture Rufio's face between them and kiss him on the lips, already feeling my gift killing his. Leaning my forehead against his, I whisper, "I love you. Please forgive me."

"I love you too."

He grunts, shutting his eyes. I close mine too, because I can't bear to witness his suffering. His struggle becomes more acute until he lets out a scream. With a cry, I attempt to let go of him, but my muscles are locked; no amount of struggle can separate me from him now. Rufio lets out a final pain-filled yell, then grows silent and still. I don't sense his essence ebbing away anymore. The power that kept me linked to him recedes, and I'm finally able to pull away.

I stagger back, feeling drained and wretched. Rufio's chin is dipped low, but the rise and fall of his chest tells me he's not dead.

"Rufio?"

Slowly, he lifts his head. The moment our gazes connect, I know the truth.

He's unmade.

40

BRYCE

Not only is the whip around my neck nullifying my powers, but it's also choking me to death. Curling my fingers around the cord, I attempt to break free. During my struggle, I catch Morpheus ducking just in time before he gets ensnared too.

Fuck this shit. I'm a level seventeen Idol; I won't be rendered useless by a damn Neo God. Instead of struggling to remove the whip from around my neck, I whirl around and pull the motherfucker holding the end of it toward me, using the little bit of telekinesis I still have in my system.

He staggers forward, getting close enough to receive a roundhouse kick to the side of his head. He falls to the side, releasing the whip in the process. I yank the leather cord from around my neck and use it against the asshole on the floor, tying his hands together.

In my peripheral vision, I see another Neo God running toward me. In his hand is a lightning-glass dagger, poised to strike. *Not today, asshole.* Angry as hell, I don't hold back as I unleash a bolt of energy strong enough to fry the circuitry of an entire building. It hits the man straight in his chest. He convulses for a few seconds, dropping his weapon in the process, before he collapses to the ground.

Not wasting any time, I look for Morpheus, Phoenix, and Soren in the melee. Soren is free from the Neo God's hold and moving so fast I can barely see his shape. Morpheus isn't too far from him, doling out ass kickings and a good dose of fear to any Neo God who comes near him. But I can't find Phoenix. *Damn it.*

I'm about to search for him with my senses when someone drops next to me. I tense on the spot, preparing to engage in battle, but it's Stephan.

"Where the hell did you go?" I ask.

"I had to check what was coming for us. A heavily armed group of Fringes is hacking up Norms left and right at the outer perimeter. They're armed with lightning-glass daggers and wearing protective vests."

"Fuck. Do you think they're working with the Neo Gods?"

"These attacks are too coordinated. They must be."

Hell and damn. This changes everything. The Neo Gods preach Idol supremacy, but if they have Fringes in their ranks, then it means they're not taking any chances. They'll exterminate every single Norm at all costs if we let them.

Soren stops in front of us, a little out of breath. "Where's Andromeda? We could use her chains."

"She's dealing with the Fringes," Stephan replies before his focus changes. He pushes his brother out of the way, preventing him from being skewered by a Neo God.

The dagger meant for Soren strikes Stephan's forearm, eliciting a wild scream from him. Before I can react, Andromeda's golden chains swoop in and run through the Neo God's chest like he was made out of butter. Blood sputters from his wounds, splashing my face.

I don't worry about wiping it off as I spin around and try to locate Phoenix. It's hard to find him in the chaos, but eventually I sense his signature. He's almost at the edge of the crowd.

Before I take off after him, I check to see if my companions need assistance. Stephan's wound seems superficial, and all the Neo Gods gunning for us have been taken care of.

"All good?" Stephan asks Andromeda.

"Yeah."

"Let's find Phoenix and get out of here," I say.

"He's helping calm down the crowd," Andromeda replies.

I stop and pay attention to my surroundings. Indeed, people are no longer screaming and running in a frenzy. They're now walking leisurely, almost as if nothing amiss.

"We should regrou—" Morpheus starts, then stops midsentence with a wince.

"What is it?"

He presses the heel of his hand against his forehead and lets out a grunt in response.

"He's not coming back, is he?" I ask.

"Who's not coming back?" Soren looks at me.

Andromeda's eyes begin to glow, and her chains react as well, as if they're sensing something. "Something terrible has or is about to happen."

"It's Daisy and... Rufio. Your father has them," Morpheus grits out.

"Where?" I grab his forearm, forcing him to look at me.

Morpheus opens his eyes finally, but I don't like the glint I see shining there. "I don't know."

"How are we doing here?" Phoenix asks as he joins our group. "Oh shit. What happened?"

"My father has Daisy and Rufio," I reply.

Phoenix's expression turns into one of horror as he processes the news. "He's going to kill her."

Fuck, like don't I know that?

"Andromeda, can you find Daisy?" I ask.

"I can try." She lowers her chin and a bright glowing light surrounds her. Her chains form a tower around her, rattling as they move in a circle.

A minute passes by, but it feels like an eternity. My heart is stuck in my throat and my chest is about to cave in. The longer Daisy is in my father's grasp, the more chances he'll have to harm her.

The light surrounding Andromeda begins to dim, allowing me to see the crestfallen expression on her face. She failed.

"I'm sorry. She's either too far or blocked from my reach."

Phoenix lets out an enraged scream and punches the air. An abandoned bus in the vicinity flies into the distance and crashes against a storefront.

"You have to try again," I urge.

"I can keep trying, but my powers can only do so much."

"What if you borrowed from us?" Morpheus suggests.

She pinches her eyebrows together. "I've never done that before, but it could work."

"How in the world are we going to lend her our powers?" Soren asks.

"We form a power circle," I reply.

"You've done this before?" Stephan asks.

"Once." On the island of horrors when we were trying to survive the night. At the time, we acted on pure instinct. But I don't tell him that.

Soren checks our perimeter. "Is it safe to do this here?"

"I don't sense any threats from Neo Gods or Fringes now. We don't have time to waste. If we're doing this, it has to be now," Andromeda replies.

"Okay, what do we do?" Stephan asks.

"Form a circle around her and then project all your power outward," I instruct, taking my position.

Morpheus and Phoenix stand at my sides. Stephan and Soren complete the circle. Andromeda's chains shoot up to the sky before coming down to form a circle around all of us. The girl is glowing again, and soon the world disappears as we're enveloped by her power. Fuck. I'm not sure if she's an eighteen or more. I've never felt so much raw energy before, not from an Idol anyway. But I don't dwell on the thought. I need to concentrate on my own essence, give as much as I can to her. My powers mingle with Morpheus's and Phoenix's first, linking them together. After a minute, I sense the circle has closed. We're all joined and feeding Andromeda's chains.

Suddenly, my mind is linked to hers too, and I see through her point of view. It's strange to be connected to another Idol like that, especially one who lacks sight. But in this plane, Andromeda can see as well as me. We're all soaring high with her, searching for Daisy's and Rufio's signatures. Time ceases to have any meaning. I have no clue how long we search for them until finally I see Daisy's bright spark.

"I found her," Andromeda announces.

"I know where she is," I reply, opening my eyes and severing the link with her. "Grab any lightning glass weapon you can find and let's go."

41

RUFIO

I feel nothing. No swirling in my chest, no tingling sensation at the tips of my fingers. As I stare into Daisy's sorrowful eyes, I know she can tell I'm no longer an Idol. I'm unmade, but I don't feel hollow or incomplete.

"Rufio, I'm so sorry," Daisy whispers, crying.

"Don't cry, my love."

The sound of slow clapping breaks our moment.

"Isn't this touching?" my father sneers. "I spent my entire life teaching my sons the importance of legacy only to have them betray me for a lowly, dirty Norm."

Daisy whirls on the spot, and a gust of air surrounds her. Her long hair whips in every direction, and despite me lacking my Idol powers, I can sense her gathering every ounce of juice she has.

"Oh, I'm sorry. *Former* Norm. So what, sweetheart? You think you can best me just because you got a taste of Idol life?"

"You'll pay for what you made me do." She pulls her hand back, ready to unleash her fury on Dad, but he simply points at Rosie, who's being held at knifepoint.

"I wouldn't do that if I were you. She'll be dead before you strike."

"You got your revenge. Now let us go," I say.

"Oh, I don't think so. Now that I've seen what Daisy can do, I think I'm going to hold on to her for a while longer. Despite her heritage, she's indeed a magnificent weapon."

"She's not a thing you can use at your beck and call!" I scream, frustrated that I can't break from my bindings.

The power I sense from Daisy recedes. She lowers her arm but doesn't lose her defiant posture. "I'll help you if you let them go."

My father laughs. "What do think this is, a negotiation? Your sister and your stupid friend are staying. As for my son...." He pauses and looks me in the eye. At the moment, I know exactly what's in store for me. "I have no more use for him."

From the corner of my eye, I see the shine of the blade coming for me. I close my eyes, but I don't feel the sting of the stab. I peel my eyes open and notice the Neo God with the weapon is moving in slow motion now. Daisy was somehow able to affect him with her gift despite his usage of the protective vest. She kicks the knife from his hand before time returns to normal speed.

The windows in front of us explode inward in a shower of glass shards, and in come Stephan, Andromeda, Morpheus, Phoenix, Bryce, and Soren. I have no idea how they reached the top floor, but I'm fucking glad they're here.

In an instant, I'm forgotten. Rosie and Toby are pushed aside when the Neo God handling them have to defend themselves. Andromeda ends the duo before they can even attempt anything, hitting them with her impressive chains. Bryce, Phoenix, and Morpheus are all carrying lightning-glass daggers, which they use against our enemies without mercy.

While the battle goes on, I struggle against the cords around my wrists. I won't be able to break free from them unless I cut them with a lightning-glass dagger. I search my surroundings until I find the weapon that was meant to be my demise, discarded next to its dead owner. When he bound me to the chair, he forgot to tie my ankles, so I'm able to get up, but I stop in my tracks when I catch my father and Delta running away from the fight. Of course they would. Cowards.

I can't let them get away after everything they've done. Without another thought, I charge in their direction, using the momentum to knock them both down. I fall on my side, and without the use of my arms, I hit my face straight on. The pain knocks me out for a few seconds, and when I come to, my father is standing over me.

"You little piece of shit. This is the last time you get in my way."

Something sharp and hot pierces my chest, robbing me of air. I want to shout, but I can't make any sound. Delta comes into focus with a bloody dagger in hand. He was the one who delivered the blow. Someone screams nearby, prompting my father and his minion to vanish from view.

Daisy drops next to me, propping my head on her lap. In the background, someone is shouting orders, but I can only pay attention to her.

"Rufio. No," she whimpers.

I try to speak but end up sputtering blood instead.

Bryce appears next to her. "We don't have much time. Please let me heal him, Daisy."

She moves away from me, setting my head back on the floor with care. I want to ask her to come back, but I can't do anything but stare at the exposed pipes on the ceiling. Bryce places his hand below my wound, and almost immediately the pain vanishes. My muscles relax, and suddenly I'm bone-tired. My eyelids are getting extremely heavy; the only thing keeping them from shutting completely is Daisy's voice, asking me to stay awake.

"Come on, Rufio. Don't give up," Bryce pleads.

"Trust... me. I'm not... trying to," I reply.

Slowly, my strength returns, but not the Idol kind. When Bryce pulls his hand back and the glow vanishes, I know I'm healed, but I also know I'm still a Norm.

DAISY

Rufio's father and his henchman escaped, the two Neo Gods I wanted to kill the most. But at least they didn't take Rufio from me. As soon as Bryce pulls his hand away, I know he succeeded in healing him. A little roughly, I push Bryce out of the way and bring Rufio back onto my lap.

"Is he completely healed?" Stephan asks.

"Yeah," Rufio answers, trying to sit up already.

"Take it easy, honey," I say.

"I'm okay. Bryce is once again a lifesaver." He grins, but his smile doesn't take away the sadness in my chest.

"Holy crap. What happened to his power?" Soren asks, making me wince.

"Daisy was forced to unmake me. She had no choice." He looks me in the eye, and I find nothing but love in his. How can he still love me after what I did to him?

"But if Bryce healed him, then maybe he'll also get his powers back," Phoenix chimes in.

"Yeah, maybe," Rufio replies, but I sense the lack of enthusiasm in his words.

"My father will be here in twenty minutes," Stephan announces.

"When did you call him?" I look in his direction.

"As soon as we saw the attack at the mall on the news."

Bryce unfurls from his crouch on unsteady legs. Phoenix steps in and keeps him upright. "Are you all right?"

"I'll be in a minute."

Once again, healing has weakened Bryce. He can't keep doing this.

I'm still watching him intensely when Morpheus offers Rufio and me his hands. He brushes my cheek with his knuckles and offers me a smile. His warm brown eyes are kind and comforting, and I wish I could drown in them. But I can't find solace in anything right now.

Rosie and Toby are farther back, holding each other. I stare at them, trying to capture my sister's gaze. She finally looks at me and mouths, "I'm sorry." It makes my throat tight. Despite our latest arguments and her hatred for Idols, she knows how much hurting Rufio cost me.

Andromeda moves closer. Her chains are hanging loose from her wrists, but they're short and a dull metal color instead of glowing gold.

"I'm sorry we couldn't get here sooner," she says.

"At least you got here." I hug her, sensing her tense for a fleeting moment before she wraps her arms around my back. "Thank you."

"Don't mention it."

We ease off, and she says, "This is where we part ways, girlie."

"You're going?" Stephan steps next to her.

"Oh yeah. My work here is done, and it's a school night." She smirks in Stephan's direction, and then she winks at me.

"Maybe you should stay. My fa—"

"Yeah, yeah. I have no desire to meet Mr. Pain In My Ass, Sr. See ya!" She strides away, knowing exactly where the exit is. Before she disappears through the door, she says, "Call me when you get back home, Daisy."

"I will."

Andromeda lifts her hand over her head and waves as she leaves.

"Why didn't she stay?" Rosie asks.

"Because she's a weirdo," Soren replies with derision.

Stephan doesn't offer a retort to his brother's remark, but I can see in his expression that he didn't like the comment. I'm so not buying that there isn't something going between him and Andromeda.

Rosie and Toby stop next to me, still hugging sideways. By the way Toby's arm is curled around his middle, I get that their stance is more out of necessity than the desire to be close to one another.

"Are you okay? They didn't hurt you, did they?" I ask her.

"Aside from some shoving and rough handling, I'm okay. How about you?"

"My wounds aren't the visible kind." I look in Rufio's direction. His arms are crossed and his chin is dipped low. My heart breaks even more.

"I'm sorry about him. But I'm sure he'll recover his powers in no time. If Bryce can turn you and Toby into Idols, no doubt his healing powers also restored Rufio's."

Rosie's logic is sound, but I have the feeling no one can restore what I took. I smile just the same, though, grateful that she's trying to cheer me up.

Around fifteen minutes after Andromeda left, Mr. Silverstone comes in accompanied by four other men I've never met, Xavier, and—color me surprised—Principal Fallon. Before anyone can say anything, Xavier strides toward us and pulls Rosie and me into a tight hug.

"I'm so, so glad you girls are okay."

"And I'm happy you came," I say, burying my face against his chest.

Shady or not, Xavier is family. I had to be tough for Rosie's sake, but I've missed having someone to look after me.

"Of course I came." He pulls back and looks us in the eye. "I may not be the relative you wished for, but I'm here for you. I'm sorry my fears kept me from doing more."

I don't realize that I'm crying until my cheeks turn wet.

"Why is she here?" Rosie points at Principal Fallon.

We face her, and immediately I notice the tension among our party. Phoenix and Morpheus are openly glaring at her. Stephan's and Soren's animosity isn't as obvious, but there's no denying they don't like her either.

"Jodie is here because I asked her to come," Mr. Silverstone replies.

She takes a step forward and glances in Rufio's direction. Her jaw clenches as she realizes what's happened to him. Nostrils flaring, she turns around to face me. I try not to flinch under her cold, accusatory stare, but it's hard. I deserve it.

"I'm here because the Neo Gods have declared war not only against Norms and Fringes but also against everyone who opposes their nefarious ideas. It was naïve of me to think I could eliminate their poisonous reach with stealth alone. We need the numbers, and that's why I've decided to join forces with the Knights."

I trade a worried glance with Bryce. Does Mr. Silverstone know what kind of snake he's inviting into his midst?

"What does that mean for us?" Bryce asks.

"The Neo Gods have armed high-level Fringes despite the fact that they abhor everyone who isn't an Idol. They're not playing to lose, so we can't either. We need every recruit we can get, but especially you and Daisy."

Bryce lets out a derisive laugh. "Let me guess. You want me to build you an army of newly turned Idols."

Principal Fallon nods. "Exactly."

"Every time Bryce used his healing powers, it cost him. We still don't know that the constant use of his healing abilities won't leave permanent damage."

"Oh, such as what you did to Rufio?" Principal Fallon retorts cruelly.

"It wasn't Daisy's fault." He moves closer to me. I appreciate his support, but her words cut me nonetheless.

"You need to keep doing what Jodie had in mind, Daisy. Now more than ever, we have to strike the Neo Gods, weaken them by taking out their top dogs," Mr. Silverstone adds.

"You don't have to use your recruitment spiel to convince me. I'd go after them with or without your help."

Bryce looks at me, then at Rufio, before he faces his mother.

"I don't care about the consequences. I want Dad and all his friends to pay for what they did."

"Bryce, what are you doing?" Rufio asks, staring at him with a sheen of fear in his eyes.

He doesn't answer Rufio, though, continuing to address his mother and Mr. Silverstone. "You want more Idols. I'll give you more Idols. I'm in."

TO BE CONTINUED IN BROKEN KNIGHTS.
AVAILABLE NOW

MORPHEUS
GIFTED ACADEMY

ALSO BY MICHELLE HERCULES

Paranormal Romance:

Dark Prince (Blueblood Vampires #1)

Wild Thing (Blueblood Vampires #2)

Forgotten Heir (Blueblood Vampires #3)

Savage Vow (Blueblood Vampires #4)

Reckless Times (Gifted Academy #5)

Savage Games (Gifted Academy #6)

Contemporary Romance:

Wonderwall (Love Me, I'm Famous #1)

Sugar, We're Going Down (Love Me, I'm Famous #2)

Wreck of the Day (Love Me, I'm Famous #3)

Devils Don't Fly (Love Me, I'm Famous #4)

Love Me Like You Do (Love Me, I'm Famous #5)

Catch You (Love Me, I'm Famous #6)

All The Right Moves

Heart Stopper (Rebels of Rushmore #1)

Heart Breaker (Rebels of Rushmore #2)

Heart Starter (Rebels of Rushmore #3)

Reverse Harem Romance:

Wicked Gods (Gifted Academy #1)

Ruthless Idols (Gifted Academy #2)

Hateful Heroes (Gifted Academy #3)

ABOUT THE AUTHOR

USA Today Bestselling Author Michelle Hercules always knew creative arts were her calling but not in a million years did she think she would become an author. With a background in fashion design she thought she would follow that path. But one day, out of the blue, she had an idea for a book. One page turned into ten pages, ten pages turned into a hundred, and before she knew, her first novel, The Prophecy of Arcadia, was born.

Michelle Hercules resides in Florida with her husband and daughter. She is currently working on the *Blueblood Vampires* series and the *Rebels of Rushmore* series.

Join Michelle Hercules' Reader Group:
https://www.facebook.com/groups/mhsoars

Connect with Michelle Hercules:
www.michellehercules.com
books@mhsoars.com